The Guitar

H.L. Wood

Copyright © 2025 H.L. Wood

All rights reserved. This book or any portion thereof may not be reproduced or used in any manner whatsoever without the express written permission of the publisher except for the use of brief quotations in a book review or scholarly journal.

First Printing: April 2025

ISBN 9798307269831

Contents

Contents	1
Introduction	5
1 The Crossroads	7
2 Last Bus To Memphis	13
3 Pawnshop Blues	19
4 Court-Martialed	33
5 Fly On My Sweet Angel	37
6 The Londoner	45
7 Another Piece of My Heart	55
8 Camp Malibu Shalom	61
9 The Talent Show	71
10 Borrow or Steal	77
11 Ashes to Ashes	83
12 The Elders	85
13 Take It Away	87
14 The Hamburgers	91
15 The Capital Tower	97
16 The Intern	105
17 Poor White Boy Blues	109
18 Dark Side Of The Moon	123
19 The Dreamers	127
20 Prime Time Television	131
21 The Safari Inn	141
22 Artificial Intelligence	145
23 On The Spectrum	151
24 Old School Analog	155
25 Channel Islands Institute	159

26	Magic Swirling Ship	161
27	FDA Approved	165
28	Perfect Pitch	173
29	One	179
30	Secrets & Confessions	181
31	Lab Rats	185
32	The Leap of Fate	189
33	The Magic Key	197
34	The War Room	203
35	Blue Glass	213
36	Ancestry	217
37	The Juke Joint	223
38	The Hitchhiker	229
39	The Ash Tray	237
40	Raw Sexuality	239
41	Moonlight Lynching	247
42	Up Up and Gone Gone	261
43	The 27 Club	267
44	Ribbons in Time	273
45	The Butterfly Effect	279
46	Resurrection	283
47	Road Trip Blues	293
48	Catrina	303
49	Intensive Care	311
50	The Rescue	321
51	The Dark Web	331
52	Forgotten Generation	337
53	One	347

54	Pretending	355
55	Corporate Greed	367
56	Real Guitars	373
57	Violet	381
58	Dead Wood	387
59	Montana	393
60	Voodoo Child	401
61	Lost In Time	411
62	Blues Man	417
63	Jimi	421
64	Bunkers	429

Introduction

The hollow chamber within the acoustic guitar, from the beginning of its creation, was crafted to absorb all energy passing by strings of catgut, nylon, and steel, outside its shell of aged wood, and to amplify and sustain that energy for as long as possible. All human experience requires energy, channels energy, releases energy. Even when energy in the form of resonating sound within the acoustic guitar becomes no longer detectable by the human ear, the energy still sustains. The length of sustain is determined by the quality of the instrument, the age and type of wood, and the soundness of the guitar's construction. Some say the resonating sound never goes away but continues to resonate within the individual cell bodies of the wood. The master luthier, a skilled artisan who makes violins, cellos, guitars, and other stringed instruments, spends a lifetime perfecting this sustain.

Pick up a well-made acoustic guitar, rest your chin on the body, close your eyes, and firmly pluck any string. Hear the sound, but more importantly, feel the sound energy penetrate through your chin and teeth, along your jaw, into your skull. Count how long that one plucked sound, that vibrating energy, truly lasts. Count until you no longer feel a single vibration. No other instrument, when perfectly crafted, can absorb and sustain energy like an acoustic guitar can.

A one-hundred-year-old guitar contains within its emptiness, through the darkened sound hole, all energy and every sound it has ever witnessed. The plucking of its strings by a new student, a baby crying for attention across a nearby bed, the slamming of a door when a drunken man staggers into the room and throws an empty whiskey bottle into the sink, demanding, "Where's my fucking dinner?"—all of these create reverberations.

Regardless of how dissonant, in tune, or harmonious the energy that enters through its sound hole and bridge, the guitar makes no judgement but only envelopes and secures that energy. Forever.

All sounds, spoken or otherwise, are captured, sustained, and enveloped within the guitar. The guitar sits in the corner witnessing everything it hears. And it will never forget. Even a guitar that has been broken to pieces still contains those enveloped sounds in the empty places of every cell.

Energy cannot be destroyed; it can only be transformed.

1

The Crossroads

When a man has no shadow, he is dead. There was no shadow at the feet of the man standing motionless on the dusty crossroad, beaten down by the sweltering sun overhead, where no wind dared blow. Robert wore a leather 'voodoo pouch' hung around his neck and a tobacco-stained acoustic flat-top guitar was slung high on his back, secured by a worn leather strap.

Robert was seventeen, but he looked forty. He weighed one hundred and thirty-five pounds, and his ragged sharecropper clothes hung loosely down his boney frame. His mind was foggy from the heavy drinking he'd done the night before as he stammered through the night to reach this point in the Mississippi Delta. He had stood motionless in this spot since daylight, swaying, wondering, pondering as men do, about women, money, music, and the guitar. The stifling heat and sweltering humidity reminded Robert that he was in hell. A single bead of sweat inched slowly down his face. He licked his dried lips, but his swollen tongue offered no relief. He longed for one shot of whiskey, bourbon, or gin. If offered a single shot of rubbing alcohol from a dirty glass, he would drink it without hesitation.

Robert's eyelids fell slowly across his dry, bloodshot eyes as he passed out and crumpled to the dusty ground; this was the spot where he had chosen to arrive and then die waiting. For what, he knew not. But for something.

The guitar on his back is what drove him in desperation to this dust-laden crossroad. He had tried in vain to play it for more than two years with modest progress. Fellow musicians had begged Robert to 'give it away' because he played it so dreadfully. The six strings and twenty-two frets along an ebony fretboard confused and confounded him to where he could not comprehend the guitar's structure nor decipher its alure. He owned a harmonica, which he played exceptionally well because it was a simple instrument, no confusing positions and never a note out of place. A harmonica made in the key of C only played notes that would sound at home with a song in the same key. When Robert played harmonica, he could hear the words to songs he wanted to sing in perfect tone and pitch. He could hear every note, every bend, every yearning plea; but he could not sing the words he longed to express with a harmonica stuffed in his mouth. Robert had experimented with other musicians, allowing them to sing the words to his songs while he played harmonica, but their tone and nuance never matched what he heard in his own head. Robert's voice was the only voice that could satisfy him. And so, he faced a conundrum: either give up playing his songs with his words and play the harmonica for someone else or figure out how to play the God-damned guitar so he could sing his songs. So he could sing the blues.

In 1928, there were two types of musicians playing in the Deep South. There were gospel musicians, full of 'praise God, Jesus, and his angels' and respected in the community as God-fearing Christians. And there musicians who sang the blues, or better known as blues men, 'filled with the Devil' and a 'destroyer of Christian souls,' scorned by the community. Robert knew every gospel song and could certainly sing them when forced to, but he felt no love toward God, Jesus, and those 'fucking angels' that never once appeared to help him or his family in times of dire need.

Robert had married when he was sixteen years old, but his wife died while giving birth to Robert's son, who also died that day. The death of his teenage bride and newborn son happened while Robert was far away, searching to become a blues man, riding rail cars and singing in juke joints and shanties across the South. When Robert finally returned to visit his wife and newborn child, they had already been buried for more than a month.

On that day, and many others throughout his life, Robert cursed God so vehemently, those around him scurried away fearing God would strike him down from the heavens. But no matter how vile he spoke to God, no matter the blasphemies that came from Robert's mouth in anger toward God, the blackened sky never parted, and a lightning bolt never descended to hush the blues man.

Robert was the youngest child born of eleven to his biological mother. His biological father had no clue that his wife was sleeping around. But that knowledge wouldn't have bothered him greatly; he was busy fathering many children with other women while married to Robert's mother. Later they would divorce, and both would remarry and have more children. Robert's life in this family meant a life bound to share cropping, poverty, hunger, and despair. He saw music as his only ticket out of bondage.

Robert's life to that point had focused on three things. One: Picking cotton all day in the stifling heat, to earn a token that could only be used at the local farm store and would barely provide a full meal. Two: Having sex, or rather, 'fucking,' to satisfy the carnal itch constantly gnawing at Robert's brain. Although he loved beautiful women, he didn't discriminate when it came to fucking; they could be short, tall, ugly, pretty, fat, or thin. Sex was sex and part of his daily quest. Three: Singing. Robert sang hauntingly. Those who heard his voice could never forget it. He sang blues because he *lived* the blues. He would hang around the porches, parlors, shanties, bedrooms, and bathrooms of every musician he knew, hoping for a chance to sing and play the blues. When he did get a chance to play with someone who could play the guitar while he sang, he made more money playing blues in a few hours than working an entire day picking cotton.

When Robert performed to a crowd or audience, he would focus his entire performance toward a single woman in the audience. Husbands and boyfriends didn't pay Robert any mind because he appeared hardly a threat. He was thin and had an odd physical deformity in the way he moved. People seeing him couldn't really describe his oddness in a conscious way. Despite the oddness, many women, after being wooed by Robert's evening of direct attention through his haunting songs, slept with him willingly. Three hours of foreplay through his music left some women helpless in his presence later that night. Most women would learn first-hand that he was a masterful seducer with his voice but a failure when it came to delivering the goods. Robert's fingers were meant to touch the sweat-soaked ebony fret board of his guitar and nothing else.

As the sun set and kissed the horizon across the barren field, Robert slowly awakened. He was lucky not to have been run over by a passing truck. He pushed himself off the ground and looked around, in search of his only important possession. In the ditch beside the road lay his guitar, face up on a bed of dry grass as if someone had caught it and placed it there for safe keeping as Robert crumpled to the ground. Sunlight reflected off the worn steel strings rubbed clean daily of possible rust from Robert's incessant playing and plucking. A small twig, lay neatly over top of the six strings, precisely over the sound hole. Robert looked around suspiciously, wondering who could have placed the twig in such a particular manner. Robert searched the trees across the barren fields for signs of movement.

And then he saw it. Along the tree line across the barren field. A moving shadow.

Robert placed the twig inside his voodoo pouch, picked up the guitar, and stumbled across the dusty field toward the tree line, leaving a trail of dust curling up behind him.

At the tree line, Robert pushed past low hanging branches and penetrated the darkened forest beyond. His feet crunched through the dried leaves and dead foliage. Branches struck the side of the guitar, thumping the body, vibrating the strings, and creating an eerie sound that filled the quiet forest. *Bang, twang, sustain!* It was as if a cowbell was tied to Robert's neck to signal anyone of his location. The further he penetrated the dense forest, the darker it became, until no light could be found. Although Robert could hardly be seen, the branches striking the guitar confirmed that Robert was still on the move.

Bang, twang, sustain!

***

Robert sat cross-legged on the ground inside a perfect circle of moonlight with his shadow falling across the body of the guitar and onto the gray dry grass beyond. The guitar lay across his lap. The forest was silent; not a critter or creature moved to disturb Robert's trance as he hummed softly and held the twig in his fingers, rubbing it gently, as if summoning a genie. The voodoo pouch hung open around his neck.

Robert dropped his thumb downward, striking the top of the guitar body. The thud reverberated and echoed, breaking the silence within the nearby forest. He dropped his thumb again, in rhythm, as he rubbed the stick in his other hand. A few moments later, a dried branch broke on the ground only a few feet away. Robert's heart began to race; he hit the guitar body harder, with fearful strikes to match his beating heart. A figure appeared from the shadows. A creature, a woman, hidden beneath a hooded robe, now sat across from him just outside the moonlight circle.

As Robert's thumb beat steady on the guitar, she reached across the moonlight with long fingers and curled nails and took the twig from his hand. She placed it in the dirt as if it were a birthday candle on a cake. Then touched it with an extended boney finger. Her fingernail glowed with a pulsing energy The twig began to smolder, smoke curling off its bark, until it burst into a single flame. Robert watched as she carved the number twenty-seven in the dirt nearby. She looked up and waited for him to acknowledge her offer. Robert nodded in agreement.

She pinched dirt from off the ground and dropped it across the burning twig, dousing the flame. As the twig smoldered, she placed it over the strings where the smoke eerily reversed direction and penetrated, disappearing inside the sound hole.

The woman ran her curled finger along the bark of a nearby tree, collecting amber sap into her palm. She lifted the smoldering twig from the sound hole and rolled it inside the thick amber sap in her palm then slid the coated twig between the strings and deep into the sound hole. She nodded as she secured it to the underside of the bridge, then lifted the guitar for Robert to hold.

He pulled the guitar against his body and looked at the sound hole to see smoke vapors swirling gently inside. The woman nodded and smiled, signaling Robert to form a chord on the neck. He placed his fretting hand into an E minor chord shape as she reached across, and using the back side of a gnarled fingernail, strummed her middle finger across each of the six strings. The forest filled with a perfectly formed E minor chord. The sustain was haunting.

She nodded for Robert to play, although the guitar strings were still vibrating in the moonlight. As Robert strummed his finger across the strings and filled the forest with a perfect E minor chord, the woman was stepping into the trees, vanishing into the darkness.

Robert's life would never be the same.

The guitar would never be the same.

2

Last Bus To Memphis

"Fucking no music on the streets of Austin!" the police officer shouted, billy club drawn.

Robert was playing his guitar on the sidewalk outside the Moonlight Jazz Club. At the officer's voice, he turned and quickly held up his arm, but the two officers proceeded to strike him repeatedly, violently. He rolled to the ground and shielded the guitar as they beat and kicked him into unconsciousness. He was later transported to jail where he was dragged into a dirty cell and pushed onto a cot for the night.

***

Robert was released from jail with a warning the following day after proving to the police that he was visiting Austin to perform at a legitimate recording session, at the Gunter Hotel. Now, in the sweltering heat, he sat in room 414, having taken several shots of whiskey to numb the pain in his riddled body. He sat silently in the modest soundproofed room wearing a black wool suit and smoking a cigarette; his hat tipped forward, hiding his black and blue eyes. He exhaled slowly. Smoke swirled around his face, beneath the brim of his hat, then upward across a recording microphone suspended overhead.

The guitar rested in its open case nearby. Cosmetically, nothing about the guitar had changed since that day at the crossroads, ten years ago, where it lay on the clump of grass in the ditch. But now, held inside the soul of the guitar, were thousands of songs, conversations, train whistles, and other memories it had experienced with Robert since that night in the moonlit forest when a desperate, willing man strummed a perfect E minor chord. Now, so many years later, the man and the guitar, although in the same room, were at odds with each other; as if they were a married couple outwardly celebrating decades of marriage but inwardly seething with hatred. Neither wanted to be looked at nor touched by the other, but divorce was not an option. So, in this makeshift hotel room turned recording studio, they came together, man and guitar, to fulfill the bargain made in the moonlight. The cost of becoming the greatest blues man would be his very soul.

Vincent, the recording engineer, sat at the kitchen table filled with recording decks and microphones. He signed a check and handed it to Robert: nine hundred dollars for exclusive recording rights. Robert stood and looked out the window at the street below, watching people walk along the sidewalk, as he folded the check and slid it into his coat pocket.

"Make sure you leave down the back stairs," Vincent insisted.

"In the back, out the back. Next time, I'm jumping out this goddamned window," Robert slurred.

"Better cash that check first, Mr. Johnson."

Robert reached down to pick up the guitar case but missed the handle and grabbed thin air.

"Fucking guitar!"

"Come back when you got more songs, Mr. Johnson."

"I done sang all the songs I ever known."

Robert grabbed at the handle and caught hold. He stammered from the room, hitting the door frame with the guitar case, then walked down the hallway, bumping walls as he headed to the back stairs. Vincent shook his head in pity.

"You take care, Mr. Johnson."

***

That night, Robert, twenty-seven years old, played six hours at the Moonlight Jazz Club on Main Street. He would certainly not be stopping to play on the sidewalk again after last night's greeting party from the Austin police. In the audience, a woman named Carol fixated on Robert. She smiled and winked at him, making sure he was aware of her desire to spend time with him. She accompanied Robert back to his hotel room where she aggressively, sexually, dominated him. She hit him, pushed him around, and slapped him across the face. Still intoxicated from a full day of drinking, Robert couldn't control her, so he took whatever it was she was dishing out. When she was finished, she left him bruised, scratched, scraped, and bleeding. First a night of beatings from Austin Police and now a beating from Carol. Something had to give.

On his third and final night of performing at the Moonlight, Robert escorted a young woman named Jamie to his hotel room. They fucked for an hour and then Robert passed out. When he woke to piss three hours later, Jamie was gone, but Carol sat in a chair across the living room smoking a cigarette and waiting for Robert to wake up. She took what she wanted, dished out what she wanted, and even stole two hundred dollars from Robert's wallet before leaving three hours later in the early morning hours.

***

"Blues man, blues man! Wake up!"

Robert awakened late the following morning to frantic knocking on the hotel room door. He moaned with pain as he crawled off the bed and limped to the door. He opened it to see the hotel porter in a frenzy.

"Blues man! Wanna live? You better pack your bag and be downstairs in one minute! Word on the street is Carol's husband is on his way to kill you!"

Robert quickly packed his suitcase, grabbed the guitar, and slipped into a waiting taxicab hailed by the watchful hotel porter. Later that night, when Robert was long gone from Texas, Carol's husband walked soberly into the Moonlight and saw Carol at a table near the stage watching the musicians. He removed a revolver from the waistband of his pants, walked calmly passed tables filled with patrons, then smiled as Carol looked at him.

"Go home," Carol said calmly.

"After you," he replied.

He pushed the revolver forward, resting the barrel on the skin between her breasts.

"You're blocking my view," she said coldly.

He pulled the hammer back with his thumb.

"See you in hell," he said.

He pulled the trigger, shooting the bullet meant for Robert through Carol's heart at point-blank range. The sound of the gun could barely be heard amidst the loud music being played. Barely anyone reacted as Carol looked down to see blood oozing from her chest onto her dress as her husband turned and walked away. When he exited the Moonlight, he turned the gun toward his throat and pulled the trigger one last time. He fell into the gutter and bled out.

***

The following day, with the foul smell of urine and body odor penetrating Robert's nose, he stood at the bus station ticket window. Behind him where fifty-one passengers waiting for the next bus to Memphis. The mostly poor men, women, and a few children sat on the benches, fanning themselves with folded newspapers and handkerchiefs. Flies crawled across bare feet of sleeping men and women huddled against the walls.

"Memphis, one way."

The station attendant was busy tuning the radio and turned up the volume. A song began to play as Robert placed two dollars on the counter and rang the bell.

The attendant slid the money into a drawer, placed two dimes on the counter along with a paper ticket.

"Last ticket to Memphis, your lucky day."

Robert placed the ticket into his hat band as the radio played a blues song with slide guitar.

"You know who that is?" Robert asked.

"Hell, yes! That's Robert Johnson, greatest blues man that ever lived."

Robert nodded but refused to smile. "Is that so?"

"Oh, yes!"

"Maybe someday you're going to meet him," Robert said.

"That'll be my lucky day for sure."

Outside, the porter loaded luggage onto the bus. There were duffle bags, twine tied boxes, worn and tattered suitcases, and a single guitar case with a worn handle and a locking latch with a tiny keyhole—Robert Johnson's guitar. That night, fifty-two passengers boarded the bus to Memphis, and as it pulled from the station, it left a trail of black smoke hanging in the stagnant heat. When the bus arrived in Memphis eighteen hours later, having made several stops along the way, only fifty-one haggard passengers staggered down the stairs in the dark. Each took their luggage and boxes and left the platform for parts unknown. But the guitar case, along with a tattered suitcase, sat abandoned on the platform, unclaimed. Two days later, a porter tripped over the suitcase and fell to the ground. In frustration, he carried the suitcase and guitar into the station and placed them into the storage room.

***

Robert Johnson was never seen or heard from again. Speculation and rumors circulated quickly among fans, haters, and fellow musicians as to what became of him. Many believed he was murdered; poisoned and buried in an unmarked grave by a vengeful husband. Others claimed he started playing under a different name and that he only appeared in the darkest, most seedy juke joints to avoid being killed by jealous husbands and boyfriends of the women he had bedded. But no one really knew what had happened to the greatest blues man to ever walk the dusty roads of the Deep South.

But the guitar, it knew everything.

3

Pawnshop Blues

It was a hot summer day when Penbrow Jamison, injured in a boyhood hunting accident, limped past the waiting lines snaking toward the recruitment office, full of young men, fit and looking to defend their nation against the Nazi and Japanese aggressors. There were two lines, one for Whites and another for Colored, and the latter had almost double the number of men waiting to enlist. As Penbrow limped between the two lines, nearly every man acknowledged his pathetic state. The year was 1942 and patriotism filled the headlines of every newspaper across America. Although Penbrow was as strong a patriot as any of the men standing line, he was told there was no place in the service for a man who couldn't storm a hill or fire a rifle at a German or Japanese enemy.

Penbrow hobbled into a Memphis Pawnshop to find it vacant.

"Any brass or metal to donate to the war effort?" he called, not seeing anyone manning the shop.

"Give me a minute," a voice came from the back room.

A few moments later, the manager appeared carrying a half-dozen cases holding various instruments, mainly horns and brass, and gave them to Penbrow. He looked inside the various cases as the manager returned to the storage room. Inside he found trumpets, saxophones, and flutes.

"I might need to make a few trips," Penbrow told the manager.

"Hold on, I got one more."

The manager stepped into the back room, then soon emerged and placed Robert Johnson's guitar case on the counter.

"Good luck on this one. She's locked up tight."

Penbrow tried to force the latch open, but it wouldn't move.

He spent the next hour carrying each instrument to the war effort donation center at the armory. When all the instruments made of metal had been taken in, Penbrow carried the guitar case to the downtown locksmith, a tiny, darkened store, that smelled of cutting oil and shaved metal. Robert placed the guitar case on the counter, and the locksmith, wearing magnifying glasses, came over and looked at the latch mechanism near the handle of the guitar case.

"Rare. Must be diamonds inside."

He stepped to a rusty file cabinet and opened a squeaky drawer. He dug around, clanging keys, then returned with two in hand.

"Whoever put that latch on it didn't want people getting inside."

He inserted the first key but no luck. He inserted the second key and *CLICK*. The latch sprung open.

"There you go, son."

Penbrow lifted the lid, revealing the worn guitar laying inside. He was mesmerized by the six steel strings running from the headstock to the bridge passing over the aged wood. He looked deep inside the sound hole, into the darkness. The locksmith tapped the body of the guitar with his finger.

"Keep the key, kid."

Later that night, Penbrow sat on the porch of his family home cradling the guitar in his lap, as if it were a newborn child and he didn't know how to hold it for fear of breaking it. With his right thumb, he gently strummed the six strings from top to bottom. They were horribly out of tune. He twisted one of the tuning pegs and listened as the pitch changed from high to low then back to high. A smile came across his face.

***

The following morning as the sun was peaking over the tree line, Penbrow hobbled back into town carrying the guitar. He entered the music shop, where a man, a luthier, sat at a workbench working on a violin. He was surrounded by all sorts of tools, chisels, stains, and lacquers. The smell of violin varnish and hide glue filled the room.

"Can you help me?" Penbrow said, placing the case on the counter and opening the top to reveal the guitar as the luthier stepped up to investigate.

"Wow, she's had the hell played out of her." He ran his hand along the strings from headstock to bridge. "Strings haven't been changed in years."

"Don't change them, don't change anything if it isn't broken," Penbrow insisted.

"Okay. How can I help you?"

"I think I'm...*supposed* to play her. Can you teach me?"

"Let's see if she can hold a tune first." The luthier rotated the tuning pegs, tuning each of the strings one by one. He formed a D shape and strummed the strings with is right thumb. The chord was solid and clear and the sustain filled the music store. "Wow, that's nice," the luthier said, nodding. He formed a G chord and strummed.

Penbrow smiled in appreciation as the man played a series of chords, and the guitar responded with perfect tone. "So, she's playable?"

"I tell you what, kid—I'll let you trade this beat up old guitar straight across for one of these brand-new beauties right here," he said, pointing to several shiny new guitars on the wall.

Penbrow reached across and took the guitar from his hands. "This one suits me just fine. When can you teach me to play?"

The man looked at Penbrow from head to toe. "You got all the time in the world, don't you kid?"

"Yes, sir."

***

For the next six months, Penbrow hobbled into Memphis twice a week for guitar lessons. He played incessantly, until his fingers either bled or were swollen to the touch. Once calluses formed, he made fast progress, forming clear chords and learning various strumming patterns. One day, as Penbrow was passing through the lines outside the recruiting office, a colored man stopped Penbrow.

"Hey guitar man, can you play us some blues?"

Penbrow was suddenly nervous, shaken by the sudden stop and request as he felt all eyes turn on him, waiting for his response. He looked down and considered whether to open the guitar case or not.

"I know a few blues songs," Penbrow offered humbly.

Penbrow lifted the lid and removed the guitar. His hands were shaking as he placed the leather strap across his shoulder. He strummed the guitar to check the tuning. He adjusted the G string peg and strummed a clean C chord.

"You know any T-Bone Walker?" a recruit asked.

"I know 'Mean Old World.'"

"Hell, yes!"

"But I don't sing so well yet, so you gotta help me."

Penbrow played the song and soon the colored recruits started dancing to the rhythm. When it came time to sing, the colored recruits, along with several White recruits, began singing passionately. Penbrow shuffled along the sidewalk as the men in line moved closer and closer to the recruit office main door.

When he finished the song, another man, farther back in line, called out to him. "Hey, guitar man, play that same song for us now."

Penbrow obliged, hobbling back up the line then launching straight into the song once again. Ten times he played that same song to the recruits as they moved along. And with each passing time, he became more committed to playing and performing. He needed to learn more songs.

***

Over the next year, Penbrow returned nearly every day, playing songs outside the recruiting office. He sang blues and patriotic songs to patriotic young men volunteering for the war. One afternoon, a stern-looking recruiter in full uniform stepped out of the office.

"Hey kid, you're getting pretty good."

"Thank you, sir."

"Would you be interested in joining the U.S. Navy orchestra? You can entertain the troops."

"The Navy has an orchestra?"

"Come on inside, let's get you signed up," the recruiter insisted.

Penbrow smiled the size of Tennessee.

***

Penbrow was assigned to attend the U.S. Navy School of Music in Norfolk, Virginia for eighteen months. While there, he also learned to play drums. There were several types of bands and orchestras formed, ranging from twelve to sixty-four musicians. Dance band became his preference and passion.

Soon enough, Penbrow was stationed on a destroyer traveling with a Navy orchestra in the South Pacific. They played a daily noon day concert and a short concert every night before the evening movie. on Friday and Saturday nights they played a six-hour dance band configuration.

While playing in a dance band in the main dining hall one night, Penbrow saw Charles McVay III, the captain of the ship, escorted to his VIP table. Throughout the night, Penbrow noticed Captain McVay watching him intently. On a few occasions, he would raise his glass and smile, toasting his performance. Captain McVay began returning regularly to see the band and, every time, he would acknowledge Penbrow with a raised glass and smile.

***

One night, shortly after retiring to bed around midnight, Penbrow was awakened by Captain McVay's secretary who then escorted him and his guitar to the captain's quarters. There, the captain sat in a lounge robe adding sugar cubes to his teacup. His hand trembled as he lifted the cup and sipped it slowly. The room was impeccably neat and tidy, with not a bit of clutter.

"The captain requests you to play a couple of your favorite songs," the secretary politely asked.

Penbrow nodded in agreement as he sat on a footstool and began tuning strings.

"It's the fourth string from the top," Captain McVay advised.

Penbrow smiled, impressed that he knew. "It's the G string. It has a mind of its own."

"Why don't you fix it?"

Penbrow didn't reply. Instead, he strummed the strings and formed a C chord. "Here is one of my favorite songs."

"I asked you a question."

"With respect, sir, some things can't be fixed."

"Perhaps you don't want to fix it because you like the attention it brings you."

"I certainly have other things that bring me much more attention, sir. I'd rather remain anonymous."

Penbrow began finger rolling the strings into a soothing, although sad, cadence. The captain settled as he sat back and placed his hands in his lap. Penbrow began to perform a pleasant ballad. With each passing verse and chorus, the captain seemed to relax more and more. When he lifted his cup to drink more tea, his hand was much steadier, although some trembling was still present. Penbrow smiled as he began to play his next song. With each passing song, the captain became more relaxed, and his eyes grew heavy.

An hour later, the secretary held up his hand. "Thank you, that will be enough."

As Penbrow nodded and stood to leave, the captain stared peacefully into the distance as if he could finally see something he had been searching for. The secretary motioned toward the doorway leading into the main ship. Penbrow stepped outside the captain's quarters and the secretary closed the door, leaving Penbrow standing alone in the cold corridor of the mighty steel ship. It was 0200 hours. He walked back to his bunk in the stern of the ship. When he arrived, all his bunkmates were asleep. He slid the guitar inside the case, locked it, then climbed into bed where he quickly fell asleep.

***

The following night, after playing a full set at the Saturday night dance, Penbrow carried the guitar through the ship corridors on his way back to his sleeping quarters, longing for a good night's rest. As he passed by the infirmary, he saw several wounded and sick men laying in beds.

One man raised his hand, attempting to get the attention of the nurses, who were attending to a man in severe pain. "Please help me!" he called out. Just then, the man looked over and saw Penbrow lurking at the door "Hey, guitar man, can you help me?"

The sight of the wounded men and the cries of pain made Penbrow hesitant to respond.

"I'm shitting my bed here; can you please get me that bed pan?"

Penbrow looked down to see the bed pan full of urine and excrement.

"Fucking hurry up!"

Penbrow set the guitar on the bed and quickly looked under the adjoining beds for a clean bedpan. He found one half full, dumped it quickly into another, then rushed it to the man's bed.

"Put it under me!"

But Penbrow hesitated as he saw the man's missing arm and the bloody bandages across his shoulder and chest.

"Jesus Christ, man," the soldier shouted.

Penbrow pushed the bedpan under the sheet, but he was too late; the man had already shat his bed and was now laying in it.

The soldier kicked the bedpan to the floor and turned away.

"Worthless piece of shit."

Penbrow stood silently, paralyzed with indecision.

"Just take your guitar and get the fuck out!"

Penbrow nodded, knowing that, to these men, he was a worthless piece of shit. Even though he was a cripple himself, and despite his gift of playing guitar and singing songs for the entertainment of the troops or singing to the captain to calm his mind, he and his guitar were worthless.

But he did not go. Instead, Penbrow slowly unbuttoned his jacket, placed it over the guitar, then looked up at the group of wounded men with a determined expression.

Without saying a single word, Penbrow went to work. He took bed pans from each bed, dumped them into the main toilet, then washed them thoroughly clean with soap and water. When that task was complete, he continued his work as the wounded men watched him replace all the soiled sheets with fresh linens. After that, he filled a bucket with warm water and soap and proceeded to give every soldier a sponge bath. Some men tried to refuse his gesture, but Penbrow ignored them and bathed them anyway. One man wept as Penbrow bathed him.

When he had serviced every man in the infirmary, when the bedpans were all cleaned and stacked neatly, when the bloody linens had all been sent to the laundry, Penbrow stood before them again. This time, he saluted them.

"This piece of shit will be back again tomorrow."

One of the doctors began to applaud. Nurses and the men soon joined and added their applause as well. For several moments, Penbrow allowed them to express their gratitude. Penbrow smiled, retrieved the guitar from its case and sat down on the bed.

"Tell me what you want to hear."

"'As time goes by,'" one man replied.

Penbrow nodded as he checked the tuning.

"Soldier, you really don't need to do this," a doctor said politely.

Penbrow smiled as he played the sweet opening to the song. "It would be my pleasure."

Everyone settled, sat on beds, leaned against hatchways, and listened as he began to sing sweetly:

"You must remember this,

A kiss is just a kiss,

A sigh is just a sigh

The fundamental things apply

As time goes by."

A nurse, in a blood-stained uniform, cried.

Penbrow played several more songs until he was too exhausted to sing another. He placed the guitar in the case, secured the latch, then stood to leave. He looked across at the first man he came in to help and nodded respectfully.

"Thank you for inviting me in," he said jokingly.

Penbrow saluted the man, gave a wink of his eye then walked away carrying the guitar. Everyone acknowledged the calm that now permeated the room.

***

That night, July 30, 1945, two Japanese submarine launched torpedoes that struck the warship's hull. The *USS Indianapolis*, carrying a classified payload on passage from San Francisco to Leyte Gulf in the Philippines was quickly sinking into the Pacific Ocean. Panicked soldiers, crew, and musicians threw everything that might serve as a flotation device into the ocean. They threw seat cushions, duffle bags, suitcases, and musical instrument cases overboard and then abandoned ship by jumping into the inky darkness.

Illuminated by the flames of burning spilled diesel, the surviving soldiers grabbed hold of anything that floated. Some donned inflatable life preservers, which made them bob up and down in the troubled seas. Within twelve minutes, the mighty warship, the *USS Indianapolis*, with giant gashes in its hull, took in water then slipped beneath the waves and sank quietly to the ocean floor.

Men began to call out, giving names and their physical condition. Many were in horrible pain; some struggled to stay upright. Two soldiers clung to the guitar, in its locked case. For six hours, the men talked, offered words of encouragement to each other and those around them. When the daylight dawned, and the light illuminated the groups of men who had survived the attack and sinking, the soldiers began to take heart and talk confidently of a quick rescue.

But as quickly as the daylight appeared to give hope, the sharks began to appear. When the first man was attacked and pulled under, screaming and shouting and beating on the shark's head, the men were confused and unsure what was happening. The survivors began huddling together, pulling wounded soldiers into tight groups with the men on the outside facing the sharks defensively with kicking legs. Every time they saw the large dorsal fin of an approaching shark protruding out of the water, the men would rally and kick wildly. What they didn't realize was that the frenzy on the surface may have abated the approaching shark, but it only made the hundreds of sharks below attack aggressively from directly below. The sharks attacked with wild abandon, ripping men's legs off, dragging them under.

Groups quickly disbanded amidst the pools of blood. Those men who swam frantically away were attacked and quickly dragged under. Those that moved slowly, as if already dead, drifted into the open water where the sharks mostly left them alone. Everyone stopped shouting and calling out the position of sharks. It made no difference; there were so many sharks and so much blood and so much fear. Only the cries of those being taken by the sharks could be heard throughout the day. The attacks subsided for an hour or so in the middle of the day, giving hope to the men in the water. But by midafternoon, the sharks returned, and the attacks continued.

The guitar, inside the locked case, heard every cry, every scream of the men being attacked by blood-thirsty sharks. For four days, the wounded men who had survived the initial blast treaded water, waiting to be rescued. And with each passing day, their hopes disappeared. Many cried outwardly, fearing death. At first, men would tell others of their wishes should they die and others survive. They talked about wives and girlfriends, mothers and fathers. But soon, nobody held hope of rescue, and talk about family and friends turned into talk of heaven and hell and what waits for the dead.

By day three, all rations were gone. Some men voluntarily drank seawater, knowing they would become sick and soon die. Some men voluntarily moved into open water and then thrashed about, wanting a shark to attack and take them from their misery.

Four long days in the water later, the *USS Cecil J. Doyle* arrived along with several other rescue boats. The process of hoisting the survivors from the water would take several hours; many men died waiting for their turn to be hoisted form the water, from shark attacks and exposure. In the end, three hundred and sixteen men of the original crew of over one thousand souls were lifted to safety. All others died from exposure, saltwater poisoning, or shark attacks, Eight hundred and seventy-nine lost in total.

The last man in the water was Captain McVay. He clung tightly to the guitar case as the three hundred and fifteen other survivors were lifted skyward, placed on deck, and attended to. Captain McVay showed no sign of fear as he watched each man lifted to safety. In his last minutes in the water, when the lifeline was finally offered to him, he prayed out loud, begging God to keep the sharks at bay, to spare his life. He quickly wrapped the lifeline around his chest and was then hoisted out of the water by soldiers pulling him hand over hand toward safety. Captain McVay clutched the guitar case tightly across his chest. The moment his feet touched the steel deck of the ship, Captain McVay collapsed to his knees and sobbed uncontrollably.

Penbrow Jamison, the patriotic crippled boy who wasn't fit for service because he couldn't storm a hill or fire a rifle, was never accounted for.

He was not among those rescued and none who survived remember seeing him in the water.

But the guitar knew what happened to young Penbrow Jamison. The guitar knew everything.

4

Court-Martialed

Captain McVay looked closely at the blade of his sword-shaped letter opener as he stood at his desk in his personal study. The guitar case, which he had never attempted to pry open, lay on the desk. The study was perfectly organized, adorned with a vast number of books, military medals, awards, and war memorabilia acquired over his years of naval service. One wall was dedicated to the books on war and strategy and included the greatest works of military generals throughout history. Because of the tragedy of the *USS Indianapolis*, Charles McVay would never be considered one of those great leaders in wartime history.

After the rescue and the weeks of recovery in the hospital, Charles McVay had carried the locked guitar by his side every moment, day or night. It was there at his feet when he sat in front of a military tribunal and was court-martialed for hazarding the *USS Indianapolis* by failing to zig-zag. On that fateful day, in his arrogance, having completed the classified mission given him, Captain McVay had thought it unnecessary to use the zig-zag maneuver. He had no idea that Japanese submarines had been silently tracking the mighty warship hoping to attack it for several days. The penalty for a court martial could range from death by firing squad at worst, to reprimands and demotion at best. Captain McVay was sentenced to lose a hundred numbers in his temporary rank of Captain and a hundred numbers in his permanent rank of Commander—a slap on the wrist. Although he was now court-martialed and eight hundred and seventy-nine men had lost their lives due to his poor judgement, Charles continued serving in the Navy. But he would never be considered a great.

Now, Charles slid the blade behind the latch securing the lid of the guitar case, and jerked it forward, causing the latch to snap open reluctantly. He placed his hands on the lid and took a deep breath, then exhaled and lifted it to reveal the guitar inside. It was untouched by seawater, diesel fuel, or the blood of dozens of men, pulled away and torn apart by sharks. How had this guitar, inside a case that didn't appear watertight, survived the tragedy? It didn't seem possible. Nonetheless, there it sat. The life preserver for many men, including Captain McVay, over that five-day nightmare.

Charles lifted the guitar from the case and examined it closely. He looked at the neck, the headstock, the steel strings, and the bridge. The wood body was worn and discolored by the sweat of a thousand performances. He looked inside the sound hole, into the darkness, where all memories were stored and hidden. He placed his ear on the body of the guitar, closed his eyes and listened. He tapped on the side, listening to the echo.

Then, he gently lifted the guitar from the case and held it suspended in air as if he were about to make a holy offering to the gods. He walked slowly to his mantle, where he placed the guitar in pride of place, overlooking his private study, like a tragic trophy. From that day on, Charles dusted it regularly. He kept a daily routine of coffee, a single cigar, and thirty minutes of reflection while staring at the guitar. He could never forget the tragedy aboard the *USS Indianapolis* caused by his lapse in judgement. He had successfully delivered the uranium to power the weapon that killed hundreds of thousands of Japanese citizens in seconds, but he had failed to follow standard wartime evasion procedures. There was a lot to reflect on.

Fifteen year later

Captain McVay sat in his study reading the morning's newspaper. The headline on the front page of the *Los Angeles Times* was "Viet Crisis Grows." As he turned through the pages, he heard a clear and distinct voice.

"Worthless piece of shit," the voice said.

Captain McVay lowered the paper and looked around the room only to find he was alone.

"Hello?"

Now he could hear the familiar sounds of a ship and men moving about, clanging what sounded like bedpans. Following the sound, Captain McVay stood and approached the guitar, then looked into the darkened sound hole.

"Who's there?"

The sounds became louder, deafening, filling the room with a cacophony of reverberations and men's voices along with cries for help. Captain McVay placed his hands over his ears, but the sounds did not go away or dampen. Desperate to stop the noise, he reached out to touch the guitar, and the moment he was about to touch the strings, the sounds quickly disappeared, echoed and the room fell silent. Dead silent.

Over the next several months, Captain McVay heard more voices and other sounds come from inside the guitar. He heard bells, whistles, and the clanging of metal. He heard men breathing heavily, begging for their lives, and soon thereafter, the screams of men being dragged away by sharks.

One night he was awakened by the sound of a dance band playing. Charles scurried into the study, thinking he would see the dance band from the *USS Indianapolis* playing. As he stepped into the room, the music slowly faded away. All he could hear was one man breathing steadily.

***

Over the years, Captain McVay had received many phone calls from upset family members of lost soldiers under his command. He had been threatened with murder on many occasions. Hate letters would accumulate on his desk for months before he'd burn them in a barrel in his garden.

Now, Captain McVay could no longer bare the reminders, the sounds that came from the guitar sitting on his mantel. At the age of seventy, standing alone in his garden outside his open study door, Charles placed his .38 Colt revolver into his mouth, bit down firmly, and jerked the trigger. Nobody knew the torment and guilt that had plagued his life. But the guitar knew his guilt, the guitar knew his torment. The guitar remembered his suicide and held it deeply hidden in its body.

***

For more than twenty years, the guitar had sat alone on that mantle. Not once had it been played while in the possession of Captain Charles McVay. After his suicide, the guitar was removed from the mantel by an inventory management detail. It was placed in a military stockroom facility where it would someday be found and played by a young Black soldier who would never make it past Private First Class.

5

Fly On My Sweet Angel

Sadie blew into a harmonica secured around her neck in a steel-framed holder. She moved up and down the scale, warming up to play. She wore flowers in her hair, beads made of heishi, puka shells, and turquoise around her neck, and her dress fell loosely across her breasts, which became fully exposed as she moved. She was surrounded by thousands of hippies and music lovers who had made the trek from across the country to the Monterey, California fairgrounds to see many of the most popular bands and performers of the day, as well as some brand-new artists performing to a crowd for the first time. More than eight thousand people filled the main stage viewing area, far exceeding the limit given them by the Monterey Fair Grounds fire marshal.

Sadie sat cross-legged on the grass and began strumming her sunflower-painted guitar. There was a large crack across the sound hole. She strummed a C chord and blew the matching note on the harmonica.

"Here's a song I call, 'Forgive me, Daddy.'"

A young man in his twenties, dressed in a crude burlap shirt, bell-bottom jeans, and hand-stitched leather sandals sat on the grass staring back at Sadie. His eyes were glassed over; he was high on LSD.

"I hope he forgives you," he said.

Sadie smiled and began to sing soulfully:

"Little girl, living in a big world.

Ain't got no place to go.

I'm just your little girl, living in a big world.

Got no place to go."

Just then, a woman near the gated entrance lifted a megaphone toward the crowd. "Okay, everybody! Soundcheck is over!"

Everybody quickly gathered their belongings and rushed to the main stage viewing area. As people pushed and shoved forward, Sadie realized she was about to get trampled. She quickly stood, grabbed her pillowcase full of belongings, then wrapped her arms around the guitar. She was only five feet two inches tall and was quickly consumed by the crowd rushing en masse toward the main stage. She moved her feet quickly as she was bumped and pushed along. A large White woman in a Mama Cas-inspired dress body checked Sadie unknowingly, sending Sadie and her guitar falling toward the ground. A tall Black man lunged forward, catching Sadie in his arms. Sadie turned to see who had rescued her.

"Don't worry, I got you!" he exclaimed and smiled broadly.

"Jesus Lord!"

The man lifted Sadie and curled his arm up and around her as she sat on his shoulder, above the crowd. It was a sight to see, Sadie with her curly blonde hair blowing with the flow, her sunflower guitar clutched in her arms, and her rescuer, a mighty Black man carrying her above the chaos toward the main stage. Sadie looked out over the sea of festival-goers: waves of denim, burlap, flowers, long hair, and leather. She smiled at her fellow bell-bottomed hippies as they migrated like a pack of peace-loving lemmings toward the stage of musical wonder soon to appear.

Once settled in the main stage area, no sooner had Sadie found her place near the main stage than the music suddenly began. What she was about to experience would change her life forever. For the next several hours, Sadie listened to performers take the stage and perform songs about peace, love, and stopping the war in Viet Nam. The following day, the performances were even better. Sadie didn't want it to ever end.

***

On Sunday night, the final night of the festival, there was an energy in the crowd like never before. Sadie had already been blown away with performances by Buffalo Springfield, The Who, and The Grateful Dead, and later she would see the Mamas and the Pappas, scheduled for that night.

The announcer came over the microphone. "And now, one of our next acts, one of the hottest bands from England. It's led by American, Jimi Hendrix. And here to introduce him, all the way over from London, is Brian Jones of The Rolling Stones. Ladies and gentlemen, Brian Jones."

Sadie was shocked to see Brian Jones appear and take the microphone at center stage. He smiled as he looked out at the immense crowd.

"I'd like to introduce a very good friend, their first time to your shore. The prettiest performer, the most exciting style I've ever heard, The Jimi Hendrix Experience."

As Brian exited the stage, Jimi Hendrix appeared from the darkness and into the lights. Visually, he was stunning, wearing colorful scarfs and flashy clothes including a pink ruffled shirt. Sadie had never seen so much color on a man. Jimi played the opening riff to a song called 'Killing Floor,' originally recorded by Howlin Wolf in the 1950s. Within thirty seconds of hearing his intense style of play on his colorful upside-down electric guitar, the crowd knew it was about to experience an historic performance. As for Sadie, she was mesmerized by the sounds that Jimi created with his electric guitar using his teeth, his lips, and his fingers. He made a feedback frenzy in the amplifiers that was out of this world and never heard before. With wild abandon, Jimi moved across the stage and played to the crowd. His guitar, his voice, and his artistry were captivating.

When Jimi began playing 'Foxy Lady,' he looked out and saw Sadie staring up at him with a worshipful gaze. He placed his guitar between his legs and moved his right hand along the fretboard in a show of pure sexuality. Sadie became embarrassed as he gestured directly toward her. She lifted her sunflower guitar in front of her face in hopes that Jimi would stop. He just flicked his tongue playfully, smiled, and then moved on with his performance. Sadie eventually lowered her guitar and continued watching him perform. With every song, Sadie fell more and more in love with Jimi.

As Jimi finished playing 'Purple Haze,' a well-dressed man appeared beside Sadie and offered her a drink from a glass bottle.

"What is that?" she yelled out above the deafening speakers.

"Bourbon and Coca-Cola," he shouted back.

Sadie took a quick swig from the bottle and handed it back. Jimi adjusted the knobs on his guitar, creating surreal effects and distorted echoes on his amplifier. He then began strumming the opening chords to his next song and the crowd erupted.

"I can get you backstage if you want," the man next to Sadie offered.

"Excuse me?"

"I can take you backstage so you can meet him!"

But Sadie was too riveted by Jimi to pay the man any more attention. Everything about Jimi came out in that song. Jimi knelt over his guitar and played the neck like his own erection.

The man leaned into Sadie once more and shouted. "I think you should meet him!"

Jimi poured lighter fluid over his guitar and lit a match.

"He's crazy!" she said.

"He's actually a very sweet guy," the man said as Jimi dropped the match on the gas-soaked guitar. It burst into flames. "He'd be very disappointed if he wasn't able to see you."

Sadie watched Jimi smile and warm his hands on the burning guitar as if he were a young boy at a campfire. She saw the magic in him. She saw the playfulness in him. The man offered her a white pill. She opened her mouth and stuck out her tongue. Sadie continued watching as Jimi stood up, lifted the guitar high into the air, and then smashed it again and again onto the stage floor. Sadie's inhibitions quickly drifted away as the effects of that little white pill began to take hold. Jimi continued destroying his guitar. Sadie smiled as Jimi threw smashed-up guitar pieces into the crowd. With that, she too became part of The Jimi Hendrix Experience.

Although most audience members were applauding and cheering Jimi's crazy antics and passionate performance, there were many that were stunned and stared blankly back at Jimi as he turned and walked off stage. This would be a night to remember for everyone in attendance. This would also be the last memory Sadie had of that night as she collapsed into the arms of the man who had given her the pill.

***

When Sadie finally awakened, two days later, she was lying face down on a hotel room bed completely naked. Three other women, also naked, lay asleep on a nearby bed. Jimi was on the couch, partially covered with a silk scarf.

Sadie could see her sunflower-painted guitar propped against the wall. She blinked her eyes, then lifted her head as she reached out as if to take hold of it, but the room began to spin with delirious hallucinations, and she quickly fell back into unconsciousness.

***

Six months after the Monterrey Pop Festival introduced Jimi to the world, Sadie sat at a window seat of Jimi's tour bus, looking out at the darkness as the bus moved along the highway. She pushed her blonde hair from her face, tucking it behind her ears as she stood and walked down the aisle toward the bus driver. Headlights illuminated the broken white line in the center of the highway disappearing beneath the bus.

"Where are we?" she asked innocently.

"Bakersfield."

She nodded.

"Six more hours to San Diego, get some rest."

Sadie turned and walked down the aisle, pushed back the curtain, and walked past two bunks filled with sleeping band members and naked groupies. She opened the door to the private bedroom and stepped inside. Jimi sat bare chested on the bed with the guitar in his lap. Robert Johnson's guitar. Sadie kissed him on the shoulder then curled up in front of him to listen.

"Angel came down from heaven, yesterday," Jimi sang as he strummed the guitar.

"You love that guitar, don't you?"

"She stayed with me just long enough to rescue me," he sang.

"Nice."

"She's my blues muse," Jimi replied.

"You got the blues, Jimi?"

Jimi set the guitar aside and moved over top of Sadie as she lay back and put her hands around his waist.

"Am I your angel?"

Jimi kissed her lips.

"Is that song about me?"

"When it's done, I'll let you know."

Sadie unbuttoned his pants with one hand and pushed them down with her feet as she kissed him and pulled him on top of her. Two hours later, Sadie and Jimi lay asleep on the bed, their naked bodies intertwined, as the tour bus made its way through the night.

***

Seven months later, six groupies, including Sadie, stood outside the tour bus with luggage at their feet. The tour manager walked down the line, handing each girl an envelope filled with cash. When he got to Sadie, he held out two envelopes.

"Jimi told me your arrangement. Are you clear with what Jimi's asking you to do with his guitar?"

"Yes."

He handed Sadie the envelopes and she opened them to find cash and note with a phone number written on it. The word 'London' was written above.

The manager turned and boarded the bus. The driver winked at Sadie knowingly as he reached for the handle and closed the door. A moment later, the bus pulled away, leaving a cloud of diesel smoke. The girls covered their noses and mouths as cabs arrived to take them away. Two of the girls began to sob uncontrollably as they watched Jimi's bus disappear in the distance.

6

The Londoner

Sadie rode in the back of a yellow taxicab looking up at the Hollywood sign on the hill. The two guitar cases sat in the seat beside her. When the taxicab pulled into the Landmark Motor Hotel, Sadie got out while the driver removed the guitars and set them on the sidewalk under the overhang. She checked in to her hotel room, showered, put on fresh clothes, then exited the room carrying Jimi's guitar.

Sadie walked past several hotel room doors before she stopped and knocked on room 105. She could hear chains and latches releasing from inside. She took a step back as the door slowly opened.

"I'm Sadie."

Janis Joplin looked out with bloodshot eyes and disheveled hair.

"Do I know you?"

"Jimi sent me."

Janis looked Sadie up and down. "Right, you're one of his groupies. I can see why he liked you."

"Jimi asked me to bring you his guitar," Sadie offered.

Janis looked at the guitar case. "Why the fuck would Jimi do that?"

"I'm just doing what he asked of me."

Janis opened the door and Sadie was shocked to see the room in complete disarray. It was filthy.

"Maid's day off, come in."

Sadie stepped inside as Janis closed the door and secured all the locks. Used syringes and spent vials of heroin lay on the nightstand nearby. A large glass ash tray held dozens of crushed out cigarette butts. Janis placed the guitar case on the bed and flipped the latch. When she lifted the lid, she looked down to see the well-worn Gibson guitar.

"Why the fuck would Jimi give me this guitar? This was his prize acoustic, makes no fucking sense."

"He said was it was 'your turn.'"

"My turn for what?"

"I don't know."

"Motherfucker was so tight with his instruments. Now he just up and gives it to me?"

"He said, make sure 'little girl blue' gets this guitar."

Janis lifted the guitar from the case and placed it in her lap. She held it close, hugging it.

"Motherfucker," she said softly.

Janis strummed the guitar, changing chords and picking melodies.

"I saw you at Monterrey," Sadie told her.

"He burned his fucking Stratocaster on stage. Now, *that's* the guitar I want," Janis said and started to laugh.

"I thought you were fantastic."

Janis looked at Sadie and her face turned solemn. "I'm fantastic, but you're fucking Jimi?"

"It's complicated."

"Oh, trust me. I know all about complicated. Janis strummed the guitar and hummed a simple melody, "Do you like me?" Janis asked.

"Yes."

"Me or the way I perform?"

Sadie didn't know how to respond and remained silent.

"Spend the night. We'll get to know each other."

Sadie considered her offer for several moments. Janis stopped playing and waited for her response.

"I don't think Jimi would want that," Sadie said finally.

"Do you know Jim Morrison?"

"Of course."

"Of course," Janis said coldly. "Groupies always know."

"But I've never met him."

"I'm working with Paul Rothschild now. He produced the Doors, now he's producing me," Janis said proudly.

"When will your next album come out?"

Janis didn't reply. Instead, she handed the guitar to Sadie then reached for a pack of cigarettes. "I want you to take that guitar back to Jimi and personally shove it up his tight ass!"

As Janis lit the cigarette, Sadie placed the guitar in the case and closed the lid.

"I don't want his fucking charity."

Sadie exited swiftly, leaving Janis sitting alone on the edge of the bed smoking and shaking her head in confusion.

"Fucking Jimi!" Sadie heard her shout as she retreated down the walkway.

***

One week later, Sadie stood in a phone booth in the Soho district of London the receiver to her ear. The phone rang and rang, but nobody picked up. She hung up and dialed the number again, thinking she might have dialed incorrectly. Still, nobody picked up on the other end. Sadie finally dialed the operator.

"Hello, can you tell me who owns this phone number?" Sadie repeated the number.

"I'm sorry, ma'am," said the operator (though to Sadie, her English accent made it sound like 'mum'). "That's a dead number. Hasn't been used in years."

"Fuck," Sadie said under her breath.

"Excuse me, ma'am?"

"By chance would you have the number for Jimi Hendrix?"

"Can you give me the spelling please?"

"Jimi Hendrix, the most famous guitar player in all of London?"

"I'm sorry, ma'am, I don't play guitar and don't know who he is. Can you spell his name?"

Sadie spelled out his name.

"I'm sorry, ma'am. I have no listing."

"It might be unlisted," Sadie offered.

"Well, in that case, I wouldn't be able to verify it for you, ma'am. I'm sorry."

Sadie hung up and rested her forehead against the glass and sighed desperately. She was now completely on her own.

"Fuck. Fuck. Fuck."

Jimi was most definitely in London, and it shouldn't be that hard to find the now ultra-famous Londoner, Jimi Hendrix. Word had spread about his horrible concert performance in Denmark where he'd told the crowd to "Fuck off!" and then walked off stage after only playing a couple of songs. Gossip papers all carried stories about Jimi now spending time recuperating from the pressures of touring. Apparently, he was with Monika Danneman, the Danish figure skater, at her flat in London. Sadie opened the phone booth door and stepped out onto the streets of Soho determined to find Jimi.

Later that night, Sadie walked into the Ship, at 116 Wardour Street in Soho, where many popular band members, groupies, and fans gathered after a performance at the nearby Marquee Club. She figured it would only be a matter of time before she recognized someone familiar with Jimi. After several nights of return visits, Sadie's patience paid off. The Danish figure skater, Monika, walked through the front doors and looked around. Sadie recognized her from tabloid photos and a polaroid that Jimi kept in his tour bus photo collection of girls.

Sadie kept her distance, watching throughout the night as Monika ate dinner and mingled with a few acquaintances. She was praying Jimi would walk through the door and join her but at the end of the night, Monika left all alone. Sadie followed Monika through the streets of

London until she reached her flat at the Samarkand Hotel. She stood outside in the darkness and watched Monika enter the flat, turn on the lights in the living room, then sit alone drinking. Three was no sign of Jimi anywhere. Sadie returned night after night, watching from her darkened vantage point among the hedges.

***

Finally, on September 15, Jimi, appeared. He wore a long London Fog raincoat and flat brimmed hat to conceal his identity as he approached the Samarkand Hotel and proceeded to Monika's flat. Using his own key, he opened the door and quickly closed it behind him. Moments later, he appeared in the living room, placed his raincoat on a rack and removed his hat. His big wild hair stirred emotions inside Sadie that made her cry.

Later that night, after Jimi had gone to bed and the lights were out in the flat, Sadie placed the guitar in front of the flat door, with a note attached to the handle.

The following night, at the Ship, Sadie sat at the end of the bar in her usual spot, watching the front door. At 10 PM, the main door opened, and Jimi appeared carrying the guitar in hand. The host escorted Jimi to a private booth near the back. Sadie waited several minutes, finished her gin and tonic, then approached Jimi's booth. Jimi glanced up to see Sadie staring down at him and shaking her head.

"I told the tour manager you'd find a way," Jimi offered.

"Bastard!"

She sat across the table and nervously folded her hands on the table in front of her. "Did you know that was a bogus number?"

"Yes. I'm sorry." Jimi looked haggard and emotionally disconnected.

"I did what you asked me to do, Jimi. I took it Janis."

"What did she say?"

"Word for word?"

"Sure."

"She said, 'Keep your fucking guitar, I don't need your charity.'"

Jimi remained silent as he fidgeted with his glass of beer.

"Then she told me to take the guitar back to you," Sadie concluded.

"Those were her words?"

"I'm supposed to personally shove it up your tight ass!"

"Wow. I'm sorry I put you in that position, Katie."

Sadie shook her head, disappointed.

"My name is, Sadie—not Katie."

Jimi rubbed his eyes and pushed his hair back "I'm so fucking tired." He took a long drink, nearly finishing the beer in his glass.

"I spent my own money for the ticket to bring back your blues muse," Sadie pointed out.

"I think you should just keep it."

Sadie sat silently considering, confused.

"Please, Sadie—keep the guitar, it's yours now."

"I can't have Jimi, but I can have his favorite blues guitar?"

"It's all I can give."

She looked at the guitar case beside him and considered his offer. Then she asked, "Are you with Monika now?"

"No. I'm just hanging out with her at her flat. I'm seeing this chick from Denmark; her name is Kirsten,"

"Are you *sure* that's her name?" Sadie said coldly.

Jimi slowly picked up his beer and tossed it into Sadie's face. She calmly took a napkin and wiped her face and hair dry.

"I deserved that. You've been nothing but good to me."

"Take the guitar, Sadie—it's your turn now," Jimi insisted.

"Play it one last time for me?"

"Here?"

"Play 'Angel.'"

"Are you sure?"

"Play my song."

Jimi removed the guitar from the case and began to play gently. Sadie began to cry softly as Jimi started to play and sing:

"Angel came down from heaven, yesterday. She stayed with me just long enough to rescue me."

"I love you, Jimi," Sadie said softly.

"And she told me story yesterday, about the sweet love between the moon and deep blue sea."

He fumbled with the chords, forgot lines, then stopped altogether.

"Jimi, you're so tired," Sadie sighed.

"It's your turn now, Angel. I want you to have it."

She smiled through her tears, as her heart was breaking into a hundred pieces. She reached out and touched his arm.

"I fell in love with you the first time I saw you up on that stage, Jimi."

Jimi smiled as he tried to remember. "Monterey?"

Sadie smiled, pleased that he at least remembered that correctly. "I'm going to think about it for a few days, if that's alright with you."

Sadie stood and walked away, leaving Jimi surprised. He watched her walk to the door, open it, and without a glance back, disappear into the night. Jimi sat silently, alone in the darkened booth, considering his actions. He looked over at the guitar resting in the case.

"Blues muse," he muttered to himself.

***

Three days later, on September 17, Sadie walked along the darkened streets toward Monika's flat, arriving just after 11 PM. She had made up her mind that she would take the guitar and go back to California. But when she turned the corner to arrive at the Samarkand Hotel, she saw an ambulance with its lights off parked outside the flat. Paramedics were pushing a gurney with a body beneath a sheet out the main entrance doors to the waiting ambulance. The sheet was partially off, revealing the corpse's head. Sadie could see the hair...Jimi's hair. She began to cry as they loaded him into the ambulance, closed the doors and slowly drove away.

Seeing that nobody was around—no police, no fans, no groupies—Sadie approached the main door and entered the hallway leading to the flat. The door was open, so Sadie stepped inside. The lights were on, the room was in disarray, and the bed was covered in dried vomit. The guitar lay on the couch nearby, the case open on the floor beneath.

Sadie hesitated to move, thinking Jimi somehow might be in the next room and could suddenly appear. But the silence reaffirmed to her that this was the place that Jimi had died. She recalled the first time she had set eyes on Jimi and now, she was the only one besides the medical personnel who had seen him carried away beneath a white sheet.

And then, as if a someone had flipped a switch, Sadie picked up one of Jimi's colorful silk scarfs off the floor near the bathroom, placed it inside the guitar sound hole, then set the guitar inside the case and closed the latch. She rummaged through Jimi's overcoat hanging on the coat rack, removed his wallet, and took several hundred-pound notes from within the folds. She threw the wallet on the bed, picked up the guitar by the handle, and quickly exited the flat through the front door.

Outside, Sadie passed beneath the streetlamps, through the rolling fog, on her way toward the unknown. Now it was her turn.

Nobody knew exactly how Jimi died that night. But the guitar, the 'blues muse'?

It knew everything.

7

Another Piece of My Heart

Sadie stood alone at Janis's motel room door holding the guitar, just like she had done several weeks before. Only this time, when Janis opened the door, they both looked at each other and began to cry. Janis pulled Sadie into the room, closed the door, secured the locks, then reached out and held Sadie in her arms. Sadie, having kept her emotions inside while traveling, closed her eyes and dropped the guitar to her feet.

"Fucking Jimi," Sadie said softly as she sobbed.

That night, Janis and Sadie held each other throughout the night as they cried and talked and eventually fell asleep together.

***

The next day, Sadie, covered by a white linen sheet, was awakened by the sounds of Janis singing in the shower. The guitar sat against the wall as Janis walked into the living area naked and dripping wet.

"Good, you're awake."

"What time is it?"

"Who the fuck cares, now get up. We leave in fifteen minutes."

Janis playfully pulled back the sheet revealing Sadie completely naked.

"Don't make me spank that ass of yours!"

Janis raised her hand to spank her, but Sadie quickly scurried into the bathroom.

"Can you at least throw me a towel?"

Sadie tossed a white towel onto the bedroom floor, then closed the door and locked it.

"Hot water runs out quick!" Janis yelled as she picked up the towel.

Janis and Sadie were a blur of color and their hair blew freely in the wind as Janis's colorful flower-painted convertible Porshe raced down the coast highway toward Malibu.

"How fast are we going?" Sadie shouted.

"Not fast enough!" Janis laughed as she shifted down and accelerated.

Sadie clutched the door handle as they sped past breaking waves and sandy beaches.

At the end of Alice's pier, Janis and Sadie leaned against the white-painted handrail and looked out at the surfers riding the waves and walking the noses of their surfboards. After several minutes of silence, Janis began to laugh at a thought that crossed her mind.

"I hated him so much."

Sadie looked over, wondering if she really meant what she said. "Why?"

"Because he respected me."

Sadie considered her words.

"I don't even respect myself."

Janis took a long drink of whiskey from her flask as Sadie stood quietly.

"I should have been the one to die on that fucking bed, not Jimi," Janis said, tossing the flask into the wave as it curled beneath the pier.

In the recording studio later that night, Sadie sat in the mixing booth behind the mixing engineer, Paul Rothschild the producer, and Jim Morrison as they watched Janis perform on the other side of the glass. She was very emotional, completely intoxicated, and was screaming into the microphone.

"Lord fucking buy me a Mercedes Benz.

My friends all drive Buicks, I must make amends!"

"She's just getting worse. Kill the recording," Paul told the engineer.

"Let me go talk to her," Jim said.

Jim exited the recording booth and passed into the sound stage as Paul muted the sound coming into the recording booth, lit a cigarette, and began pacing the floor. Sadie watched as Jim approached Janis, who was still shouting lyrics into the microphone. As Jim tried to console her, Janis began shouting obscenities at him. But Jim remained calm and opened his arms to embrace her.

Janis would not be consoled. She picked up a microphone stand and threw it across the room. Jim grabbed hold of her from behind and picked her up off the ground as she kicked and screamed at him. She pulled her hair and scratched at her arms as Jim began singing to her.

"What is he saying?" Paul asked.

The engineer unmuted the studio microphone and Jim's soothing voice filled the room.

"Don't ya love her madly? Wanna be her daddy? Don't ya love her face? Don't ya love her as she's walkin' out the door? Like she did one thousand times before."

Janis began to calm herself as she recognized his words.

"All your love. All your love. All your love. All your love."

Janis turned and embraced Jim while he hummed softly to her. Paul watched Sadie shed a tear. Jim looked back into the recording booth and made eye contact with Sadie, then gave her a tender wink.

***

One week later, Sadie sat on a stool on stage at the Whiskey a Go Go playing the guitar and singing. Two men sat at a table reviewing her performance, as a bartender watched from across the room.

"Angel came down from heaven yesterday. She stayed with me just long enough to rescue me. And she told me a story yesterday. About the sweet love between the moon and the deep blue sea. And then she spread her wings high over me. She said fly on my sweet angel. Fly on through the sky. Fly on my sweet angel, forever I'm going to be by your side..."

Sadie stopped playing and looked out at the men. The bartender gave her two thumbs up.

"All right, Sadie," said one of the men. "You'll be the warmup for the main acts. Six to seven PM. Seven covers, one original—that's it. You'll serve drinks the rest of the night."

Sadie sat motionless and numb.

"Sadie," added the other man, "are you good with that?"

"Seven covers, one original. Thank you," she said softly into the microphone.

***

The following morning, Sadie awakened to the sound of a guitar being played. She was in bed, but it wasn't Janis's bed. She got up, put on a man's robe laying across a chair and walked into the next room. Jim Morrison sat naked on the couch playing a guitar.

"Good morning," he said.

Sadie leaned against the doorway and watched him play simple chords and then start to sing:

"Touch me, babe

I am not afraid.

What was that promise that you made?

I'm going to love you

'Til the heavens stop the rain

I'm going to love you

'Til the stars fall from the sky

For you and I."

***

Sadie arrived at the motel by cab later that day and walked quickly to Janis's room. She noticed her flowered Porsche parked sideways, taking up two parking stalls. When Sadie arrived at the room, she found the door partially ajar.

"Janis?" Sadie called out.

Sadie slowly pushed open the door to see Janis laying on the floor, her head wedged between the nightstand and the bed. In one hand she clutched a pack of cigarettes; in the other she clutched twenty-two dollars. Sadie stepped inside and quickly closed the door. She stood quietly for nearly a minute, hoping Janis was just passed out or sleeping. There was a heroin vial nearby on the floor and a needle resting on the nightstand beside an ashtray filled with spent cigarette butts. As Sadie watched Janis's body closely, she realized that Janis was dead.

Sadie saw the guitar resting in the chair across the room. The case was open on the floor nearby.

Sadie knelt beside Janis and pushed the hair from her face. Her eyes were open, her face swollen, and her lips purple. She was clearly dead.

"Little girl, blue."

Sadie began to cry.

8

Camp Malibu Shalom

It was early afternoon with the sun high overhead, hardly a cloud in sight. Sadie sat on a split-log bench next to an empty campfire with the guitar in her lap. Camp kids, ages ten to fourteen, sat on log benches facing Sadie, forming a kind of campfire classroom. They wore handmade name tags on their shirts. Some Jewish boys wore yarmulkes, and the girls were conservatively dressed.

"Welcome and good afternoon," Sadie began with a big smile.

"Good afternoon, Miss Sadie," the kids replied in unison.

"Today is music appreciation class."

Sarah raised her hand.

"My father is Vice President of Capitol Records; may I return to my cabin now?"

"No, Sarah, but thank you for reminding me about your father once again." Sadie strummed a B7 chord. "How many of you have heard of The Beatles?"

Every kid raised their hands.

"Okay, ten bonus points for all of you. What about Jimi Hendrix?"

All the students kept their hands up.

"Elvis Presley?"

Everyone kept their hands up.

"Jefferson Airplane?"

A few hands went down.

"Hank Williams?"

Every hand went down, except for that of Ethan, a quiet kid with curly blonde hair.

"BB King? Otis Redding? Buck Owens?"

Ethan did not raise his eyes to meet Sadie's but kept his hand high with an air of confidence that said, "You can't stump me."

"All right, Ethan, impress me."

"Do you know, McKinley A. Morganfield?"

"Actually no, is he a musician?"

"Yes. His street name is Muddy Waters. Do you know him?"

"I've certainly heard music by Muddy Waters, but that's the first time I've heard his real name."

"Mr. Morganfield was born in 1913 to Berta, who was thirteen years old, some say twelve, in Rolling Fork, Mississippi. But really Jugs Corner. His grandmother was Della, she was thirty-two," Ethan said softly.

Sadie was awestruck. "Class, I think I've just been replaced."

"Ethan is the smartest boy I've ever met," Sarah announced.

"Thank you, Sarah—I think you're smart too," Ethan said, looking up for the first time.

"His dad is a label producer at Capital Records. Ethan has a photographic memory. He pretty much knows the lyrics to every song he's ever heard twice."

Ethan nodded in confirmation but didn't speak.

"Ethan, do you know how to play the guitar?" Sadie asked.

"Yes."

"I was going to play a song by Bob Dylan to the class, do you happen to know 'Tambourine Man'?"

"I know all eight versus."

"Wow, I'm not sure Bob Dylan knows all eight versus."

"He's a very poetic writer. But he's middle of the road on guitar," Ethan added.

"Oh, really—why do you say that?"

"He's more of a troubadour, less a musician. It would be easier if I just show you," Ethan replied, reaching out for the guitar.

"Class, Ethan is about to teach us all, including Bob Dylan, how 'Tambourine Man' should be played."

Ethan cradled the guitar against his chest, then finger picked the strings with amazing precision.

"For me, I would have chosen a lighter approach to the beginning verses."

He played a sweet melody in the key of D for an intro.

"Hey mister Tambourine Man, play a song for me. I'm not sleepy and there is no place I'm going to."

Ethan's voice was eerily identical to Bob Dylan's though his performance was slightly enhanced. Sadie was stunned by how he mimicked Bob Dylan in the way he performed and sang. The camp kids sat mesmerized through all eight versus of 'Tambourine Man.' By the time Ethan played his last chord, Sadie was deeply moved.

"That's how I would have played it," Ethan concluded.

He promptly handed the guitar back to Sadie and started drawing on a notepad.

"Where did you learn to play like that?"

"I had teachers here and there when I was a child. I kind of just teach myself."

"Can you play any songs by Muddy Waters?"

"Of course."

"Will you play one for us right now?"

"No, I'd rather finish my drawing first."

Ethan continued sketching on his notepad as Sadie tuned the guitar.

"That's a nice guitar, by the way. Where'd you get it?" Ethan asked.

"My friend Jimi gave this to me."

"Jimi Hendrix?"

Sadie smiled at his guess.

"Yes, as a matter of fact. Sweet, Jimi Hendrix."

"That's sad what happened to him," Ethan said softly.

Sadie shook her head, trying not to become emotional at the thought of losing Jimi.

"All right, does anyone here know Joni Mitchell?" Sadie asked.

Ethan quickly blurted out:

"They paved paradise and put up a fucking parking lot!"

Camp kids laughed and applauded.

"Exactly! How rude is that?" Sadie replied affectionately.

Sadie played the song on guitar, keeping a close watch on Ethan as he sketched in his notepad while singing along.

Sadie sat at the dinner table with Rabbi Michael later that evening along with and other camp counselors. The mess hall was filled with camp kids eating dinner, playing board games, and teasing one another. Two girls chased a boy who had stolen dinner rolls along the back wall. Rabbi Michael picked at his food like he dreaded the thought of eating another camp dinner.

"Tell me about Ethan Klein," Sadie said.

"Intelligent. Non-compliant. Anti-social," he said.

"Non-compliant in what way?"

"Is he here?"

Sadie looked around the dinner hall and could not see him.

"He eats in his room. French fries and pizza. Cheese only. He goes to school but thinks most of the teachers are idiots. And, as you can see, keeps to himself unless forced to socialize," he finished.

"Today he performed all eight versus of 'Tambourine Man' to the class on my guitar. Did you know he plays perfectly?"

"No. But I'm sure his father would love to hear him play at the talent show. Convince him and you might win some major points with a Capital Records producer!"

With that, Rabbi Michael stood and carried his tray to the kitchen. Sadie looked to the other counselors.

"This is Ethan's last year, so good luck," one of them offered.

Sadie knocked on Ethan's cabin door later that night, carrying the guitar. Ethan opened the door and looked up at her.

"Hello," Ethan said.

"Good evening, Ethan."

"Is something wrong?" Ethan asked.

"No. Everything is fine."

Ethan looked down at the guitar then said, "I finished my drawing; would you like to see it?"

"Sure, I'd love that."

Ethan stepped back to his bed and retrieved his notepad. He held it up for Sadie to see. She was stunned.

"Ethan!"

"Do you like it?"

It was a sketch of Sadie playing guitar and it was incredibly good.

"That's me!"

"Yes, it is. I hope that's okay."

"I had no idea you were drawing me!"

"I think you're very pretty and I like your curly hair."

Sadie was embarrassed but so grateful.

"I showed it to Sarah, and she said you'd love it."

"Sarah was right. I love it."

Ethan gently tore the page from his notebook and handed it to her.

"I signed the bottom of it; that's my signature right there."

Sadie took the picture and held it up to look at it closely. "I'm speechless."

"Why?"

"Nobody has ever done anything like this before for me."

"Well, it's about time, don't you think?" Ethan looked down at the guitar again. "Do you still want me to play a Muddy Waters song for you?"

"I would love that, but first I have a favor to ask."

"What?"

"I feel so guilty now that you did this amazing drawing of me."

"What is the favor?"

"I would love to see you perform at the end of summer talent show."

Ethan's face turned solemn as he considered her ask. "You want me to play 'Tambourine Man' again? The kids in class already heard it."

"No, play something new. Play an original if you have one. I'd just love to see you perform on stage. And Rabbi Micheal thinks your father would love to see you perform as well."

Ethan nodded as he considered her request. "Can I use Jimi's guitar?"

"Jimi would be honored," she replied.

"Any song I choose?"

"Yes. Well, try not to say 'fuck,' Shalom parents are a little uptight about words like that."

"Okay," Ethan said as he reached for the guitar.

"You'll do it?"

"Of course I'll do this for you, Miss Sadie. I love you."

She smiled as she handed him the guitar. "I love you too, Ethan. You're a gift."

"Okay, bye." Ethan stepped back and abruptly closed the door.

"Bring it to class tomorrow," Sadie called out through the door.

Sadie looked at the sketch, smiling in awe, then stepped off the porch and walked to her cabin in the moonlight.

***

Ethan sat cross-legged on his bed with the guitar laying face up in front of him. He had two pencils and was tapping out a beat on a top of the guitar with the eraser ends. He began to hit harder, then faster, changing his rhythm. The percussive sounds amplified through the guitar and filled the room. Suddenly, the door blew open with a mighty gust of wind and swirled dried leaves everywhere. Frightened by the sudden intrusion, Ethan pulled the guitar against his body and retreated to the end of his bed as he looked through the open door into the darkness. He sat silent for several moments, waiting for someone to appear.

"Hello?"

The wind subsided, and the leaves settled onto the floor. The moonlit shadow of a tree outside danced slowly in the doorway, spilling across the cabin room floor.

Ethan stood, cautiously approached the door, and then gently shut it and secured the latch. He returned to bed, picked up the guitar, and placed it in his lap. He sat still, contemplating, considering.

"Oh, you want me to play 'Tambourine Man' by Bob Dylan again? Okay," he said.

Once again, he began: "For me, I would have chosen a lighter approach to the beginning verses."

He played a sweet melody in the key of D for an intro.

"Hey mister Tambourine Man, play a song for me. I'm not sleepy and there is no place I'm going to."

Sounds projecting from inside the guitar began to powerfully fill the room. Ethan's voice rang out in unison with the sounds from within the guitar as if it were amplified from an exact recording. The room transformed into the classroom surrounding the empty campfire earlier that day, with Ethan seated on the split-log bench, singing 'Tambourine Man' to Sadie and the camp kids. He looked down at the guitar as he continued to replay every word and every note precisely as they had been played earlier that day. Ethan watched everything play out exactly as before as he sang the next verse and chorus. He became frightened and confused at the sights and sounds surrounding him. He knew he was in his cabin sitting on his bed, but everything around him was the campfire classroom earlier that day.

Desperate to stop the scene, Ethan struck the guitar firmly across the strings with the palm of his hand and immediately the experience ended. The kids disappeared; Sadie disappeared. Ethan was suddenly transported to his cabin room at night where he sat alone on the bed. He immediately placed the guitar face down on his bed and stood up. For several moments he remained motionless, expecting something to change in the room again.

When he was convinced everything had settled, he asked softly, "What the fuck was that?"

He stepped forward and looked directly into the darkened sound hole.

"Play 'Tambourine Man,'" he instructed, thinking his command would initiate the transformation once again.

But the guitar did not comply with his command. The room did not change. Everything was quiet and still as Ethan stood alone, confused.

But the guitar was not confused.

It knew everything.

9

The Talent Show

Counselors, camp kids, parents, and friends gathered in the main stage area as preparations for the talent show continued. A sound technician checked microphones securely attached to mic stands stationed across the stage.

"Check, one, check, two."

Behind the main stage, camp attendees practiced their various talents and routines. Performers were dressed in colorful costumes and dance attire, except for two girls dressed as mimes. They mimicked and mocked other performers who were warming up. They were quite funny and never broke character.

Sadie stood near the back watching several high-power Hollywood executives and music industry moguls being shown their seats. Ushers positioned them in the VIP seating area where white sheets were placed over split log benches along with padded seat cushions. These VIP guests wore hats and sunglasses, although it was a cloudy afternoon, and sipped fruity drinks with paper umbrellas.

Rabbi Michael stepped to the microphone on center stage.

"Ladies and gentlemen, please find your seats as the Camp Malibu Shalom Talent Show is about to begin."

Sadie scanned the crowd and walked the backstage area looking for Ethan, but he was nowhere to be found. She hurried to Ethan's cabin and knocked on the door.

"Ethan, are you inside?" She knocked loudly on the door once more. "Ethan, it's Counselor Sadie. May I come in?"

She tried turning the door handle, but it was locked. She peered into the window but couldn't see past the curtains. Hearing a rise in volume, from in the main stage area, she sensed the show was about to begin. After one last glance in the window, she turned and rushed back.

"Good afternoon everyone! Welcome to the Fifteenth Annual Camp Malibu Shalom Talent Show!" Rabbi Michael said over the loudspeakers.

Sadie stood at the back of the crowd watching kids take the stage and perform. One kid juggled a football, a basketball, and a tennis ball. When he attempted to juggle two bowling balls, he wasn't strong enough to keep them from falling through his fingers and they crashed onto the stage. Fortunately, he missed his toes and escaped injury. A boy and girl performed the magic box trick with him cutting her in half with a carpenters saw while she lay on a black draped table. Two boys strapped to homemade stilts, making them ten feet tall, danced on stage to circus music. A camp counselor randomly rode a unicycle across the stage in between the acts.

With each passing performer, Sadie became more anxious about whether Ethan would show at his scheduled time. She wanted to see him perform with the guitar that meant so much to her. She wanted him to experience the applause of the parents and visitors.

"All right everybody, next up to perform is our very own singer songwriter and guitar player, Ethan Klein. It's his first time on the big stage, give a warm welcome to Ethan Klein."

Sadie prayed for a miracle as the crowd waited patiently for Ethan to appear. And then, from beyond the stage, among the cabins, Ethan stepped into the open, carrying the guitar across his back. He wore blue bell-bottom jeans, a white ruffle shirt, a leather tassel vest, and a black hat. He was his own version of Bob Dylan, Jimi, and a bit of Malibu surf with his curly blonde hair sticking out from under his hat. He was making a big entrance. Sadie smiled as she saw him approaching the stage. The every-other-day camp kid Ethan was now transformed into a rock star.

"Ethan, the stage is all yours!" Rabbi Michael said as he applauded.

Ethan stepped from behind the curtain and stood at the back of center stage. The audience applauded politely as Rabbi Michael stepped away and walked backstage.

Ethan stared at the shiny microphone, blinking. He bit down on the back of his hand. He wanted desperately to return to his cabin and close the door.

Eleven steps to the microphone, stop, adjust the guitar, adjust the microphone, announce the song, he thought.

Sadie intertwined her fingers on her lap as Ethan walked forward, audibly counting each step as he progressed to the microphone.

"One, two, three, four."

His head was down, hiding his eyes from the audience beneath the brim of his hat.

"Five, six, seven, eight."

As he reached the microphone, he stopped and adjusted the guitar across his body. He placed one hand on the microphone and pulled it to his mouth. He saw his father in the audience smiling up at him. He saw Sadie and he gave her a wink.

"'Malibu Blues,' in A minor," Ethan said assuredly.

He placed his pick on the top string then began to sing. No guitar, just his voice.

"Lord, if I had million dollars, I'd move on down to Malibu," he sang in a soulful, yearning voice.

He began strumming a twelve-bar blues rhythm.

"I said, Lord if I had just one million dollars I'd move on down to Malibu. My feet are so cold here, baby—I don't know what to do!" he sang.

Sadie smiled.

"Jesus just left Chicago, and he moved on down to Malibu. Yes, Jesus just left Chicago, and he moved on down to Malibu. You can see him at Alice's pier, trashing and getting totally tubed!" Ethan continued, singing to perfection.

The audience clapped to the rhythm.

"Lord I'm gonna buy me a surfboard and take me a lesson or two. Yes, I'm gonna buy me a big old surfboard and take me a lesson or two. I'm gonna walk right onto that nose and hang my toes into the blue!" he sang out.

Ethan improvised a solo and Sadie cheered. Others stood and joined her.

The performance was passionate and performed with perfection; all the while, Ethan's feet remained glued to his spot on the stage. Ethan finished 'Malibu Blues' with a surf riff slide. The audience gave him a standing ovation. He looked out at the crowd, genuinely surprised at their reaction to his performance.

Ethan's father was glowing with pride and applauding. He looked toward Sadie and acknowledged her with a nod of appreciation. Sadie smiled and gave a small wave.

Ethan grew uncomfortable with the attention, so he ducked his head toward the audience then turned and walked off stage.

10

Borrow or Steal

Inside his cabin, Ethan sat on his bed cross-legged while Sadie sat on a chair facing him. She was finger-picking a folk song. He watched her picking hand alternate her thumb to the E and A string.

"See how I do that?"

Ethan moved his head with the rhythm of the song. His picking hand moved against his belly. "I've got it," he said impatiently.

Sadie passed him the guitar and Ethan tuned the G string to its correct pitch. "Try half speed at first."

He fumbled, missing the A string and hitting the D. He started again.

"Like a slow train," she said.

"I hear the train coming."

"Folk music. Steady and true," Sadie offered.

"It's rollin' round the bend."

Ethan was doing well.

"Stay there."

"Can I ask you a question, Miss Sadie?"

"Of course."

"Was Jimi Hendrix your boyfriend?"

Sadie hesitated to answer.

"No."

"But you wanted him to be, right?"

"I would have loved that."

"Where did you first meet?"

"The Monterey Pop Festival."

"Where he burned his guitar on stage."

"Yes. It was a crazy night, for sure!"

"Did you go on tour with him?"

"Yes."

"Did you have sex with him? I mean, were you his groupie?"

"Ethan, I'm your camp counselor! There are subjects that I really don't feel comfortable talking about," Sadie replied.

"I know how it works, Sadie. Sex is not a big deal."

"I'm not talking about my sex life with a fourteen-year-old boy," Sadie insisted.

"Why not?"

"Ethan, please."

"I know how the world works. I'm not like other boys my age," he persisted.

"I realize that. Let me think about this for a minute."

Ethan finger picked the guitar, adding embellishments to what Sadie taught him. "Who played this guitar before it belonged to Jimi?"

"He said he found it in a storage room when he was in the army. He borrowed it and never gave it back."

"I'm playing stolen government property," Ethan joked.

"He called it his 'blues muse.' He told me to guard it with my life as we went from show to show."

"It's magic."

"Yes, it is."

"No, I mean it really is magic," Ethan repeated.

"What do you mean, Ethan?"

"Remember when I played 'Tambourine Man' for the class?"

"Yes."

"The next night you brought me the guitar and asked me to play in the talent show. I sat down to play. I just started to play what I played for the class. A few bars into the song, everything in the room suddenly changed. Sounds were coming from inside the guitar like an amplifier. This entire room changed, and I was right back at the campfire classroom. I was playing the song again," he said.

"Music can bring back memories in an instant," Sadie explained.

"This was not a memory. This was real. I was there, at that time. You were here watching me," he said flatly.

"Me?"

"Yes. The sights, the smells, the sounds, the people; nothing was different. We were literally back at that moment," he insisted.

"I don't understand."

"I played the same song. I was back in class with you. I saw myself. I saw you," Ethan added.

Sadie remained quiet, confused and wondering.

"It wouldn't stop. I got really scared. So I hit the strings with my palm and the entire setting shifted. You disappeared, so did the other kids. I was swept back to my room at night, right back to this bed. Just me alone, with this guitar on my lap. Like right now. Only my hands were in front of me, shaking," Ethan concluded.

He was clearly upset as he bit down on the back of his hand.

Sadie touched his leg. "Ethan, listen to me. I've taken some serious drugs and gone places I never thought possible, and it all seemed pretty God damned real to me too. But it wasn't."

Ethan took her hand and squeezed it hard. "What I told you really happened. This guitar is magic."

Sadie sat quietly considering his story.

Ethan began to play, improvising on what Sadie had taught him.

"How old are you, Miss Sadie?"

"I'm already an old woman, I'm twenty-seven."

Ethan nodded as he played. "The same age my mom died."

Sadie remained quiet, not sure how to respond.

"I barely remember her."

"Ethan?"

"Yes."

"I believe you."

"That this guitar is magic?"

"Yes."

"I don't care if you believe me or not. I know what happened."

Ethan continued playing the guitar as Sadie sat quietly and watched his fingers slide up and down the fretboard, improvising, picking notes, strumming; exploring just like she used to watch Jimi do for hours.

"Jimi would have loved to hear you play."

11

Ashes to Ashes

Sadie sat on the bed with the guitar in her lap, strumming, finger picking, searching for inspiration. She rested her chin on the body of the guitar and closed her eyes.

"Jimi."

She continued playing the same pattern for several bars then slowly stopped playing. She opened her eyes and looked around the room. She was done.

Sadie placed the guitar in the case then proceeded to gather and pack her personal belongings into a duffle bag. She cleaned the room, gathering scribbled-on pieces of paper and tossing them into the garbage can. When she finished cleaning, she stood in the middle of the room and looked around at her duffle bag, the guitar case, the neatly made bed, the clean bathroom.

The door rattled as if someone was shaking it. Sadie walked over and opened the door slowly. A gust of wind blew dried leaves and flower petals across the floor.

"How rude," she mused.

Ethan slept peacefully in his cabin room. The bright moon cast a gentle shadow of the trees through the window, dancing slowly throughout the night, sweeping across the wood floor, Ethan's bed, and eventually into the blackness. The sun appeared to rise and cast a golden glow into his room…but it wasn't the sun. A fire alarm suddenly blared over the camp loudspeakers! Ethan sat up quickly and covered his sensitive ears with his hands.

Camp counselors and kids emerged from their cabins as the alarm continued to alert the camp to the emergency. Sadie's cabin was engulfed in flames, leaping skyward with black smoke pouring from the windows. The rafters were glowing red and white hot with ferocious force, warning all to stay away.

Ethan emerged from his cabin holding his hands to his ears. He saw Sadie's cabin engulfed in flames. He grabbed a bucket and filled it with water, but as he ran to the cabin, the heat forced him to stop and cower. He threw the water at the flames, and they vaporized with no effect. As the siren blared, he placed his hands back over his ears and moved quickly away.

"No, Sadie! No!"

There was nothing anyone could do to stop the fire. They watched the flames consume every bit of the cabin until it was reduced to ashes. All anyone could do was stand in horror and cry. Ethan cried throughout the entire ordeal until daylight eventually dawned and counselors were able to console him.

Later that morning, after all the camp kids, counselors, and staff members had traveled down the canyon toward their homes, Rabbi Michael stood alone at Sadie's smoldering, burned out cabin. He was shocked at what he now witnessed in the ashes.

The guitar case had survived the blaze while everything around it was reduced to ashes.

12

The Elders

Rabbi Michael drove down the canyon in a passenger van filled with belongings and supplies from camp. The guitar case sat in the seat behind him. He gave the scorched case a worried glance in the rearview mirror.

When he arrived at the Temple, he brought the Elders into the assembly hall where everyone looked suspiciously at the guitar.

"There is no way that a leather case and wood guitar could have survived that furnace," Rabbi Mark declared, stroking his beard.

Rabbi Michael flipped the latch on the case, and it popped open. As he lifted the lid slowly, a puff of gray smoke seeped out. The guitar lay fully exposed on the table for all to see. It was untouched, not a hint of damage.

He touched his hand to the strings as if feeling for a heartbeat.

"Was anyone upset with her, or angry for some reason?" Rabbi Mark asked.

"I don't think it was intentional," Rabbi Michael replied. "Sadie brought out the best in them; in all of us."

They all considered the miracle before them.

13

Take It Away

Ethan, Rabbi Michael, and Ethan's father, John, sat in the living room. Before them, unopened on the coffee table, lay the guitar case. Ethan was biting the back of his hand nervously.

"I'm not going to play it."

"We don't expect you to, Ethan," John said calmly.

"We just wanted you to see what we found," Rabbi Michael explained.

He reached forward and opened the lid to reveal the perfectly preserved guitar. Ethan stared at it, looking up and down the fretboard, the body, at the sound hole.

"It's a miracle," Rabbi Michael said solemnly.

"There are no miracles. There is only science," Ethan remarked.

Rabbi Micheal looked to John for guidance on what he should say. John shook his head, letting him know he should just remain silent.

"There must be some element in the case that protected it from the heat," Ethan concluded. "A compound that would keep it safe from a four-hundred-sixteen-degree temperature. Maybe a ceramic compound used on the Apollo rockets. We should have the case analyzed so we can know for certain."

"Rabbi Michael wants you to have the guitar," John told his son.

"I believe Sadie would have wanted you to have it, Ethan," Rabbi Michael added.

Ethan looked at the guitar for several moments. "NASA could figure this out, they would know."

"Ethan," Rabbi Michael said gently, "You knew Sadie best. Who would she want to have this guitar?"

Ethan considered his question for several moments before looking up solemnly "Sadie is dead. He reached up and closed the lid onto the guitar and secured the latch "Take it away."

Ethan stood and walked out of the living room. Rabbi Michael turned to John. "Keep it for a few days and think about it," Rabbi Michael told him.

John pulled a wad of twenty-dollar bills from his pocket and discreetly handed them to Rabbi Michael.

"Ethan wants it taken away. Have someone bring the guitar by my office at the label this week. Ethan will come around. I want it to be here for him when he does," John said.

"I can't accept this money, John. It's unnecessary."

"It's for the temple, Rabbi—put it to good use."

Ethan entered his room and sat on the edge of his bed. His emotions mounted as he shook his head in confusion. His mouth began to quiver as tears formed in his eyes.

"I love you, Sadie," he said softly.

14

The Hamburgers

Inside the Troubadour in West Hollywood, John sat at a dimly lit table accompanied by two beautiful women in their twenties. One blonde, the other brunette, both were dressed in white knee-high boots, leather mini-skirts, and glittering tops. They sipped drinks slowly, while John smoked cigarette after cigarette as he watched bands perform on stage. This band, The Hamburgers, were playing 'Light My Fire' by The Doors. The lead singer sang a decent imitation of Jim Morrison but fell far short of his good looks and charisma.

Still, John was assessing The Hamburgers for a possible label offer. He watched each member closely, observing their abilities and looking for elements that would help the label market the band if a deal was struck. The guitar player was good, the bass player kept a good groove, and the drummer was the most entertaining to watch as he smiled while flipping and twirling his sticks. Many bands were hitting the clubs of Los Angeles with regularity, trying to land record label deals. Bands knew that if they could play the Whiskey or the Troubadour on a Saturday night, there would most likely be record label executives gathered at the rear. It was strict policy at the Troubadour that band members were never allowed to approach any of the back tables where VIPs camped out.

The Troubadour was filled with repeat fans who were enthusiastic to support any band who made it to the stage. Bands would typically do one or two covers songs to warm up the crowd, then start playing originals, hoping the crowd would react with equal enthusiasm.

On the table was the set list, which one of the girls had stolen from the stage in between acts. John was bored of the covers and eager to hear the original songs coming shortly. The Hamburgers had t-shirts for sale at the merchandise table with a silk-screened logo of a deranged looking hamburger holding a guitar.

Clark, the lead singer, stepped to the microphone as the band changed their positions on stage. The acoustic guitarist sat on a stool as the bass player stepped back near the drummer.

"Can we turn the lights a little lower, please," he asked.

The house lights dimmed, and the spotlight illuminated Clark. The drummer clicked his sticks marking time for the beginning of a rock ballad entitled, 'Drive Me Crazy.'

After a simple acoustic lead in, Clark began to sing. The two women nodded in approval as they performed a very impressive ballad. After three more songs, John had made his decision.

John sat with the band in the green room later that night and made them the standard first-time recording contract with the label. It was certainly an offer that any smart band would jump on. John and the two women sat and waited for a response from the band.

"No, thank you," Clark said confidently.

"Is there something you didn't like about the offer?"

"It was a good start," Clark replied.

"I thought your songs were really good!" one of the women interjected.

Clark shared a look with the other band members. "We think they're great."

"It's a great offer for first time bands," John pointed out.

"Are you a musician, John?" Clark asked.

"I'm a label producer, Clark. My job is to help bands like yours record their music, tour, and become successful."

"And make a lot of money."

"That's right. For the label and all of you," John said.

"But most of it goes to the label."

"The label funds the entire album and tour. It's an investment in your band."

"Our songs came first; your money came second."

"What are you asking, Clark?"

"I think it should be a fifty-fifty contract."

"With all due respect, there has never been a fifty-fifty contract at any label, let alone Capital."

"Well, the times they are a changing'" Clark said with a grin.

"Even Bob Dylan can't get a fifty-fifty contract," John replied with his own grin.

Clark and the band sat still with nothing more to say. John looked at the two women and they both nodded.

"I wish you all the best, I retract the offer."

They stood to leave.

"Wait, wait!" Clark said.

"We'll never get to fifty-fifty, Clark." John extended his hand. "Best of luck."

"How about a second meeting?" Clark insisted.

"There's no use dragging this on."

"Mr. Klein, please. Take a seat," Clark said calmly.

John remained standing as he pulled his hand back.

"The Hamburgers brought you here to the green, this is our office. How about you return us the same respect, tomorrow afternoon in your office?"

"You want to come to my office at the Capital Tower?"

"I think it only fair that we come see where you do your work," Clark said.

"There will be no fifty-fifty contract."

"There must be some room for negotiations, am I right?"

John was amused at Clark's supposed negotiation tactics. "I'll see what I can do."

"Fantastic!" Clark said, offering his hand to John.

John took Clark's hand. "I'll know if you take another meeting."

"We won't, I swear," Clark committed.

"I'll have my office call you."

"Can the girls stay?" Clark asked with a smile.

John walked away, leaving the band ogling at the women, eager for their response.

"Ladies?" Clark asked.

The women smiled in unison and stepped forward.

15

The Capital Tower

On the ninth floor of the Capital Records building, The Hamburgers stood with John at his office picture window, looking up at the Hollywood sign. John was dressed neatly in a suit with white shirt and tie; the band members looked to be wearing the same clothes they performed in at the Troubadour the night before. John's office was adorned with artist autographed gold records on the walls along with several guitars and other musical instruments with placards beneath each one.

"That's one helluva view, John. I guess you never forget where you are," Clark remarked in awe.

"It would be nice to see the ocean once in a while," John said, taking a long drag on his cigarette.

Toby, the intern, and Camille, John's executive assistant, stood at the credenza preparing coffee, bagels, and donuts.

Clark started checking out the gold records on the walls.

"Impressive, John. You really produced all these records?" Clark asked.

"I contributed."

"Country, rock 'n' roll, blues. Nat King Cole, really?" Clark asked.

"Before my time at the label. He signed it for me."

"I'll bet he's managed by whoever occupies the mother ship office on the thirteenth floor," Clark said.

John crushed his cigarette in the ash tray as Toby began to fill a cup with hot coffee from a pot. As he poured, he heard a sound, like a train whistle, coming from his left. He quickly turned and saw the guitar hanging on the wall. The sound was coming from inside the guitar. Scalding hot coffee spilled across Toby's hand.

"Oh, shit!" he cried out.

He dropped the overflowing cup onto the serving platter and hot coffee splattered everywhere.

"Shit, shit!" Toby exclaimed.

Camille stepped in to block the view from the guests.

"There's some burn ointment in the supply room, behind the door."

"Fuck! I'm so sorry."

"Go!"

Toby ducked out of the room holding his hand as Clark watched him leave.

"I hope he's not in charge of our tour."

"Interns," John said, brushing it aside.

Camille added cream and sugar into a fresh cup of coffee for John and brought it to him.

"Bagels and donuts for everyone," she announced.

The band members converged on the serving platter and made their selections.

In the supply room, Toby applied burn ointment liberally across his blistered red skin. He winced in pain as he wrapped it with white gauze then secured it with medical tape.

Meanwhile, in John's office, everyone sat around the main table with their coffee and pastries as John stood leaning against his desk.

"I was able to get some accommodations. An extra point for the credited writers on each original song. One half percent producing credit and studio time fees for each of you as contributing artists," John offered.

"I'm listening," Clark said.

"You'll each be provided the use of a car and driver during the weeks of the recording sessions."

"That way you know our comings and goings," Clark pointed out.

"We certainly want to know you'll show up to play at the recordings," John said with a smile.

"Severe penalties if we show up late or can't perform," Randy, the drummer said.

"You read the contract."

"Extra points and the cars. There must be a catch," he said.

"The Hamburgers—people love them because they taste good. It's not a good name for a debut album."

Toby entered and stood beside Camille, showing her his professional-looking bandaged hand.

"You've obviously done this before," Clark said to him.

"My dad was a doctor."

Clark returned his attention to John. "How committed is the label to changing the band's name?"

"It's non-negotiable."

"Fuck, John, if you had told us last night that we'd have to change the name of the band, I wouldn't have wasted my fucking time coming here today."

"You needed more; the label needs the freedom to market your music well."

"Freedom or absolute fucking control? I won't do it!"

With that, Clark placed his coffee cup on the serving tray and stood to leave. "Come on guys, we're out of here!"

Nobody moved.

"Randy?" John asked.

Randy looked up at Clark "I always hated the name."

"Are you fucking kidding me? You designed the logo for the t-shirts!"

"We're talking about an album, Clark. A real goddamned album."

"You're fucking killing me, Randy!"

"There's four members of the band, Clark."

"But I write the fucking songs!"

"And you'll get an extra point because of it," John interjected.

"Stay out of this, John!"

"Those in favor of signing a deal today and renaming the band?" Randy asked.

Everyone but Clark quickly raised their hands.

"Fuck you, and you and you! Fuck, fuck, fuck!" Clark ranted as he began walking the room, holding his hand to his head.

Toby smirked at Camille and rolled his eyes.

"And especially, fuck you, intern! You don't even know how to pour coffee!" Clark said, pointing his finger at Toby's face.

"Leave the intern out of this, Clark," John said half-heartedly.

"The Hamburgers got us here today, right here in the Capital Records Tower! The Hamburgers did this, don't you all see that?" Clark insisted.

"Your songs got you here, Clark, *in spite of* the name of the band," John countered.

Clark sat back in the chair and sulked for several moments as everyone waited.

"Hamburgers are a fucking American tradition," he said introspectively.

"There's more coffee if anyone needs a refill," Toby offered.

John shook his head at Toby; poor timing.

Clark looked at John, sizing him up with a steady stare as John held his gaze.

"I'm in."

The band smiled and applauded.

"Welcome to Capital Records, fellas, I'll have contracts drawn up."

"Don't any one of you ask me to eat a hamburger again!" Clark declared to the rest of the band.

Toby smiled at Camille.

In the mix studio, later that afternoon, John sat with two other Capital Records Executive Producers, Sandy and Frank, listening to a mix of 'Silver Wings' by Merl Haggard.

"I don't hear the variations." John said.

"We added trumpets and pumped up the percussion snare. Only a die-hard listening to them side by side would notice," the engineer responded.

"I'm good with that."

"Same here," Sandy replied.

"Approved, next," Frank echoed.

John crushed out his cigarette as the engineer loaded the next reel.

"*The Best of Merle Haggard*, *The Best of Nat King Cole*, they're fucking killing us, guys! Why aren't WE on the Pink Floyd album?" Frank asked.

"Because the has-beens work on the has-been albums, dip shit," Sandy told him.

"I'm no fucking has-been," John insisted.

"Jesus Christ, John, name the last top ten group you produced for the label?" Sandy asked.

John couldn't provide an answer.

"Maybe we should start looking elsewhere," Frank mused.

"I'm not leaving Capital, no way in hell!" John replied.

"Nobody leaves Capital. Capital leaves you," Sandy stated flatly.

Frank gave him the middle finger as 'Oakie from Muskogee' began to play over the studio monitors.

"Here we go, track three for *The Best of Merl Haggard*," the engineer announced.

"God, I hate country music," Sandy muttered.

"Thank you, country music fans everywhere, for paying my fucking mortgage," John said, raising his empty glass.

Sandy and Frank raised their glasses in token.

16

The Intern

Toby stood at the serving area near the guitar, gathering soiled napkins from the spill and putting used coffee cups on the serving tray. He carried it to the coffee table then returned and wiped down the spill area. As he wiped the surface, he heard distant whistles and blowing wind coming from the guitar. He stopped and looked at the guitar. The sound was clearly coming from inside.

Toby set the cleaning rag aside then gently lifted the guitar off the wall.

"Um, excuse me!" Camille cried out.

Toby turned to see Camille lurking in the doorway.

"What are you doing?"

"It's making sounds at me."

"We don't touch things hanging on John's wall!"

Toby placed it across his body.

"Put it back, Toby—right now!"

He strummed it slowly.

"Toby!"

"Ten minutes, that's all!" he begged.

He walked to the couch and sat down. Camille closed the door and looked at her watch.

"Ten minutes, not one second more!"

He placed his bandaged left hand on the neck, wincing from the pain as he formed a D chord and plucked three strings in unison. The guitar produced a warm tone that filled the room. He smiled at Camille then began strumming.

"Holy wood!"

He played an elaborate classical piece of music, which included finger picking, strumming, and harmonics.

"You can play guitar like that, but you can't pour a cup of coffee?"

"Fucking hurts like hell!"

Toby winced with the pain, experimenting with various progressions and styles, as Camille checked her watch. He plucked a harmonic chord and let it ring out. The sustaining note filled the office.

He put his strumming hand across the strings and looked up at Camille. "Wow. This is one helluva guitar."

"Put it back."

Toby reverently placed the guitar back on its perch.

"THIS never happened," Camille warned him.

"THAT guitar does not belong on a fucking wall," Toby shot back.

"Jimi's guitar stays on that fucking wall unless I say so, you got that, intern?" Camille demanded.

"Jimi?"

"Yes, Jimi. That Jimi."

Toby smiled as he looked at the guitar, considering everything he just experienced.

17

Poor White Boy Blues

At the Melrose Recording Studio, John stood at the window of the stage six recording booth and looked out at the band members of the Hamburgers. They were donning headphones and performing a final mic check. The assistant inside the recording stage made a final adjustment to a microphone, then gave a thumbs up to Barry, the mixing engineer seated behind the massive mix console.

"Ready on stage."

"Let's do this. We've got two hours; not two minutes more," John announced. "Okay, fellas, first up is 'If Only.' Give me a thumbs up if you hear the click track."

Each musician responded with a thumbs up.

"Stay on click track, stay on budget," John told them.

Camille and Toby sat in chairs behind John as he lit a cigarette and sat down to supervise the recording.

"Welcome to your first recording session, intern," John said.

Toby nodded nervously to John then smiled at Camille.

"Count us in when you're ready, percussion," Barry said.

"One, two, three, four," the drummer said, clicking his sticks together.

The band played the first bars of the song then Clark stepped to his microphone with his electric guitar.

"It was so many years ago."

The guitar cable popped out of the guitar and fell to the floor, causing horrible feedback in the amp. Everyone pushed their headphones from off their ears to stop the screeching noise.

"Through the strap!" Barry instructed.

The sound assistant fed the cable through the guitar strap then into the pickup and the screeching stopped. Everyone returned their headphones over their ears.

"Percussion, when you're ready."

"One. Two. Three. Four," the drummer said.

Camille watched Toby writing a note on a legal pad. His hand was no longer bandaged. It looked completely normal. She wrote a note on a buck slip as the musicians finished the take with a final drum flourish and guitar strum.

"And cut," Barry said.

"Fucking yes!" the guitar player said proudly.

"Fucking, no," John said flatly.

"Sorry, boys. Stay on that click track. We're going again. Ready percussion."

"One. Two. Three. Four," the drummer counted.

Camille handed Toby the buck slip. It read: *Where are your bandages?*

"The guitar player is killing us," Barry said.

"Fuck," John replied.

Toby wrote a reply then passed the buck slip to Camille.

I think the guitar healed me, Toby had written.

Toby lifted both hands to show her they were identical and healthy. No blisters, no burned skin.

"He's getting worse," Barry said.

"Make the call."

"Fellas, we need to take a ten-minute break, but sit tight, don't leave."

He picked up the phone.

"I need Franco in studio six, Stratocaster, single coils."

Minutes later, the door opened, and Franco entered.

"Here's what we got, Franco."

He cued the song and let the guitar play through. While Franco listened to the song, the assistant in the recording stage brought in a Fender Stratocaster and placed it on a stand beside him. He plugged it in and pulled a chair close by.

"Not bad, okay licks," Franco said.

"Go make it great, Franco," John replied with a smile.

Franco exited and a few moments later, he appeared in the recording studio and sat down with the Stratocaster.

"Hey, John, what the fuck?" Clark yelled.

"Guys, this is Franco. He's here to give you a visual reference just like you were on stage," John replied.

"Okay, fellas, this one will be perfect, I feel it," Barry said.

Franco smiled assuredly at the guitar player.

"Percussion."

"One. Two. Three. Four."

The band began to play, with Franco's guitar clearly dominating the sound in the booth. His performance and timing were flawless. Toby smiled as he watched them perform together. The guitar player clearly believed Franco helped him nail the take as they finished the song and waited for Barry in silence.

"Franco's track for final?"

"As always," John replied.

"Nailed it that time. Moving on," Barry said to the band.

"Fucking yes!" the guitar player shouted as he raised his pick high.

The band members applauded each other as Franco sat quietly waiting for the next song.

Later that day, Toby stood in the archives vault in the basement of the Capital Records Tower with Camille by his side. More than one hundred file cabinets sat beneath rows of interrogation lights dangling overhead. Stacks of unfiled lyric sheets and loose folders lay atop the file cabinets.

"You want me to alphabetize everything in this room?"

"You do know the alphabet song, right, intern?" she joked.

"This could take me weeks."

"Oh, it will take you much longer than that. The last intern quit after two days," Camille smiled.

A rat scurried across the floor and disappeared behind a broken wall.

"I haven't had my rabies shot this year!"

"I'll let you play Jimi's guitar if you do a good job."

Camille exited the vault, leaving Toby alone with the past. He stepped to the nearest first file cabinet and pulled open a drawer.

"Holy shit."

There were stacks of lyrics and music sheets laying loosely in the drawer, not a single file folder or indexing method in place. Toby lifted a song sheet from the drawer and held it under the pulsing light.

"Mississippi John Hurt, 'Avalon Blues,' Avalon, my hometown, always on my mind, Avalon, my hometown," Toby read out loud.

Toby took a file folder and labeled it *M. John Hurt* with a pencil then slid the song sheet inside. He picked up the next song sheet in the file cabinet and held it under the light.

"Nat King Cole, 'I heard you cried last night,'" he read out loud.

He read the lyrics and nodded in approval with each verse he read. He labeled a file folder, *NK Cole*, and placed the lyric sheet inside.

***

A cab pulled up outside the Rubaiyat Cocktail Lounge on Western Avenue where a line of musicians and fans, mostly Black men, were waiting for entry into the evening's show. Toby exited the cab onto the sidewalk and looked at the marquee as he closed the door. Eddie 'Cleanhead' Vinson was playing along with The Blevins Brothers and Ayoka Ayana. The Sunday Jam session was scheduled from 6 PM to 2 AM. Toby walked to the back of the line and waited.

Later that night, Toby stood at a table near the back nursing a bottle of beer as musicians played a full-on jam session on the small stage. The talent was amazing. Every musician on stage was Black and it was pure magic to see how every musician interacted with each other. Everyone got a turn; everyone gave respect to the other. Everyone tried to one-up each other with fierce competition. Toby was riveted by every lick.

A woman serving drinks approached and stood beside Toby.

"Do you play?" she shouted in his ear.

"I play the guitar," he returned.

"How come you never get up there?"

"I'm embarrassed to say."

"Tell me," she insisted.

"I don't own a guitar," he replied.

The woman stared at him blankly as if he was joking.

"White boy like you ain't got no guitar? Bullshit!"

"It's true. It's a long story. When my parents died I had to move and well…"

She held up her hand to stop him. "Not the kind of story I wanna hear."

She walked away leaving Toby completely embarrassed. He sucked air from his empty beer bottle as he returned his attention to the blues being played on stage.

"Poor White boy ain't got no guitar. I said, poor White boy ain't got no guitar. Daddy and Mommy done got killed now I drink from a mason jar."

***

By the end of the week, Toby had managed to sort and index nearly half of the files in the archive. Camille opened several drawers and inspected Toby's work, smiling as she saw how organized things were getting.

"Good, good. You're making progress."

Toby handed her a folder with several songs inside. "I found some pretty good songs. I'd like to try these out on Jimi's guitar."

Camille opened the folder to see the selected songs.

"Maybe you could supervise me while John's in New York."

"On Jimi's guitar?"

"In his office, just like before."

Camille looked over each of the songs, nodding her head as if to say 'yes.' "These are interesting choices."

"I can't believe they haven't been recorded."

"I like what I see."

"Then I can play them, on Jimi's guitar?"

"No."

"I've been working my ass off here! Throw me a bone!"

"I already made plans this weekend and they don't include babysitting you. Maybe next week."

She handed him the folder and walked away. Toby considered what he should do.

***

When the city bus pulled away from the front of the Rubaiyat Cocktail Lounge on Saturday afternoon, Toby stood on the sidewalk with Jimi's guitar case in one hand and the folder of music in his other. He looked up and down the street, half expecting Camille to have somehow discovered his shenanigans and followed him. He took a deep breath and walked past the bouncer and through the lounge door.

Toby sat on stage with three musicians and two singers, all Black. Sitting across from him was Sam, holding a black Gretsch electric guitar. Catrina sat on a stool in front of a microphone as Toby looked at his folder.

"This one is sort of a blues but not quite your traditional twelve-bar."

Sam snatched the music sheet from his hand and showed the musicians beside him.

"Piece of cake," Sam boasted. He started playing an opening blues base pattern as Toby reached out and gently took the sheet back.

"I know that's how it's written, but I don't want to play it that way."

"You don't want us to play it like you wrote it?" Sam asked, confused.

"These aren't my songs. I like the lyrics, but I hear a different arrangement."

Toby handed the lyrics to Catrina for her to read as he began to play Jimi's guitar. He finger picked an opening to the song and within moments of his playing, the other musicians realized Toby was quite good.

"Okay, boy's got chops, keep it going," Sam commented.

Sam joined in and improvised, following Toby's direction. After going through the progression a few times, Catrina moved up to the microphone to take her cue.

Toby nodded as everyone worked in the right direction.

"And this is you," he said to Catrina.

Catrina looked at the lyrics and started to sing.

Her voice was pure and poetic. Her delivery was controlled and full of feeling.

Sam looked at Toby and nodded in approval. "Is that what you heard?"

Toby nodded as he continued playing the guitar.

"We can harmonize on the chorus next time around."

Catrina smiled broadly at Sam as she prepared for the chorus. When she sang out, everyone in the club stopped and looked toward the stage. Something magical was clearly happening. The woman serving drinks—the one who had previously asked Toby about his guitar—smiled and nodded in approval as she watched near the bar.

That night, Toby stood outside the lounge waiting for the bus to arrive. It was two o'clock in the morning and the streets were empty of vehicles. A country squire station wagon pulled from a nearby parking area onto the street and approached Toby. Sam rolled down the passenger window and shook his head.

"You serious?"

"Serious about what?" Toby asked innocently.

"Bus don't run this late. You get beat up if you stand out here."

"Can't get beat up if nobody is around," Toby pointed out.

Catrina rolled down the passenger window. "Put your guitar in the back and get in."

"I gotta get back to Hollywood. Capital Records."

"We'll take you, now get in."

Toby slid his guitar through the back window of the station wagon then bailed inside.

As Sam, Catrina and the other musicians lay their heads back and closed their eyes, Toby snuggled in between guitar cases, closed his eyes too, and fell asleep.

Catrina nudged Toby on the shoulder as the station wagon pulled in front of the Capital Records Tower.

"Hey, guitar man, stop dreaming, we're here."

Toby awakened to see Catrina smiling down at him. "You were talking in your sleep! In French?"

"What did I say?"

"Well, I don't speak French."

Toby climbed through the back window, grabbed the guitar, and stepped to the curb. "Thanks for the ride!"

"Any time," Catrina replied as the station wagon pulled away.

"Tomorrow, don't forget!" Toby called out.

Catrina waved goodbye as they drove into the night.

Toby ran to the back door of the tower and used his key to get inside. After returning the guitar to John's office and hanging it neatly to the wall, Toby made his way to the archives where he fell asleep on a couch stored amongst old office furniture.

The following morning, Camille sat next to Toby organizing the mail at John's desk. Toby was sleepy and having a hard time keeping focused on sorting the mail.

"You played it, didn't you?"

"No."

"Don't lie to me, Toby."

"I might have played it."

"Where?"

"Out."

"Out where?"

"Does it really matter?"

"Toby, you don't understand what's at stake here?"

Toby grabbed hold of her hand and stopped her from sorting mail. "I took two songs from the archives and did a collaboration. I want you to hear them, tonight!"

"Where?'

"The Rubaiyat Lounge on Western."

"That's an all-Black club."

"No, it's not."

"Yes, it is. People get stabbed there all the time."

"I was there, so it can't be all-Black. Come with me, you need to hear us play these songs."

John entered, put his coat on the couch and sat down to do mail.

"I've got fifteen minutes before my next meeting. Intern!"

Toby prepared coffee for John as Camille pushed the stack of correspondence across the desk.

"Finance approvals on top, contract updates in the middle, rejections on the bottom."

Toby adjusted the guitar on the wall to signal Camille. She rolled her eyes as Toby poured coffee and brought it to John.

"Two sugar, one cream, sir."

"Thank you." John sipped from the cup as he read the first invoice.

"That's the session man invoice for the Hamburgers," Camille told him.

"I don't want this on our books. Bill it to Pink Floyd as mix overdub. They've got plenty of budget."

John signed the invoice and handed it to Toby.

"Camille can show you the back door to the Pink Floyd account."

"Creative accounting. Yes, sir."

Toby winked at Camille, mouthed the word 'Tonight,' and strummed his hand. She shook her head, noncommittal.

Later that night, Camille sat at a table in the Rubaiyat Lounge and watched Toby, Sam, and Catrina play the songs Toby was raving about. She was the only White girl in a sea of Black men and women enjoying the music. A server brought her two drinks and pointed to two men at a nearby table smiling at her. She took the drinks and nodded 'Thank you.'

Toby's ensemble group was amazing, and the audience was riveted. Camille was surprised by the lyrics, the arrangement, and especially how well Sam, Toby, and Catrina harmonized and played off each other. It was as if they had been playing together for years; they had a chemistry that was undeniable. When their songs were over, and the audience was applauding and cheering, Toby looked at Camille as he leaned into the microphone.

"Do you see this?"

Camille smiled and nodded.

"Magic," he concluded.

"Yes, magic," she agreed as she raised her beer bottle and toasted them.

18

Dark Side Of The Moon

"John will never approve this!" Camille insisted.

Toby, Catrina, and Sam sat with her in the country squire station wagon at the Capital Records' back entrance. Sam smoked a cigarette.

"He might if he comes to the lounge and sees how people are reacting!" Toby replied.

"Capital doesn't produce Race records, Toby. Plain and simple. We'll have to go somewhere else."

"But we're playing Capital-owned songs."

"I know, that's the problem. We're between a rock and deep shit here."

"What if John didn't know?" Catrina asked innocently.

"He's my boss, he'll expect to know," Camille told her. "If I hide this from him I'll get fired and they'll sue us all."

"What I meant was, what if he didn't know we were Black?"

Everyone looked at Catrina.

"Maybe he hears the song without being able to see us."

"Like we play behind a curtain? I'm not fucking doing that," Sam sneered, taking a drag of a cigarette.

Camille looked up at Toby and smiled.

"Pink Floyd."

Toby shook his head, not knowing what she was referring to.

"Catrina is right," Camille said. "John needs to hear the song without being able to see the trio. Let him hear the songs just like everybody else in the world would. Already recorded, on the radio, so to speak."

Toby smiled when he realized what Camille was saying.

"Fucking Pink Floyd."

***

Two nights later, Camille stood in the mixing booth at Melrose Studios beside Barry. He smiled broadly, holding a work order in his hand.

"Dark Side of the Moon?" he asked.

"Completely confidential," Camille told him.

Toby, Catrina, and Sam sat together on the recording stage as the assistant placed the microphones.

"All right, time is money, are you guys almost ready?" Camille asked.

"Give us two minutes," Toby replied.

"First time in a studio for all three of them?" Barry asked.

"Should I be scared?" Camille replied.

Barry smiled and cued his microphone. "Can you give me some strums and picking please?"

Toby began strumming chords and finger picking.

"Wow. Good tone. Can you strum a B7 and let it sustain?"

Toby gave a thumbs up and nodded.

"You can speak, we hear you."

"Here's B7."

He strummed firmly, letting the sound ring out. Barry tapped his finger on the mixing board, silently counting. "Old wood. Is that his guitar?"

"No, it belonged to Jimi Hendrix."

"Jimi's guitar on a Pink Floyd recording," Barry mused.

Camille looked at the clock on the wall. It was 9.30 PM.

"Give me a mic check, Toby."

"Check, check. *All you need is love. Love is all you need*," he sang, smiling at Camille.

"If that were only true," she said.

"Catrina," Barry instructed.

"Love, love, love," she sang.

"Holy shit, she's got pipes," Barry gushed. "Sam."

"Ain't no Sunshine when she's gone," he sang with passion.

"Another holy shit," Barry said.

The studio assistant gave a thumbs up.

"Bringing in the click track at ninety beats. Take your time and lock in."

"Can I say something?" Camille asked.

"Sure."

She pushed the button and leaned forward. "Intern?"

"Yes, babysitter."

"This might be the last time either of us sees the inside of a studio, so sing these Goddamned songs like they were your last."

Toby smiled at Sam and Catrina then nodded.

"It's all yours, kids." Barry said.

Toby looked at Sam and tapped his foot, counting them in.

Two hours later, Sam, Toby, and Catrina held a harmony on the last few words of the song and let it ring out until dead silence.

Barry leaned into the microphone with a smile on his face. "That's a wrap."

Camille sat in her chair staring out at the studio with her hands clenched under her chin. "How soon can we play this for, John?"

"I'll mix all night if you tell me to. That was good shit."

Camille smiled as she watched Toby hug Sam and Catrina in the studio.

19

The Dreamers

John sat in the mix room listening to the fully mixed songs being played over the studio monitors. Camille and Toby were nearby, watching him intently.

John nodded in approval as the last song finished.

"Those songs came from the Capital Archives?"

"I found them myself."

"Fucking fantastic," he exclaimed.

"That's what I said," Barry added.

"Session players?"

"No. All unsigned artists," Camille replied.

"First time in the studio?"

"All three of them."

"Enough with the suspense here, when do I meet this amazing trio?"

Camille nodded to Toby.

"I'll go get them."

Toby exited the mix room as Camille looked at John. "Promise me you won't freak out."

"Why would I freak out? Those were great songs."

"Just promise me."

Toby entered the recording stage and sat in the chair where he had recorded the songs.

"Are you ready meet the talent?" Toby asked.

"Yes," John replied impatiently.

Toby reached his hands out as Sam and Catrina stepped into view and stood on each side of Toby.

"Are you fucking kidding me?"

"John, I'd like you to meet Catrina on vocals, and Sam on vocals, guitar, and bass. We call ourselves The Dreamers." Toby said proudly.

"Pours one bad cup of coffee. Plays one helluva guitar," Camille added.

John folded his hands across his lap and looked over at Barry. "Capital doesn't do Race records."

"You should see them in front of an audience," Camille offered.

Barry pointed his finger at John. "If anyone can figure out a way, you can."

John nodded in agreement as his mind churned a hundred ways to promote the songs. "Who paid for this?"

"Billed it all to Pink Floyd." Camille confessed.

"Good, good," John said, nodding in agreement.

"Excuse me? We can see you all talking in there." Toby said from the recording stage.

"What do you think, John?" Camille asked.

After several moments of consideration, John looked up. "We'll figure out a way."

Camille leaned into the microphone and said, "The Dreamers, come meet your new executive producer."

20

Prime Time Television

The Dreamers arrived at Studio 41 at CBS Television City in a stretch limousine. A security detail of four men surrounded the car as it pulled to a stop, and they opened the doors. Backlot personnel rushed around them as Toby, Sam, and Catrina stepped out and looked up at the massive rolling stage doors.

"Hello, I'm Jonathan, please follow me," a production assistant called from the opening to the stage.

Sam and Toby took their guitars as they were removed from the trunk of the limo.

As they passed inside, Catrina peered up at the high ceilings overhead to see men and women working along the catwalks, adjusting lights and securing rigging.

"Oh, my God, I'd pass out if I were up there!"

"Heh, yeah," Jonathan replied. "So, we'll do a quick sound check on set then I'll take you to hair and makeup."

He led them across the stage floor toward the studio audience area and main set. It was hard to see details as most of the set lighting was turned off.

"Watch your step," Jonathan warned them and shined his flashlight at the floor where large cables lay neatly strewn.

After passing through several darkened hallways, they finally arrived at a dimly lit set where they would be performing for the show.

"Please set your cases over here, then take your place on stage as you would normally perform. Catrina, I believe you will be front and center here," Jonathan said, pointing to a t-marker on the floor.

Toby and Sam placed their guitar cases on a large table, opened them, and removed their guitars. Technicians appeared and quickly plugged them into the mixing console off-stage as they took their places.

"Do you have a warmup song you can play so we can get levels on everyone?" a sound technician asked.

"'Proud Mary'?" Sam asked Catrina.

"Sure."

"Start whenever you're ready."

Sam played the opening lick and Toby jumped in as the techs quickly adjusted sound volumes and mix settings. Catrina started singing, timidly.

"Don't hold back," the technician said politely.

Catrina began singing with full force.

"Nice, nice," the technician nodded. "Alright everybody, play it strong and hard."

Toby and Sam played with force as the console tech dialed in the mix. After a minute more, the technician held up his hand for each of them to stop.

"Place your guitars in their stands and please exit carefully. When you return to play, DO NOT touch a single knob or tuning peg."

Sam and Toby did as instructed and stepped carefully away.

"Everyone, this is Chet," Jonathan announced.

Chet, wearing a red flannel shirt and suspenders, stood with his arms folded across his belly and chewing gum aggressively.

"I'm head of property," he said abruptly. "Once you finish performing, place the guitars back on stage, right where they are right now. I'll be moving them to the cage area where they will remain under lock and key for the next forty-eight hours. I'm the only one with a key."

He jangled the keys on his hip for effect.

"Once the show is locked, probably Sunday morning sometime, I'll let you know so you can come pick them up. Is that clear?"

"Yes," they replied.

"All right, The Dreamers, follow me."

Jonathan escorted them away. Sam looked back at his guitar and saw Chet, chewing his gum and watching him. Sam nodded and waved politely, but Chet did not respond.

Two hours later, Catrina, Sam and Toby, looking utterly fantastic and nervous as hell, stood in the greenroom waiting for a set call

"National television, holy shit," Toby said.

Seconds later, Jonathan appeared and looked them up and down. Catrina smiled broadly.

"Oh, my God—you're going to kill them!" Jonathan enthused. He tightened Toby's necktie and buttoned Sam's jacket. He looked Catrina head to toe and nodded in approval. "You're perfect."

"Thank you," Catrina returned.

"Is everyone ready?"

Toby offered his hand to Catrina. She took it, then took Sam by his hand.

"The Dreamers, please follow me to your destiny."

"The Dreamers," Catrina sighed.

Jonathan led them from the green room into the hallway. When they arrived on stage minutes later, everyone took their positions as technicians visually checked the instruments. The stage lights suddenly illuminated and blinded them from seeing the audience. Toby held up a hand to block the lights.

The assistant director stood by their dedicated camera and held up his hand to focus their attention. The Dreamers looked over and watched his five extended fingers. The main camera on the adjoining stage was pointed toward the hosts of the show with a red light illuminated on top.

"Cher, did you know we have a very special musical segment for our audience tonight?" Sonny asked.

"Well, of course I do, Sonny. I was at the rehearsal, remember? Are you losing your memory already?"

"No, Cher, I'm not, I was just reading the cue cards placed in front of me," Sonny replied, garnering a laugh from the audience.

"Now I know how to keep you focused. I'll have a set of cue cards made up for our bedroom later tonight," Cher said, winking at the audience.

The audience laughed robustly.

"Debuting right now, their very first song on *The Sonny & Cher Show*, give a warm welcome to The Dreamers," Cher announced to the camera.

The assistant director counted down from three, two, one, as the red light on top of the camera illuminated and he signaled The Dreamers to begin performing.

Toby smiled as he tapped his foot: one, two, three, four. They came in on the first beat perfectly in sync with each other. Catrina smiled as she watched Sam and Toby play the opening to the song with complete confidence, as if they'd played it a hundred times together, because they had. They appeared to be lifelong best friends just jamming in their living room. Sam played a memorable melody lead in as Catrina turned to the camera and started to sing. Not a single waver in her voice, she was crushing it. Her voice was pure and powerful, and every word had meaning.

The audience was riveted by what they were seeing before them, live. With each passing verse and chorus, more members of the audience began moving to the groove. By the time the final verse came around, everyone in the audience had joined in. Toby and Sam were playing in perfect unison as Catrina poured her soul out, pleading with every word, inviting everyone in the audience, and everyone watching at home through the close-up camera affixed to her, to come together, celebrate, heal.

For the final chorus, Toby and Sam stopped playing altogether and they sang in perfect three-part harmony. The audience was stunned as they held hands, cried, and closed their eyes. Just before the last few words, Toby and Sam played their guitars with gentle ease and then let them ring out as they sang in harmony with Catrina's final words. As the audience erupted in applause, the Director cut back to the camera focused on Sonny and Cher.

Cher was crying. She could not speak. She put her hand to her lips to stop them from trembling. Sonny took her hand and looked into the camera.

"Ladies and gentlemen, who would have ever thought that my wife would be speechless. The Dreamers, ladies and gentlemen. They made Cher cry on national television. You'd better get your tickets now, because they're coming to a town near you. That says it all. You have an open invitation to come back any time you like," Sonny concluded, with a glance towards the band.

Cher and Sonny applauded The Dreamers as the audience rose and gave a standing ovation.

"I cannot believe what I just saw and heard," Cher offered, wiping her tears.

"We'll be right back, folks, after these commercials," Sonny said into camera.

When they cut to commercial, Cher approached The Dreamers with outstretched arms. They stood and embraced her in a group hug as Toby held the guitar securely in his hand.

John and Camille stood backstage applauding, taking joy in witnessing something they helped create. Chet stood in the shadows with his hands deep in his pockets, his jaw locked, clearly agitated.

The assistant director broke up the group hug and moved Sonny and Cher back to the main set. Sam and Toby placed their guitars back in the stands as Jonathan waved them in his direction. The Dreamers hugged each other as they walked past Chet and followed Jonathan to their dressing rooms.

"Stay with them, things might heat up fast," John said to Camille as they passed by.

Minutes later, inside the shared dressing room, Catrina, Sam, and Toby were having makeup removed by the staff when the telephone began to ring. Camille, stationed nearby, took a breath and lifted the phone.

"The Dreamers," Camille said, smiling at the trio.

She listened to the voice on the other end.

"Right now? Okay, no problem," she said, then hung up.

"The head of CBS Television wants his picture taken with The Dreamers."

"Oh, shit," Toby replied.

"Let's get them photo-ready!" the head makeup girl announced to the staff.

They converged on The Dreamers like bees swarming a hive. They fixed and applied makeup, curled hair, pressed shirts, and straightened neck ties as fast as possible.

Five minutes later, there was a knock at the dressing room door. The Dreamers, Catrina, Sam, and Toby, stood in front of the lighted mirrors looking fantastic.

"Catrina, big smile. Boys, stay stoic," Camille instructed hastily.

Catrina smiled her full beautiful smile as Toby and Sam attempted stoic.

"Close enough."

She opened the dressing room door to see John standing side by side with Herb Weisman, head of CBS Television, dressed in a snappy suit and wearing a big smile. He greeted each of them, gushed over The Dreamers, complimented them profusely, and posed for dozens of pictures. The photographer moved around the room as if he were floating on air. Flashbulbs popped and dropped for ten minutes until, just as suddenly as they'd arrived, John escorted Herb Weisman out of the dressing room. Camille watched them go and once she was sure they were gone, she closed the door and turned around.

"On Monday, that man will be hanging your pictures on his wall and claiming he was the one that launched your career."

"And we'll let him do that, all the way to the bank!" Sam declared as he lifted a glass of water. "To The Dreamers."

Everyone lifted a nearby glass and toasted. "The Dreamers," they all said in unison.

The Dreamers were escorted through the backstage passage later that night by the security detail.

"Stay close, don't reach out or take anything handed to you. If Elvis wants to take your picture, do not stop!" the lead security guard insisted.

Toby took Catrina's hand as they followed the security detail out the back door and into the wave of fans going crazy. Dozens of cameras flashed as The Dreamers moved in tight formation through the crowd. People jumped up and down, trying to see who they were.

"Is it Sonny and Cher?" one called out.

"It's the musical guests," another fan replied.

"Who are you?" a man shouted.

Nobody replied. A Black woman reached through and grabbed hold of Catrina's wrist and stopped her. Toby held firm to her hand.

"Who are you?" the woman begged.

A security guard took hold of the woman's arm. "Kindly remove your hand, ma'am."

"Who are you?" she repeated

"The Dreamers," the guard told her.

"The Dreamers?" the woman responded warmly.

"Yes, we're The Dreamers," Catrina said sweetly.

"The three of you, just like this?" the woman asked as she looked at Catrina's hand in Toby's.

Before she could answer, security whisked them toward the waiting limousine, and they were pushed inside.

"Are you any good?" the woman shouted after them.

With Toby, Catrina, and Sam secured inside, security closed the doors to the limo and tapped the top of the roof three times.

The limousine pulled away as the guards held the crowd at bay.

Inside the limousine, John and Camille faced The Dreamers.

"Everyone okay?" John asked.

"That was crazy," Toby mused.

"That woman grabbed my arm."

"Did she hurt you?" Camille asked.

"No. She said something I didn't understand."

"What did she say?"

"'The three of you, just like this?'" Catrina said pointing her finger at the trio.

"I was holding her hand," Toby added.

"What did she mean by that?" Catrina wondered.

"It means she's seen a lot of chocolate and a lot of cream, but she's never seen an Oreo cookie," Sam replied happily.

"That's a good thing, right?" Catrina said nervously.

"The answer to that question comes on Sunday night when twelve million viewers see The Dreamers make Cher cry on national television," John replied confidently.

Toby looked at Camille and smiled as everyone settled in for the ride. "Thank you for sending me to the archives with the rats and moldy bread."

She smiled and nodded. "Thank Pink Floyd."

21

The Safari Inn

"Somebody already picked them up," Chet said, matter of fact.

Toby and Sam stood at the check-out counter in the props warehouse late Sunday morning.

"How can that be?" Toby asked.

"I don't know, says here in the log that some guy named Tony and some guy named Stan picked them up two hours ago."

"He's Toby, and I'm Sam. And we're here *now* to pick up our guitars because you called us and told us to come."

"Wasn't me, my shift just started."

"Chet—is this some kind of friendly prank you guys are pulling on us?" Toby enquired with a smile.

"I'm not your friend, and I don't have time for pranks. Log says two guys named Tony and Stan picked up your guitars at 10:32."

"Fuck." Toby said under his breath.

"Oh, and this note was left." Chet handed Toby a folded yellow notepad page. "Good luck, boys."

Chet walked away as Toby looked at the note and then showed it to Sam.

Outside the studio, Sam and Toby climbed inside a cab. Toby pulled out the note and handed it to the driver.

"Safari Inn, Studio City."

"Fucking hell is going on?" Sam said under his breath.

"I can't lose that guitar, Sam. I swore I'd protect it with my life."

An hour later, the cab pulled into the parking lot of the Safari Inn.

"Wait here, we'll be right back."

They exited the cab and walked quickly to the stairs leading to the second floor. Sam pulled a pistol from his waistband and slipped it inside his jacket.

"What the fuck are you doing, Sam?"

"Backup."

When they arrived at room 211, Toby knocked on the door. The door opened and a girl with disheveled hair and wearing a halter top and blue jeans greeted them.

"Are you the musicians?"

"Yes. Who are you?" Sam asked.

"There should be three of you, where's the other one?"

Toby gave Sam a look of concern.

"She's waiting in the cab, now give us our guitars!" Sam insisted.

The girl pushed the hair from her face as she looked down at the cab in the parking lot. "Okay, fine. Your guitars are in the bathtub," she said.

As Toby and Sam entered and crossed the room the girl stepped out, closed the door behind her, then ran down the stairs toward the parking lot.

Confused, Toby and Sam entered the bathroom to see the two guitar cases floating in the bathtub.

"Fucking no!"

Sam pulled them from the water as Toby grabbed towels off the shelf and rushed into the bedroom. They placed the guitar cases on the bed and quickly dried them off. They unlatched the cases and opened the lids.

Minutes later, Toby and Sam lay face down on the floor, unconscious and paralyzed, life ebbing away.

***

At John's house in Malibu, later that night, Ethan celebrated his birthday with many of his friends including some from Camp Malibu Shalom. As kids played 'pass the orange,' balloon games, Twister, and danced to records playing on the stereo, Ethan wore headphones to protect his ears.

The doorbell rang. When John opened it, he saw Camille and Catrina flanked by two police officers. Catrina cried as the officers told John about finding Toby and Sam dead at the Safari Inn. John embraced Catrina and they stood in silent shock.

Ethan watched his father embrace Catrina, while Camille looked over and made eye contact with him. He knew something tragic had happened as he bit down on the back of his hand.

22

Artificial Intelligence

January 11, 2025; 45 Years Later

Ethan, now fifty-nine years old, wearing noise cancelling headphones and a white lab coat, sat in a wheelchair being pushed quickly down the hallway by Yang, an Asian woman, also in a lab coat, and Stanley, a tall scientist with a goatee. Ethan drew on his iPad as Yang talked into her phone.

"Yes, yes—we're on our way!"

She put her phone in her pocket and picked up her pace.

"Fuck, Stanley, this is ridiculous! This meeting should have been in Ethan's calendar?"

"It was! He deleted it. He hates corporate review meetings."

"Today is the debut announcement! Claire will be there."

"Oh, fuck."

Yang veered Ethan around the corner with a power slide and saw that the sprawling glass walled conference room was filled with executive staff. Yang slid to a stop and backed the wheelchair against the wall.

Ethan stood immediately, put his iPad to his side, then led the way into the conference room with Yang and Stanley flanking him. He had no injury or illness that required the wheelchair; he just enjoyed being pushed around in it.

Claire Holland, CEO of Nerva Corp, stood at the head of the conference room. On the big screen behind her was an image of a spinal implant cable with twenty-six nodes extending out, looking much like a giant millipede.

"Today, we pay respect to our first-generation spinal implant, which put this company on the map, and provided critical pain management to hundreds of thousands of patients," she said, then added wryly, "It also paid for every one of your mortgages."

Ethan, Stanley, and Yang proceeded to the back wall and took their seats.

"But here at Nerva, we never rest on our laurels, on our past, or ignore our competition. That is why we have taken pain management to the next level. Take a long hard look at this implant, everyone. Say goodbye to twenty-six inches of braided cable, twenty-six double nodes, and three hours of invasive surgery. Ugh. So 2024," she groaned.

"Unbelievable!" Frank, a senior executive called out.

"Welcome to the future, today. Welcome to Nerva AI," she said with a smile.

A hologram suddenly appeared directly over the conference table of a 3D graphic body showing fifty-two pea-size receptors placed throughout the body, along the spine, the neck, arms and legs, feet and hands. Each receptor was independent of the others; there was no cable connecting any of them.

"Fifty-two fully rechargeable proximity receptors. Each receptor capable of acting as the mother ship should one go down, which they won't. And the cherry on top; minimally invasive scope installation completed in less than one hour with no general anesthesia needed," Claire reported.

Cheers erupted among the executives.

"Why is there no hideous connecting cable? Because every receptor communicates organically with each other through the body."

"Holy shit," Frank gasped.

"Where's the remote control?" an executive asked.

"Fully voice driven. Speak it, it hears it. It also learns and adapts based on activity level, heart rate, oxygen level, outside temperature; over two thousand critical parameters."

"Where does it store all the metadata?" Frank asked.

"Uploaded to the cloud while they sleep."

She changed to a slide showing a modern AI diagram in the cloud.

"This is where Nerva AI shines. Developed in house by Ethan's team of scientists in R&D, our very own, proprietary AI engine processes the data, looks for ways to improve the experience, makes decisions, and then feeds it back to the patient's local receptors," Claire explained.

Everyone applauded Ethan, Stanley, and Yang.

"Ethan, please," Claire said.

Ethan stood along with Yang and Stanley and acknowledged the applause.

"What about FDA approval?"

Ethan quickly sat back down.

"Right now, we're the belle of the ball. March is what I'm told," Claire answered.

"So, this is not 5G or Bluetooth?" Stephanie asked.

"No, this is fully organic."

"What's the cancer risk?"

"I'll let the brains in Research and Development answer that. Ethan, can you give Stephanie an easy way to describe your cell driven communication model?" Claire asked.

Ethan moved his headphones down around his neck.

"Well, it's just human science, at a very deep level, so I'll try to make this simple for you. Every cell in our body has information that it can share or not share with surrounding cells. Nerva AI receptors use the body's natural communication channels to send and receive information. There are hundreds of thousands of paths with which to communicate, so it's nearly instantaneous. There is no cancer risk." Ethan explained.

"Could it suddenly induce a coma or make someone drive off a cliff on their Segway?" Stephanie mused, grinning.

"Joking about the death of the founder of Segway isn't very funny. Conspiracy theorists believe Elon Musk hacked into his Segway and remote controlled him off the cliff."

"It was just a joke, Ethan," Stephanie told him.

"The point is, could this communication model cause any damage to organs or tissue?" Claire asked, a little exasperated.

"No. It's completely natural," Ethan confirmed.

"Certified organic," Claire insisted.

"Not like organic food, but yes, scientifically 'organic.'" With that, Ethan replaced his headphones then returned to sketching on his iPad.

"One more round of applause to research and development. Thank you, guys!" Claire said.

"Can I ask a hypothetical?" Frank asked.

"Yes."

"I'm a sixteen-year-old football player, I get Nerva AI installed while in the Chick-fila line. We're down five with twenty seconds to go in the fourth quarter."

"God, I hate sports analogies," Stephanie interjected.

"*Anyway*," Frank continued, with an annoyed glance at Stephanie, "I get hit in the quads by a linebacker; ready to black out from the pain. I say, 'Block pain in my quads' and Nerva AI grants my wish! I'm back on the field. We score and win the game!"

"Guarantee on the pain blockage. No guarantee on the win," Claire replied.

"You wouldn't need voice control. The receptors will already be on high alert, sensing the intense levels of activity parameters," Yang replied.

"But pain is what triggers the body to heal itself. Are we affecting the healing process here?" Frank asked.

"We don't touch any of that, only perceived pain by the patient," Stanley replied.

"This all seems too good to be true..." Stephanie pointed out.

Ethan removed his headphones and shook his head impatiently. "It's just science, people. We're talking pure algorithms and AI learning. Nothing more, nothing less," Ethan stated.

"Thank you again, Ethan," Claire said.

"Can we stop talking about this now?" Ethan placed his headphones back over his ears as executives around the room shared an amused look of appreciation for Ethan's ability to be bluntly honest—and get away with it!

"Enough for now, thank you, Ethan."

Claire advanced the slide presentation to an earnings dashboard.

"Frank, take us through the pipeline?" Claire asked.

Ethan stood with Yang and Stanley and exited the conference room.

"Let's start with EMEA. As of Midnight Greenwich, we're ahead of projection by 20%," Frank said enthusiastically.

23

On The Spectrum

"You do know how weird this makes you look?" Yang said.

Inside the Research and Development lab, Ethan attached Nerva AI micro-receptors onto a box of Cap'n Crunch cereal with small dabs of super glue. He had already placed two receptors onto a two-liter bottle of Mountain Dew and two more onto the second half of his tuna sandwich sitting nearby.

"I'm not weird, I'm curious. And curiosity, Yang, is how all great science is discovered."

Ethan moved a high-tech wand over the cereal box receptors as energy frequencies began emitting a series of noises over the monitors on the workbench.

Yang cupped her hand to her mouth, mimicking a play-by-play announcer. "One hundred eighty calories per serving. Oat Flour, sugar, lecithin."

Ethan moved the wand over the Mountain Dew bottle.

"Do the Dew! Do it! Don't do it! Do me!"

"Not funny, Yang," Stanley said, flatly.

"This just in, Stanley was born without a sense of humor."

Ethan moved the wand over his tuna sandwich as Stanley cupped his hand over his mouth.

"Mercury poison off the Japanese coastline, does not comply with California Prop 65 cancer warnings!"

Yang looked at him and shook her head. "You stole my bit."

"But did it work?"

"Prop 65 was a nice touch. But cancer is never funny."

Ethan continued to generate intense sporadic sounds across the auditory spectrum as he turned mixing knobs and played with reverb settings.

"Let us know if you find any life out there, boss!" Stanley said as he and Yang exited the kitchen, leaving Ethan alone with his curiosity.

Ethan sat in Claire's office later that afternoon, looking over a document inside a manila folder.

"You've promoted me three times in three years. I still don't understand why. I keep doing the exact same job."

Claire turned to Bella, Director of HR, who was seated nearby.

"The board of directors is very pleased with your work, Ethan. That's why they keep promoting you," Bella explained.

"And another bonus?" Ethan said.

"As CEO, I want to be certain you are happy working here," Claire said calmly.

"Yes, I'm happy to work here."

Ethan took his pen and signed the keyman agreement then handed it to Bella.

Claire smiled and nodded at Bella.

Ethan pointed at a professional soccer jersey hanging framed on the wall beside Claire's desk. "I know that team."

"You know the Hotspurs?"

"I've seen them play on television."

"Maybe we can get you tickets to see an MLS game live?"

"The noise in the stadium would be too much for me. I have Autism, remember?" Ethan said.

"Can I ask you a question, Ethan? About your Autism?" Claire asked.

"Sure, I don't mind educating people."

"What precisely do you hear when you're in the conference room with a large crowd of people? Is it just this big wall of sound coming at you like a tidal wave?"

"No, it's not like that. I hear everything, perfectly clear without distortion. It's hard to pick the conversation I want to follow. My brain processes them all and at some point it shuts me down. That's why headphones help. I can pick and choose who I pay attention to," Ethan replied.

"Fascinating. I did not know that!"

"There's an excellent book called *My Life on the Spectrum* by Herman Maze. I highly recommend it," Ethan offered.

"Thank you, Ethan."

"You're welcome. May I go now?"

"Of course."

"Thank you, Ethan," Bella added.

Ethan stood and smiled.

"Cheers to you both."

"Cheers, Ethan," Bella replied.

"Cheers, Ethan," Claire echoed.

He placed his headphones over his ears as he walked away.

24

Old School Analog

An elevator door opened, and Yang emerged, pushing a rolling cart filled with items covered by a shipping blanket. Waving her security badge, she passed through the double doors and into the research and development lab.

The lab area was extremely high-tech. Plasma monitor displays, glass walls, stainless steel cabinetry, and security cameras were scattered throughout. It looked much like a climate-controlled clean room for computer chip manufacturing.

Yang stopped the cart in front of a long empty workbench area then pulled back the moving blanket to reveal three vintage pieces of scientific equipment: a Heathkit IO-12 Tube Oscilloscope; a Realistic DX 100L Coverage Receiver; and a Sonar Fs-23 Tube Type CB Radio. She lifted the heavy oscilloscope onto the bench with a notable 'ugh' then placed the coverage receiver to the right of the oscilloscope and the sonar CB radio to the left.

"Welcome to the 1950s," Ethan declared.

Yang jumped at the sound of his sudden voice. "God, don't do that, Ethan! You'll make me pee my pants!"

"This is all analog. Where did you find these?" Ethan asked.

"eBay."

"I recognize the tube oscilloscope, what are the others?"

"Realistic coverage receiver, sonar tube CB radio," she replied.

Yang removed the side panel on the oscilloscope to reveal several tubes. She donned a pair of sterile cotton gloves as Ethan looked closely at the equipment.

"Looks untouched."

"I just hope it works."

She reached in and gently grasped the first tube, wiggled and turned, releasing it from its seat. She held it up to the light to see an amber glow inside.

"Can I help?"

"Did you record Cap'n Crunch and Tuna Sandwich yesterday?" Yang asked.

"Yes."

"Excellent. Go back to your office, put both wav files in the shared lab folder, then don't bother me for the rest of the day."

"The entire day?"

"Maybe more."

Ethan walked away as Yang examined another tube. A rainbow of colors passed through the glass as she rotated it against the light.

"You look pretty good for your age."

She cautiously replaced the tube into its original seat and then gently rotated the larger tube from its seat.

"Hello, Pappa Bear."

This tube was darker, more amber, like aged whiskey.

Yang inspected each tube from the oscilloscope, then moved on to examine the coverage receiver and eventually the Sonar CB radio. She cued the microphone.

"Hello, Bandit? Come in, over."

The doors to lab opened and Stanley entered, carrying two bags of Door Dash food.

"Wow, what have you got going on there?"

He set the takeout bags of food on the table.

"Have you ever used one of these before?" Yang asked, referring to the oscilloscope.

"My father was an electronic technician for the Airforce during Vietnam. I probably watched more oscilloscope than television."

"Fantastic. Consider yourself drafted."

"What are you trying to do?"

"Nerva receptors communicate organically in the body; we've already figured that one out. Now, Ethan the 'boy-wonder,' thinks tuna sandwiches and boxes of cereal communicate in similar ways, otherwise he wouldn't be recording their output," Yang offered.

"I'm listening."

"Nothing in the body is digital, right? We are entirely analog. Tuna sandwiches are analog, Crunch berries are analog. I figured we get us a bunch of old analog shit and see what we can discover."

"This will lead us nowhere fast."

Ignoring that, Yang replied, "Get your shit hooked up, and I'll get Ethan's energy readings."

Stanley pulled a chair in front of the oscilloscope as Yang opened the shared lab folder on her computer nearby.

"Get me a pen and a fresh logbook," Stanley said as he sat down.

Yang retrieved a logbook and pen from a nearby table. She wrote *Curiosity kills cats* at the top of the page, underlined it twice, then handed it to Stanley who nodded and smiled.

25

Channel Islands Institute

An elderly man sat alone at a game table, wearing a long nightshirt, his legs and feet bare below the knees. He was eighty-five years old. A chessboard sat before him, the pieces in various spots, some to the side, already captured. A nurse approached pushing a cart with medication cups for patients.

"It's your move," she called out as she touched his shoulder.

He nodded slowly as he lifted his pointer finger; it trembled terribly. He lowered his hand toward the knight and quickly grabbed it. He moved slowly, shakily, hovering his hand over the desired spot on the chessboard then slowly opened his fingers. The black knight rolled from his fingers and tumbled to the board. It landed, twirled a full turn on its base, then stopped upright. He nodded knowingly, smiled ever so slightly, then mouthed 'Checkmate.'

He lowered his shaking hand into his lap, took a deep breath in, then slowly closed his eyes. After several moments, he exhaled ever so slowly.

***

Two days later, John was hydro-cremated and his ashes scattered into the clouds by a small airplane flying over the Ventura Harbor.

Several days later, Ethan stood looking down at a four-foot square pallet package resting on the Nerva loading dock wrapped in clear cellophane. The label read. *Attention: Ethan the Mad Scientist From: John "Apple Pie."* Tears began to well in his eyes.

"'Apple Pie,' is that his nick name?" Bella asked.

"No," Ethan told her, "it was our secret code, so we'd know it was real."

"When was the last time you saw him?"

"Six years, four months, two weeks, and eighteen hours ago. Now I can stop counting."

"I can have shipping bring this up to your lab this evening if you like," Bella offered sincerely.

"Thank you." He turned and walked toward the elevators.

"May I check in with you later?"

"It's important that you stay connected with me for the first few weeks following a tragic event in my life," Ethan said as if reading from the HR handbook.

Bella smiled as Ethan reached the elevator and pressed the call button.

"The Mad Scientist," he said quietly.

And then he smiled.

26

Magic Swirling Ship

That evening, when Yang and Stanley had gone home for the night, Ethan cut through the straps secured around the packing pallet box with a pair of scissors. He removed the lid as the straps fell to the floor then pulled out sheet after sheet of bubble wrap as if there would be no end to it. Finally, he pulled the last piece out and looked inside. He stood silent, shocked to see something he never imagined he would ever see again.

It was Jimi's guitar case, a key taped to the handle, surrounded by dozens of framed pictures of his father with famous musicians and his signed gold records. Ethan's heart began beating fast as so many memories flooded over him. He wasn't sure who all the musicians were in the pictures, but many of them were holding the guitar, with John standing alongside them, pointing to the fretboard.

Ethan placed the case on the workbench near Yang's vintage electronics then unlocked it and slowly lifted the lid. The guitar lay inside; it was as if no time had passed since he played it at camp. It looked exactly as he remembered it. He lifted it gently from the case and set the guitar on a pad near the oscilloscope.

The corner of a piece of paper stuck out from behind the velvet fabric lining in the case. The lining folded back as he pulled on it to reveal the sketch that he had done of Sadie. Ethan smiled and shook his head. Somehow, it had survived over the years, hidden in the lining untouched by any other musician. Or, Ethan wondered, perhaps John had kept the drawing since camp then placed it in the case before he died at the Institute. Either way, Ethan was happy to see Sadie again.

He propped the sketch inside the case so he could see Sadie as he sat down, picked up the guitar, and placed his hands in position to play. He looked at Sadie and then took a deep breath.

He began to play.

"Take me on a trip upon your magic swirling ship. My senses have been stripped. My toes too numb to step. Wait only for my bootheels to be wandering. I'm ready to go anywhere, I'm ready for to fade. Into my own parade. Cast your dancing spells my way. I'm ready to go under it," he sang out.

Ethan looked longingly at Sadie as he rested his chin on the guitar. It was the happiest he had been in many years. He closed his eyes and remembered.

***

The next day, Yang stood in the lab looking at the guitar resting on the pad in front of the oscilloscope, receptors placed across its body, neck and headstock. A note lay across the body with the words *Good luck!* penned by Ethan.

Yang hovered over each receptor with an activation wand, triggering a notable *beep-beep* and LED lights turning from red to green. She activated all fifty-two receptors, and they began flashing in unison, cycling from red, to green, to blue, and then remaining on a pulsing soft white.

A 3D laser holographic image illuminated over top the main workbench matching the shape of the guitar. It began rendering a wireframe of the guitar body along with the glowing receptors. Yang reached into the hologram and rotated the image. Tiny blue lines began to appear representing the paths that each receptor communicated with the other receptors. Sections turned from wireframe to wallpaper and then finally the actual skin tones of the wood itself began to display. She cycled through the display modes by touching the holographic surface of the guitar.

Yang turned on the oscilloscope then moved the wand reader over each of the receptors. The oscilloscope screen jumped to life with intense patterns.

"Stanley!" Yang called out.

A moment later, Stanley appeared through the doors and approached her. "What have we got?" When Yang didn't answer, he looked at the holographic guitar image and the actual guitar laying on the bench. "What is all this energy?"

Yang held the wand over the bridge of the guitar and the scope went crazy. "It keeps changing."

Stanley adjusted the knobs on the scope as Yang moved the wand to the nut on the fretboard. A completely new set of waves appeared on the scope.

"We're recording all of this, right?" Stanley asked.

"Yes."

"Where did this guitar come from?"

Yang pointed to the packing box and scattered bubble wrap at the far end of the lab. "You need to watch the video from last night," Yang told him.

"Now?"

"Yes!"

Stanley sat down and opened the recording session from the previous night.

In fast forward, Ethan could be seen clearly removing the guitar from the packing box, placing it on the counter, then removing it and starting to play. As he sat down and played, Stanley pushed *normal speed play*.

"Take me on a trip upon your magic swirling ship. My senses have been stripped. My toes too numb to step. Wait only for my bootheels to be wandering."

"Holy shit, the boss can play Dylan perfectly!"

"I'm ready to go anywhere, I'm ready for to fade. Into my own parade. Cast your dancing spells my way. I'm ready to go under it,"

When Ethan finished singing, as he sat and looked at Sadie's sketch, Yang stopped the video and zoomed in to a close shot of Ethan's face and the sketch.

"Who is that?" Stanley asked.

"I don't know, but I know love when I see it."

"Ethan has a girlfriend? No way," Stanley remarked.

"A woman knows these things. Don't you dare say word about this, do you understand?"

"But I want to know who she is."

"Stanley!"

"Okay, I won't say word. But she's gorgeous."

Yang zoomed in to a closeup of the sketch. "I think she's from his past. And that looks like Ethan's signature."

"The mystery girl."

27

FDA Approved

Claire and the Nerva contingency of executives were being led through the glass ceiling hallways of the FDA by Charlie Smith, Director of Medical Device Compliance. As he walked, he pointed out the unique architectural design and modern structure of the building; there were vast solar panels neatly designed into almost every sun-facing surface. Ethan remained near the back of the group, wearing his headphones.

In the state-of-the-art review board room, ten FDA officials sat at a long glass table with their names appearing in glass holographic plaques in front of them.

"The FDA would like to know Nerva's commitment on sustainability and DEI," Charlie Smith stated.

Claire looked over at Bryan, her Sustainability Officer, and nodded.

"Nerva has offices in twelve countries," Bryan began, "and we face very strict CO_2 emission mandates in some places, and not so strict in others. We publish our sustainability report and reduction plan every year. Although we are not net neutral, we strive for that. Regarding DEI, we are proud to fly every color."

"In order to achieve net negative, is your company able to commit to purchasing carbon offsets as part of your strategy?" Charlie queried.

"Net *negative*?" Bryan asked.

"The FDA is committed to being fully sustainable. Are you?" Charlie shot back aggressively, the underlying threat being that he would hold back final FDA approval on Nerva AI.

Claire looked at Bryan and gave a subtle nod of her head.

"Nerva is absolutely committed," Bryan replied.

On the flight from Chicago back to the West Coast, Ethan sat against the window in first class, strumming his fingers on the tray table. Claire reached over and touched his hand for him to stop. Ethan removed his headphones and looked over at Claire.

"How do they get away with demanding we buy their stupid carbon fund?"

"It's called situational power, Ethan. They know if they give FDA approval on Nerva AI, we're going to make a lot of money. It's all part of their little global science project."

"It's not science."

"Nerva AI solves the human problem with pain management, the US Government looks good by solving the global problem, real or otherwise. It's not a fight we want to enter."

"Models are not science," Ethan insisted.

"Ethan, Nerva AI just got FDA approval. Final FDA approval, Ethan. You created that! It's not a model, it's not a theory, its Goddamned solid science."

"Fucking right it's solid science."

The airplane suddenly jolted from turbulence for a few seconds. Claire grasped Ethan's hand and held it tight.

"Ladies and gentlemen, please fasten your seatbelts," the pilot announced.

Claire let go of Ethan's hand and returned to working on a spreadsheet "Do you know our total cost of manufacturing Nerva AI receptors for one patient?"

"Well, there's the high-grade alloys, silicons, and lithium batteries…"

"Total cost. Take a guess."

"Five thousand dollars," Ethan offered.

"Not even close."

"How much?"

"The cost of an iPhone, the cheap one," Claire said, smiling.

"Then why are we charging so much to the patient?"

"Parts are cheap. Your AI technology platform costs a fortune to build and maintain. Whatever you're doing down there in the Research lab is expensive," Claire pointed out.

"Come down some time, I'll show you exactly what we do—you won't be impressed," Ethan joked back.

"Why do you say that?"

"I currently have receptors doing analysis on my tuna fish sandwich," he said seriously.

Claire laughed just as the airplane jolted severely; a passenger screamed behind them and Claire took Ethan's hand again.

"I hate the continental divide!"

Ethan looked out the window calmly.

"Doesn't this scare you?"

"No. Based on decades of good data, the chance of this airplane falling out of the sky and crashing into Mount Elbert is ten million to one."

"Mount Elbert?"

"It's the highest peak in Colorado, standing at fourteen thousand, four hundred and forty-four feet."

"Tell that to the lady in economy, I'm sure she'll calm right down," Claire replied.

***

Ethan stood in the lab with Stanley and Yang the following day. He touched the hologram, and the guitar turned to wireframe, showing the inner structure of the guitar.

"Six ribs, three cross braces. And this little bridge support. Fascinating."

He rotated the hologram and examined the wireframe of the neck and the fret wires that glowed an amber color.

"Twenty-four frets, mathematically placed."

He rotated the head stock, making it twice the normal size. Each of the metal tuning pegs could be seen secured in place with a nut on the back. The gears were clearly displayed. Ethan expanded the G string nut and saw a chink in the gear's metal.

"That's why it falls out of tune. Are we recording this?"

"We've got video and audio recording full time," Yang replied.

"What happened when you activated all the receptors?"

Yang turned to the corresponding page in the logbook. "Each receptor initiated, notable beeps, normal LED cycle went from red, then green to eventually white without fail on all receptors."

"Were there any more dominant?"

"Even distribution of all communication across all receptors. Colors are uniform and illumination clear."

"No hi-jackers?"

"None. They all played fair."

Ethan reduced the hologram to its normal size and the normal skin of the guitar rendered over the wireframe. The receptor nodes were glowing blue and steadily pulsing.

"Glowing like the metal on the edge of a knife."

"What does that mean?" Yang asked.

"Meatloaf, 'Bat out of Hell.'"

Stanley looked at Yang and shrugged his shoulders.

"Is that something you want me to put in the logbook?"

"No."

Ethan looked at the AI progress display, which was blinking *Building AI Base Language*.

"When will we start seeing AI progress?" Ethan asked.

"It's been fully provisioned," Yang replied, "but it will be a couple more days."

"How much data is in our AI base language so far?"

"About six hundred thousand terabytes."

"These are the data feeds?" Ethan asked, stepping toward the data wall.

"Fifty-two receptors converge here, normalize here, parsed into the data lake here," Yang answered, pointing at the display wall graphics.

"Six hundred terabytes?"

"No, boss; six hundred THOUSAND terabytes of data so far," Stanley corrected him.

"How can something like this old guitar contain that much data?"

"I don't know, and she's not showing any signs of slowing down."

"Is it looping, maybe creating redundant data?" Ethan asked.

"No, I made sure we bled any redundancy out before feeding the lake."

Ethan stood silently, reading the data feeds, looking at the hologram.

"So, boss. I have a question…" Stanley began.

"Yes."

Yang shot a look to Stanley, reminding him about not bringing up the picture of Sadie.

"Where the hell did you learn to play guitar and sing like Bob Dylan?"

Ethan smiled.

"You sound just like him!"

"My father was a record label producer. I met Bob Dylan at a party when I was ten years old," Ethan explained.

"No fucking way!"

"He told me to stop smoking cigarettes."

"You smoked cigarettes when you were *ten*?"

"It was a candy cigarette. I used to mimic musicians at parties for fun. I could mimic most anyone. My father paid me ten dollars if I really nailed someone perfectly. He called me his little street monkey."

"Well, you sing a pretty mean Bob Dylan, little street monkey," Stanley quipped, winking at Yang.

Yang narrowed her eyes back at him.

28

Perfect Pitch

With the guitar receptors glowing steadily on the hologram and a microphone placed directly over the sound hole, Ethan watched the oscilloscope screen as he plucked the G string. The screen responded with a four hundred and forty kilohertz wave form then slowly died as the sound faded away. He plucked the B string, and a three hundred and thirty kilohertz wave form appeared. When each string was perfectly tuned, Ethan took the guitar in his arms then sat down to play.

"Where can we go today?"

Ethan played several chords, and the holographic guitar jumped to life and sparkled with activity between the receptors.

"Okay, I think you like this."

He placed his hand over the strings to kill all sounds and the holographic guitar settled to a slow pulsing, like a heartbeat.

Ethan looked at the sketch of Sadie as he considered what to play. After a few moments, he smiled sweetly.

"I would have chosen a lighter approach to the beginning verses."

He played the memorable sweet melody in the key of D.

"Hey mister Tambourine Man, play a song for me. I'm not sleepy and there is no place I'm going to. Hey mister Tambourine Man..." Ethan sang.

Suddenly, the room memory warped as it did so many years ago, to the exact time when Ethan was singing the song to Sadie and the other camp kids.

Ethan was now back at camp, playing and singing the song. And although he was performing the song in the past when he was much younger, it was his current image as an older man that he saw playing and singing to the kids and Sadie. Ethan remained calm and observed carefully as he continued singing all eight verses of the song.

Ethan was mesmerized by what he saw; it was like a literal trip down memory lane. He took it all in, without any fear. Sadie was there. She was overwhelmed with what she heard from Ethan's performance. After eight verses were completed, Ethan finished the song and held his gaze on Sadie. She was crying.

"Please don't cry," he said to Sadie.

The moment he spoke the words, the room shifted and Ethan warped back to present day inside the lab. Yang stood in front of him, deeply concerned.

"Ethan, can you hear me? Ethan are you there?" Yang demanded.

The holographic guitar was lit up like a Fourth of July fireworks display, and there were alarms sounding in the lab.

"Ethan!"

"Yes, I hear you."

"What the fuck just happened?"

Ethan took a moment to collect himself.

"I'm sorry, Yang. What did you see?"

"I thought you were having a stroke. I was just about to call 911."

"Did you hear me play 'Tambourine Man'?"

"What? No, I saw you frozen in your chair for six minutes straight."

Ethan placed the guitar back on the pad on the workbench.

"Take me back ten minutes on our video recording. I want to see what you saw."

"That scared the shit out of me. Are you sure you're, okay?"

"I'm fine, just show me."

Yang opened the video file and scrubbed back.

"Stop, play from there."

Ethan could be seen cradling the guitar, playing chords, and then singing the song. The moment he memory-warped to Camp Shalom, he sat motionless in his seat holding the guitar. The holographic guitar began glowing with intense energy.

"You triggered some serious reactions inside that old guitar," Yang whispered in awe.

They watched the holographic guitar continue glowing with intense energy. The feeds were pouring vast amounts of new data into the data lake.

"Are you going to tell me what happened?"

"Yes, get Stanley, I don't want to repeat this."

Yang ran out of the lab passing directly through the holograph guitar, past the kitchen area, and through the double doors.

Ethan sat down and began writing in the logbook.

Seconds later, Yang came back through the lab doors. "I can't find him!"

"Check the loading dock."

"Fuck!"

She ran out again as Ethan continued writing events in the logbook.

A short time later, Stanley arrived with Yang, pushing a shipping cart. There were a couple of what looked like military-grade pieces of equipment.

"Put that shit away and get over here."

"This is Airforce Surplus shit if you don't mind showing a little respect," Stanley retorted as he pushed the cart against the back wall.

"Did you tell him anything?" Ethan asked Yang.

"No. Nothing."

Yang grabbed the logbook to take notes.

"Forget about the logbook for now, I need you to listen."

"I hate logbooks anyway," she said and tossed it back on the bench.

"I'm sure there's a scientific reason for what I'm about to tell you," Ethan began and then he told Yang and Stanley about his time at Camp Malibu Shalom in 1974. He recounted the lesson with Sadie and that she allowed him to play her guitar, this guitar.

"She wept when I played it singing 'Mr. Tambourine Man' in my mimicking voice. The next day, Sadie came to my room."

"The girl in the sketch, that's Sadie?"

"Yes, that's her."

"If she kissed you, I'm gonna freak out!" Yang warned.

"She asked if I would perform at the talent show then left me this guitar."

Ethan recounted how, as was his habit, he'd started repeating things in his head. And how as he'd started replaying his 'Mr. Tambourine' performance word for word, suddenly the room had shifted, and he was back in front of the other kids and Sadie. He told them how he got scared and stopped everything by putting his hands across the sound hole and deadening the strings.

"When I arrived back in my cabin," he went on, "it was night, and my hands were shaking."

"But it was only your imagination, right?" Stanley asked.

"No, it was fucking real. And what happened ten minutes ago was real also."

"You triggered it by playing it?" Yang offered.

"It has something to do with this guitar and my singing that triggers the memory recall."

Yang looked over at the holographic guitar that was still glowing with energy. "She's a fucking time machine."

"A rewind machine," Stanley added.

Everyone considered the magnitude of those statements.

"What other songs did you play on this guitar, back then?" Yang asked.

"'Malibu Blues,' at the talent show."

"Can you play it now and see what happens?"

"I don't see why not."

But Ethan hesitated as he looked up at the hologram and the vast amounts of data still flowing into AI data lake.

"Boss, what are you thinking?" Stanley asked.

"If we're going to do this, we must do it scientifically. I don't want to miss something important. I want every bit of data we can get out of this," Ethan explained.

Ethan drew on his iPad as Stanley and Yang looked at each other, wondering what he was about to present.

"We've got all these receptors on the guitar feeding the AI, and I have shared energy that it obviously recognizes. So, if we want to be able to translate all this data into anything meaningful, we need this."

Ethan showed the screen to them. It was a storyboard drawing of a man in boxer shorts, wearing headphones, with his arms stretched out. Tiny dots were placed all over his body.

"This is…you?" Stanley said.

"And these are Nerva AI receptors?" Yang asked.

"Fifty-two receptors on the guitar, fifty-two receptors on me. We have shared energy, I've proven that. Our new AI can do direct comparisons, linkages, translations, anything we ask."

Stanley shook his head.

"Fucking brilliant," Yang whispered.

29

One

"You're blood work came back solid as ever. I'm not seeing anything that concerns me. You'd be a perfect Nerva receptor candidate."

Ethan, Yang, and Stanley sat across from Dr. Harrison as he reviewed Ethan's chart. He shifted his glasses as he turned through the various pages of test results.

"But you're not experiencing any pain. Why would you want them installed in your body?"

"Research, we're just gathering data."

"And this requires you? Nobody else can be used?"

"No, I'm the only one who can play the way I play."

"Play?" Dr. Harrison asked, a bit confused.

"It's complicated. It must be me."

"Nerva has keyman insurance on you," Dr. Harrison pointed out, removing his glasses and setting them on the counter.

Stanley and Yang shared a look of concern.

"You're required to disclose all medical procedures before they occur."

"Okay," Ethan said, nodding as he looked at Yang and Stanley.

"I'll need an email from someone in HR letting me know they've been properly informed," Dr. Harrison continued.

"I'll take care of it," Ethan assured him.

Dr. Harrison looked at Stanley and Yang then back to Ethan. "I'll send a car to your place on Friday evening. I'll put you up in a nice hotel and we'll run some final tests in the morning. If all checks out, we'll insert the receptors on Saturday afternoon. Is that good?"

"Yes, thank you." Ethan extended his hand to Dr. Harrison. "You're part of the research team now," Ethan said graciously.

"Tell me what this all means when the time is right."

"Absolutely."

"Now go sign some autographs with my staff," he instructed, handing Ethan a black sharpie.

"I don't sign autographs," Ethan sighed.

"Yes, you do! Now go!"

30

Secrets & Confessions

The smell of freshly baked bread filled the air as Bella looked around. The color scheme on the walls, the old-school bench seating; it was as if they were back in the 1980s.

"I haven't been in a Subway for years," Bella mused.

"That sweet smell of success!" Ethan quipped.

Yang and Stanley sat across from them eating sandwiches.

"Brings back a lot of memories of late-night study groups in my college days," Yang said.

Having tired of the small talk, Ethan turned to Bella and said flatly, "I saw Dr. Harrison earlier today."

"Are you okay?"

"I'm want to have an elective procedure, non-invasive, and I need to inform HR as part of my keyman policy."

"An elective procedure?"

"Yes."

"What procedure?"

"What am I required to tell you?"

"I need more than 'this is an elective procedure,' no doubt," she replied.

"May I speak off the record for a minute?"

"I don't know what that means."

"I want to talk to you as a friend and not as the Director of HR."

Bella looked at Stanley and Yang then back to Ethan. "Okay, let's talk as friends," she replied.

"I'm having all fifty-two Nerva AI receptors installed in my body on Saturday as part of an ongoing research project," Ethan said bluntly.

Bella's eyes opened wide.

"It's not for pain management and I'm the only viable candidate."

"Is that it?"

"I'm not at liberty to discuss it at this time."

"Research and Development confidentiality," Yang piped up.

"An elective procedure on you, the scientist, confidential?"

"Yes."

Bella nodded. After a pause, she asked, "Is Dr. Harrison onboard with this?"

"Yes."

"Does this have any relation to your father's passing?"

Ethan thought for a moment. "I promise to update you as we make progress."

Bella could sense Ethan did not want to discuss his father.

"What do I need to do?"

"Send Dr. Harrison an email confirming that I told you of the procedure," he replied.

"I'll do that tonight before I go to bed."

"Awesome, would you like an oatmeal cookie? They're good!" Yang asked, holding out a cookie.

As Bella reached out, she noticed Stanley place his hand on Yang's knee. Bella smiled as she took the cookie. Yang saw Bella looking at Stanley's hand.

"Excuse me!" Yang said as she pushed his hand away.

Bella winked at Yang.

31

Lab Rats

A stainless-steel insertion rod punctured Ethan's skin near his belly button, holding a pea-size receptor in a small chamber behind the sharp tip of the rod. Dr. Harrison moved the receptor about one inch up from the insertion point then pulled a trigger-like arm that moved the receptor from the insertion rod and pressed it firmly into place within the muscle tissue. As he slowly retracted the rod, he used a laser to seal the puncture in the skin.

"And that, Ethan, makes fifty-two."

He wiped a drop of blood away and cleaned the skin with an antiseptic wipe before making three small dots around the receptor with a blue marking pen.

"Didn't wince once," Dr. Harrison added.

Ethan lay face up on the surgical bed, his waist covered by a white sheet. He wore his headphones and listened to music. Dr. Harrison tapped him on the hand, letting him know he could get up. Ethan sat up to reveal blue markings all over his body. Receptor markings were found along his spine, across his shoulders, on his chest and his hips, down his legs and arms, and at the base of his skull at the back of Ethan's neck.

Dr. Harrison removed his mask and smiled. "You're free to dress now, Ethan. No strenuous activity and DO NOT, I repeat, DO NOT activate a single receptor until I'll see you in four days. Am I clear on that?"

"Yes, thank you, Dr. Harrison," Ethan replied as he pulled his pants up, zipped and buttoned.

Later that day, Ethan stood in the lab with his arms out, wearing only his boxer shorts.

"Four days?" Stanley asked.

"I'm not waiting that long."

Yang turned on the activation wand and checked the power settings.

"You know how to work the activator, right?" Stanley asked.

"I should, I designed and built it."

"I really think we should wait on this," Stanley added reluctantly.

"If doctors ran the world, we'd be in a constant state of bubble-wrap and quarantine. There's no way I'm losing four days of research waiting for him to say it's okay to activate my technology."

As Yang approached him with the activator, Stanley powered on a second hologram projector. Ethan's wireframed image appeared next to the guitar hologram.

"Ready when you are," Yang said.

"To the end of the world as we know it," Stanley declared, raising his coffee mug.

"Let's do this," Ethan insisted.

Yang touched the activator to the first receptor on Ethan's chest. A slight twitch occurred on the skin.

"That tickled."

"Ready for the next one?"

"Keep going."

Yang proceeded to activate one receptor after the other, each one causing a slight twitch of the skin.

"Holy shit," Stanley muttered.

The hologram of Ethan's wireframe body showed the various receptors as they became active and began communicating with the other receptors with glowing lines.

"They're talking to each other already," Stanley said.

As Yang activated each receptor, she made a little smiley face with a pen over the receptor.

"Cute," Ethan remarked.

With each new receptor that became live, the hologram glowed and pulsed with more information and mapping details to Ethan's body.

Stanley reached out and touched the hologram near Ethan's chest. "Wow, look at that, the boss has a heart after all!"

"I'll cancel my trip to Oz," Ethan mused, smiling as he watched the holograms of the guitar and his own developing body right beside it. The energy pulses between receptors varied and operated independent of each.

"In your wildest dreams did you ever expect to see this?" he asked his colleagues.

"No," Yang and Stanley said in unison.

One hour later, Ethan lay stretched out on the couch, fast asleep beneath a blanket. His hologram continued to display all fifty-two receptors as active and communicating at full capacity. Ethan's heart rate, oxygen levels, and respiration numbers displayed near his ear.

Stanley was relaxing nearby, drinking coffee and snacking on donuts and left over pizza. Yang was curled up on a nearby couch with a blanket.

"Wake me up if you see any anomalies," Yang instructed him.

Stanley watched the hologram of Ethan's body as energy data flowed steadily from each receptor and into AI data lake.

"Never in my wildest dreams," Stanley sighed.

32

The Leap of Fate

"All right, enough dabbling. Let's do this!"

Yang lifted the guitar and placed it in Ethan's lap as he reclined in a lab chair with legs and arms supported with cushioning. His hologram looked like the damaged death star from *Star Wars* as it was still rendering his full body image. All the receptors were glowing and communicating with each other.

"Am I fully connected?" Ethan asked.

Yang looked at monitors above the workstation. "We added three additional video cameras and two microphones."

"'Tambourine Man'?" Stanley asked.

"I'll start with that and see what readings we get."

Ethan secured the strap across his shoulder as Yang sat down with the logbook.

"Any predictions, hypotheses?" she asked.

"I think my energy will flatline the moment the guitar takes over," Ethan offered.

"Okay, makes partial sense. I predict energy goes ballistic on both the guitar and you," Yang surmised.

"Fact: we're wasting a lot of time guessing when we should be flipping the switch," Stanley interjected impatiently.

"Well, here goes," Yang started. "Today is May 21, 2025. 11.15 in the morning,"

"For me, I would have chosen a lighter approach to the beginning verses," Ethan commenced.

He played the melody in the key of D.

"Hey mister Tambourine Man, play a song for me. I'm not sleepy and there is no place I'm going to. Hey mister Tambourine Man..." Ethan sang.

And the room memory warped as it did previously, to the exact time as before.

Ethan sang the song to Sadie and the kids. He remained calm and observant of his surroundings as he continued singing all eight verses of the song.

When he was finished, once again, Ethan held his gaze on Sadie, who was crying.

Just as she was about to speak, Ethan placed his palm over the strings of the guitar and the room memory warped back to present where Stanley and Yang stood watching him closely.

"Are you back?" Yang asked.

Ethan blinked his eyes and nodded.

Yang pointed at the holograms. "Someone took their fingers out of the goddamned dam!"

Both holograms were lit up like Christmas trees, processing data at record speeds into the AI data lake.

"We've got some serious shit going on," Stanley reported.

"It started the moment you made the jump twelve minutes ago," Yang added.

"Show me the video feed."

Stanley did a quick rewind. "This is the moment you made the leap."

Ethan appeared completely normal. The moment he warped, his face lifted slightly, and his eyes opened wide. The closeup camera showed his eyes opaque and glassed over.

"Whoa, I look possessed."

"Your vitals jumped up and stayed high the entire time," Stanley observed.

"But look at how the holograms reacted to each other," Yang pointed out.

The two hologram receptors were pulsing at the precise same time.

"Completely synchronized. Nobody predicted that scenario."

"Okay, I was there in front of all the other kids. But did I really go there or was it all just my memory playing out virtually?" Ethan asked.

"How did you stop the memory?"

"I palm muted the strings."

"Do you remember what happens next? After you finished the song?" Stanley asked.

"No, it's been way too long."

"Good. On this next attempt, don't touch the strings; let's see if the memory keeps going. Then we'll know for sure," Yang offered.

Ethan swallowed deeply. His throat was dry.

Yang handed him a glass of water. "Virtual or not, your body certainly believed it performed all eight verses."

As Ethan drank the water, Yang made an entry in the logbook.

"Can we go again, right away?" she wondered.

"Yes," Ethan replied confidently as he finished drinking water.

"We're recording and set on my end," Stanley confirmed.

"I'm going to start on the last verse of the song."

Ethan handed the partially empty glass to Yang. She accidently bumped the guitar and water spilled on Ethan's bare legs.

"Oh, shit. I'm sorry!" she exclaimed as Ethan positioned the guitar in his lap.

"Don't worry about it."

Stanley tossed her a hand towel as Ethan began to sing.

"In the jingle jangle morning I'll come following..." he sang as Yang wiped the towel across Ethan's wet legs.

"Take me on a trip upon your magic swirling ship, my senses have been stripped..."

At that moment, Ethan made the leap. His head titled subtly backward; his eyes glazed over. Yang also suddenly froze; her hand clutched the towel on Ethan's leg. Her eyes glazed over.

Ethan finished performing 'Tambourine Man' then handed the guitar back to Sadie and started drawing on a notepad.

"Where did you learn to play like that?"

"I had teachers here and there when I was a child. I kind of just teach myself."

"Can you play any songs by Muddy Waters?"

"Of course."

"Will you play one for us right now?"

"No, I'd rather finish my drawing first."

Ethan continued sketching on his notepad as Sadie tuned the guitar.

"That's a nice guitar, by the way. Where'd you get it?" Ethan asked.

"My friend Jimi gave this to me."

"Jimi Hendrix?"

Sadie smiled at his guess.

"Yes, as a matter of fact. The late, great Jimi Hendrix."

"That's sad what happened to him," Ethan said softly.

Sadie shook her head, trying not to become emotional at the thought of losing Jimi.

"All right, does anyone here know Joni Mitchell?" Sadie asked.

Ethan quickly blurted out:

"They paved paradise and put up a fucking parking lot!"

Ethan placed his hand over the strings of the guitar and was memory warped back to the lab. Both he and Yang returned to full awareness as Yang's hand finished moving the towel across Ethan's wet leg.

"Holy shit!" Yang cried out.

"What the fuck happened?" Stanley demanded.

"I was there! I saw the whole thing!"

"You were there with me?" Ethan asked.

"Yes!"

"What did you see?"

"You said 'No' then started sketching. She said this guitar belonged to Jimi Hendrix!"

"You saw my entire memory?"

"I didn't just see it. I could *feel* it. I was fucking *there*!"

"This is what I saw," Stanley offered.

He played the moment Yang wiped Ethan's leg with the towel. It was clear from the video that Ethan and Yang made the transition at the exact same time.

Stanley handed them both a glass of water. "Nobody predicted this would happen!"

The receptors on both holograms were fully engaged, communicating and feeding data into the AI data lake.

"What the fuck is going on here, boss?" Yang asked.

"You were touching me when I made the jump; logically, you were just a physical extension of me," Ethan surmised.

"Could you see Ethan?" Stanley asked Yang.

"Yes. This proves that this is not virtual; it's fucking real!" Yang enthused as she began writing in the logbook.

"Did you ever sense Yang being next to you or connected to you during the recall?" Stanley asked Ethan.

"No, I was so focused on letting the memory play out, she never came to my attention until we memory warped back here."

Stanley took the guitar from Ethan and placed it on the blanketed workbench. The two holograms stopped communicating in synchronicity and began pulsing to their own unique patterns.

"Wait, did you see that?"

"No."

"Give it back to me."

When Stanley handed the guitar back to Ethan, the holograms became perfectly synchronized once more.

Ethan handed the guitar back and the moment his hands were free, they fell out of synchronicity again. Stanley handed it back and they synchronized.

"It's like they're married now," Stanley observed, taking the guitar away.

"Proximity synchronicity, I've got it," Yang replied as she wrote in the logbook.

Ethan's hologram continued to build his full image. His vital signs showed a reducing heart rate and lowering blood pressure.

Yang looked up at the sketch of Sadie. "That was her. She was there."

Ethan nodded.

"She loved you."

"Why do you say that?"

"Every woman can recognize that look," Yang replied.

"She loved the performance, not me."

"Then she loved both."

Ethan was about to speak until Yang glared at him. "Don't argue with me."

Ethan looked over at the sketch of Sadie smiling back at him. It warmed his heart to think of Sadie having affection toward him.

33

The Magic Key

"So maybe it's like an organic hard drive that somehow remembers everything it has ever heard or experienced; songs, conversations, images," Stanley suggested.

Stanley, Yang, and Ethan sat the workbench looking down at the guitar.

"We triggered the memory recall by recreating the energy it already knows. Whoever holds the guitar takes the trip back in time," Ethan concluded.

"Or anyone touching the person holding the guitar," Yang added.

"You were a hitchhiker," Stanley agreed.

"But obviously the recreation of the energy or trigger doesn't have to be an exact match," Ethan pointed out.

"Why do you say that?"

"My adult voice mimicking Bob Dylan is certainly not the same as my fourteen-year-old voice at camp. And I'm sure I didn't match note for note the performance."

"Maybe the recall trigger only needs to be a 90% match. We can play around with that and figure out where the threshold is," Stanley offered.

"Like eighty-eight miles per hour in *Back to the Future*," Ethan mused.

Yang made notes in the logbook as Ethan looked up at the monitor showing the data stream feeding into the data lake.

"My three songs are just three raindrops of everything this guitar has ever experienced. How do we tap into all other memories, other songs, all the other musicians who have ever played this guitar?"

Yang looked at Stanley, considering the challenge.

"Why is that enticing to you, boss?" Stanley asked curiously.

Ethan thought for several moments, deeply considering his reasons.

"I'm almost sixty years old. I only know my life experience with my filter, my Autism. I have no idea how others see and feel things with whatever filter they have. I'd like to experience other people's lives, their feelings, their emotions, through their filter. I'd like to experience samples of life as my father did. I could learn so many new things, spending time as him," Ethan said poignantly.

Stanley and Yang considered his powerful observations.

"I'd like to know what Autism feels like," Yang said.

"I think this new AI might allow both of your desires to happen," Stanley remarked. "And I think this new AI can help us discover these other musicians and their songs. Now that your experience is linked directly to the guitar's energy, the AI can make the connection and start building a common language."

"It teaches us, we teach it?" Yang asked.

"Why not?" Ethan said.

"We already have a few hundred words to prime the pump. I think we're going to need a couple of language and data analysts to put this all in perspective," Yang said.

Ethan and Stanley nodded in agreement.

"I know a few analysts. Should I call them?" Yang offered.

Ethan watched his body hologram intently; it was almost completely rendered.

"Make the call," Stanley said, knowing Ethan was thinking about other things.

Yang stepped away with her phone as Ethan touched his hologram, removing his outer layer of skin. All his muscles were exposed with cartilage and bone. He raised his arm high, and the hologram followed, matching his movement. He touched the hologram again and the muscles disappeared showing his circulatory system and blood flowing throughout his body.

Next Ethan took a sip from a bottle of blue Gatorade; the hologram showed the fluid pass over his tongue, down his throat, and into his stomach where it was absorbed and passed into the blood stream and into his extremities.

"Never gets old watching what our bodies can do," Stanley mused.

"There's so much we still don't understand," Ethan stated.

Ethan touched the hologram showing only the skeletal structure, the brain, and the central and peripheral nervous systems. All fifty-two receptors glowed.

"If this guitar remembers everything it has experienced, do our bodies do the same? Does a lullaby sung to me as a child exist in a cell outside my brain?" Ethan asked.

"Perhaps," Stanley replied.

"That guitar has no brain matter, but it still retains its memories."

"Guitars are built to sustain sound."

Ethan looked over and smiled. "Exactly. And so are we as human beings."

Yang stepped back in as Stanley looked up at the spinning hologram of Ethan's body.

"Maybe these receptors can be used to reroute memories from other sources. A possible cure to Alzheimer's and dementia," Ethan theorized.

Yang shared a look with Stanley.

"You keep this up and you're going to win the Nobel Prize," Stanley mused.

"But why do our bodies retain everything, only to cast it all aside and return to dust? There must be a deeper purpose," Ethan wondered.

"Even the dust remembers," Yang offered.

Ethan nodded in consideration. "A decaying body in a coffin six feet under still remembers everything."

"Holy shit, can you imagine digging up a murderer and tapping into the stored memories?" Yang asked.

"Dark and twisted, but why not?" Ethan replied.

"I have a feeling that in the next couple of days, we're going to learn things that we never thought possible," Yang added.

"Do either of you believe in good and evil?" Ethan enquired.

"Angel on one shoulder, devil on the other?" Yang asked.

"Yes."

"I believe people can choose good or evil," Stanley replied.

"Is one always good, and the other bad?"

"Not always, sometimes one is a little better than the other."

"But sometimes one is clearly good, and one is clearly evil?" Ethan asked.

"Absolutely!" Stanley blurted.

"How?"

"Hitler made choices to exterminate an entire race. Terrorists made choices to fly airplanes into towers! People make evil choices every fucking day!"

Ethan nodded in agreement. "Perhaps."

"Perhaps," Yang relinquished.

"For more than one hundred years, this guitar has experienced good and evil, I'm certain of it."

"Does that scare you?" Yang asked.

Ethan considered the magnitude of her question.

"Absolutely."

34

The War Room

"Shamir speaks Farsi, Hebrew, French, German, and Vietnamese. Angel speaks Spanish, Portuguese, Swedish, Latin, and Southern Baptist. Carline speaks twelve Filipino dialects including Wari, Ilocano, Visayan, and Bicolano, and can code in six languages," Yang reported to Ethan. "They've all been briefed on our need-to-know war room protocols, so they won't be asking questions. Their job is to crack the first new song code by taking your existing memory recalls and marrying it to the guitars energy language and helping us find a base language for the AI to ingest."

The three specialists, wearing noise cancelling headphones, punched away at keyboards seated behind a wall of glass. The monitors above them showed the code words they were working to decipher.

"Words will start to appear up here on the gamification board," Yang said, pointing at the projection on the wall showing a dashboard of graphs, charts, and lists displaying mock data. There was a dollar sign beside each analyst's name.

"What's that?" Stanley asked.

"We give a cash bonus for every word they match. Words earn dollars, phrases earn more, song titles, musicians, and band names the most," Yang replied with a smile, then added, pointing to another glass wall, "The full library will start populating back on this wall."

"How do we know what they are finding is real?" Ethan asked.

"If someone finds a match on the name Jimi Hendrix, it would have been spoken and heard by the guitar for it to show up on our board. If we find a song, say 'Little Wing,' and the lyrics are also sourced from the guitar, then it will run a match on the actual song with Jimi's voice. It will then determine if he sang it and played it on the guitar or someone else sang it. We could find multiple matches for the same song. Each version of the song will only match the specific artist," Yang explained. "We're looking for songs that you can perform to prove our theory of doing a recall on memories that don't belong to you."

"Precisely."

"So, if you sing 'Little Wing' in the style Jimi performed on this guitar, you'll memory warp to the exact time he sang it originally," Stanley said.

"And, if our AI can make sense of this all, we will have discovered—no, *created*—a time machine," Yang concluded.

Everyone paused at that thought.

"Or more appropriately, a rewind machine. Because we only experience what the guitar has experienced," Ethan pointed out.

"That's the theory. I'll believe it when I see it," Stanley countered.

"What do we do while we wait for these analysts?" Ethan asked.

"Go sing karaoke, brush up on your Jimi Hendrix," Yang suggested.

"I don't sing karaoke."

"Go play *Mario Kart* then! Goodbye, we're doing science stuff here!"

Ethan smiled and walked away, leaving Yang and Stanley to work.

The gamification board showed the very first word: 'man.' The dollar value under Angel's name now read $10 and the word 'man' appeared in the master list on the wall.

"We have our first matched word, everyone!" Yang shouted.

The analysts cheered briefly then returned to their work as more words began to appear.

Carline's dollar value changed to $10, then $20, then to $30. Nine new words suddenly appeared on the database list. Trip, magic, ship, there, hands, feel, senses, no, tambourine.

"Houston, we have lift off!" Yang declared.

Shamir's dollar sign changed to $250 and the phrase, 'In the jingle jangle morning I'll come following you,' appeared on the database wall.

Words began populating on the database board in rapid succession. New phrases appeared, and the dollar amounts climbed. 'Mr. Tambourine Man' showed up under song titles.

Just then, George, a bearded man resembling Santa Claus, entered the lab pulling a roller bag. "I'm here to see someone named Stanley Yang?" he read from a post it note on his sleeve.

"I'm Yang, that's Stanley. Are you George, my database specialist?"

"Yes, ma'am."

"Old school," Yang said as she looked at the post it note.

"The wife."

"Perfect timing. Follow me. Ignore the big ass data lake you see over here. Right now, we're deciphering the language with AI matching words and phrases, song titles and artists. This goes back decades, so this will get pretty hairy moving forward," Yang explained.

"Are you using any outside verification? DataDNA, RingLead, Ancestry?" George asked.

"I have no idea what any of those things are, but verification sounds valuable," Yang replied.

Yang took George into the data center and placed him behind the language specialists. He unpacked his workstation and plugged in.

"Is it okay to order me an IV box of Starbucks Caramel Coffee?"

"Use the Starbucks app, hash Nerva Skunkworks. And I'd better not see a bunch of shit being ordered—I see every request."

"Roger, Wilco."

"Oh, God not another pilot talker," Yang sighed.

"Is that my dashboard on the back wall?" George asked.

"Yes. Keep things simple and concise. I don't want this to look like NASA Mission Control," Yang advised.

"What's the big picture for me?"

"That guitar, out there, is a one-hundred-year-old hard drive and we're trying to learn what it knows. What it's heard, seen, experienced. Give us perspective. Dates, people's names, places, relationships, and any gaps that we might have missed."

"I'm on it. Any questions for me?"

"Will the elves at the workshop be calling demanding Santa come home?" Yang quipped.

George touched his finger to his nose and gave her a Santa Claus wink.

Yang giggled as she exited the war room and entered the lab area.

Later that night, Ethan sat in a sound booth with Yang and Stanley, looking at them expectantly.

"Good news! The first song that came back fully formed was a song by Janis Joplin," Yang announced.

"Not surprised," Ethan said. "Janis had the guitar for at least a day or two. What was the song?"

"'Mercedes Benz,'" Yang replied.

"I've heard it before."

"Not this version. This one is highly modified."

"We overlayed her voice samples, so this isn't exact," Stanley added.

"From October 2, 1970, first some random conversation, then the song," Yang reported.

The rendered audio began playing on the studio speakers.

"God damned Mercedes fucking Benz. Last car I'd ever drive! Find me a word that rhymes with Rolls Royce for fucking sakes, you bunch of pricks," Janis Joplin's AI rendered voice spoke chillingly.

"Then there's space of about a minute with random noises. Now she sings," Stanley explained.

"My fucking manager bought me a Mercedes Benz. His friends all drive Porsches, he must make amends. He's a German motherfucker, he has got no friends. I have got no friends. Look at me, I've got no friends," Janis sang.

"Then more random sounds for about five minutes and then we hear three words," Stanley said.

"Fuck the rug!" Janis said.

And then silence.

"That's all we have," Yang said.

"Play it again."

Stanley scrolled back and pressed play. After listening once more, Ethan nodded his head.

"She acts drunk, but she sounds normal," Ethan said.

"The samples are studio recorded voice. I can apply a mumble effect and a pitch change," Stanley offered.

"I can definitely match what she played on guitar."

Ethan took the guitar as Stanley played with audio effects on the Janis voice.

"Can you put the lyrics on the monitor?"

Yang set the monitor to display the lyrics.

"This is your waveforms beneath hers so you can see how close you match," Yang said.

"My fucking manager bought me a Mercedes Benz," Ethan sang while playing the chords.

Ethan's waveform comparison showed a 59% match.

"His friends all drive Porsches, he must make amends," he sang, mimicking Janis's tone.

The comparison jumped to 65%.

"You're getting closer," Yang observed.

Stanley played a manipulated waveform with the murmur effect. Ethan tried to closely mimic Janis as it played through several times.

After nearly an hour of tweaking and performing, Ethan got the waveform percentage up to 90%.

"You're sounding really good, boss," Stanley commented.

"I could swear Janis was right here playing," Yang enthused.

"Apparently 90% isn't enough though," Ethan sighed. "We've isolated the lyrics. We've isolated the guitar. What else are we missing?"

"If this really is the last song she sang before she died, she would have been in the motel room, right?" Stanley asked.

"Yes."

"What other sounds could there have been besides her voice and the guitar?"

"Room noise. An air conditioner. People in the next room having sex," Ethan replied.

"Can you mute her singing and the guitar?" Yang asked.

Stanley muted the lyrics and guitar stems as a series of odd sounds played. There was a steady ambient sound playing throughout the sample.

"None of this has been identified by the AI?"

"No."

"Could be anything. A room fan, a neon sign."

There was a light knocking sound, like the tapping of a pencil on a table. Then it did a few double taps.

"Definitely some kind of percussion," Ethan muttered, deep in thought.

"Lay in the guitar, see if it matches the beat," Yang said.

There was no tap or echo at first, but then the tap suddenly appeared part way through the first verse.

"She's keeping time," Ethan said.

"The heel of her shoe?" Yang suggested.

"The guitar neck bumping something?" Stanley added.

"Maybe a ring on her strumming hand," Ethan offered.

Suddenly, Yang pressed pause on the playback.

"Bio-break!"

Yang and Stanley rushed from of the lab to use the restroom.

"Does she sound like she's on heroin?" Ethan asked.

"How the fuck would I know?" Stanley shouted back.

"Yes," Yang yelled.

Ethan continued listening to the track, engraining the performance into his brain.

When Stanley and Yang returned to the lab, Ethan sat silently on the couch with the guitar in his arms.

"Boss, is everything okay?"

"We're getting close, I can feel it."

"That's a good thing right?" Yang asked.

"I hope so. But it kind of scares me."

"Why?"

"I like my consistent, predictable daily patterns. If this works, we're jumping headfirst into the unknown."

Yang looked at Stanley, concerned.

"You don't have to do this," Yang said to Ethan sincerely.

Ethan strummed each note of the guitar and let it ring out.

"It's your decision, Ethan."

Ethan flattened the G string slightly then said slowly, "If Janis was on heroin…there's no way she took the time to tune the G string before playing it."

Yang smiled at Ethan.

35

Blue Glass

Two delivery men in coveralls rolled a vintage feather mattress and 1970s bedframe through the double doors and into the lab. Ethan, Stanley, and Yang sat at the table devouring lunch and didn't look up.

"Right over there, please," Yang said, pointing.

The men unloaded the frame off the pallet jack then placed the mattress on the frame. As they did so, it squeaked loudly. Ethan, Stanley, and Yang looked at each other and smiled.

That afternoon, with all cameras and microphones recording, Ethan sat on the end of the vintage motel bed holding the guitar.

"I'm ready if you are."

Stanley pressed the master record button on the mix console. "We have speed."

Ethan tapped his foot in proper time to the song, causing the bed frame to move and squeak with the rhythm.

"That's good, boss."

Ethan nodded, then began to play the guitar just like Janis had performed.

"My fucking manager bought me a Mercedes Benz. His friends all drive Porsches, he must make amends. He's a German motherfucker, he has got no friends," Ethan sang as the match meter showed 97%.

At that moment, Ethan froze on the bed and his eyes glazed over.

Ethan memory warped to the Hollywood motel room where Janis sat on the bed playing the guitar.

"I have got no friends. Look at me, I've got no friends," *Janis sang.*

Ethan could see the entire room as he sat on the bed, as if he were looking out through Janis's eyes. Janis took a long drag on a cigarette, lightly thumping the body of the guitar with her thumb, keeping time with the song.

There was knock on the door, the familiar 'shave and a haircut' pattern as Janis took a long drag on her cigarette then crushed it in the ash tray.

As Janis placed the guitar on the bed and walked into the bathroom, Ethan's perspective shifted to that of the guitar. Janis grasped the sink and stared into her reflection in the mirror, then turned on the hot water. She looked horrible—hair disheveled, eyes bloodshot—as steam began to rise and cover the mirror.

She submerged a washcloth into the hot water, then slowly lifted it by the corners across her face and over her ears. She made no reaction to the hot water as she stood silently for thirty seconds. She repeated the process twice more then turned off the water and tossed the washcloth into the bathtub.

Janis picked up her coin purse off the nightstand and walked to the door where she unlocked three locks. A dead bolt lock. A chain lock. A knob lock. Oddly, as if her name had been called, she turned and looked directly at the guitar. She squinted her eyes and held her gaze on the sound hole as she slowly exited the room. Several minutes later, she reappeared with items in her hands and pushed the door closed with her knee. But the door didn't close; the chain was jammed, leaving a half-inch gap to the outside world.

A brown paper wrapped package lay open on the nightstand. Inside was a vial of heroin and a disposable needle. After securing a length of surgical tubing around her bicep, Janis took a long drag on her cigarette, placed the smoking butt in the ashtray, then filled the needle with amber courage. A single drop of heroin oozed from the needle as she pushed the needle into her protruding vein then pushed the plunger to its final resting position. She released the surgical tubing with a SNAP, and it fell to the table.

Janis danced sporadically on the rug. The room spun, her hair whipped across her face, into air. She laughed and cried, shouted obscenities with glee toward nobody. As she reached out to embrace the guitar, her foot caught the edge of the rug, and she stumbled forward.

"Fuck the rug!" she called out.

She fell headlong toward the glass ashtray. Her face struck the corner of the nightstand forcing it away from the bed as her body fell violently into the crevice. There was a loud THUD before her body fell lifelessly into calm nothingness. No rustling, no body twitches, no moans of pain. The glass ashtray, still full of cigarette butts, teetered at the edge of the nightstand above her head.

Ethan placed his hand over the sound hole of the guitar, and he memory warped back to present day in the lab where Yang and Stanley sat watching him.

"Oh, my God!" Ethan cried out.

"Are you okay?" Yang asked.

Ethan cried softly. He struggled to form the words as he nodded.

"Boss?"

"I saw her die."

"Janis Joplin?" Stanley asked.

"Yes, she's dead."

36

Ancestry

"These are all known names spoken within listening distance of the guitar. Hundreds of musicians, fans, friends, and random people. But more relevant to your research, these are the names of every musician who ever played this guitar."

George stood at the hologram monitor displaying a genealogy diagram dashboard. He changed the display to list the musicians in a fan diagram.

"We validated every name with various ancestry meta data and they now appear in this fan diagram. Not every musician had a perfect match, so we made some assumptions to fit them into the year we suspect they played the guitar."

Ethan looked closely at the fan diagram; some sections were very detailed, others quite sparse.

"How much of the guitar's data have we processed?" Stanley asked.

"About 25%."

"The good news is, it's getting faster. It's an exponential curve; the more verified matching words we find in each song, the faster the next one will appear," Carline added.

"There's Jimi Hendrix and Janis Joplin," Ethan said, touching their names.

"This is my favorite view. Check this out," George said.

He touched the monitor to show an organic family tree diagram of the guitar. It looked very much like a tree, only the leaves and branches were individual names of people who either played the guitar or were mentioned by name. A list of songs appeared beneath each artist's leaf.

"Here we have Ethan at the very outside top of the tree. He's played the guitar most recently, so we have a branch and leaf associated with that performance. If we trace this branch all the way back down to the middle, then out a little, here is Ethan's performance in the 1970s," George explained.

"Camp Malibu Shalom," Ethan offered.

"Janis Joplin on October 4, 1970," Yang said, pointing at her orange-colored leaf.

"And her final song, Mercedes Benz. The day she died," Ethan said quietly.

Yang could tell Ethan was still processing Janis's death and that it had deeply affected him.

"If we verify the death, we paint it orange," George explained as he zoomed in on Janis's leaf.

"Which musician has the most songs?" Ethan asked.

"No doubt, Robert LeRoy or Robert Johnson, same guy. 1920s to 1930s," George replied as he enlarged the leaf for Robert.

"Robert Johnson played this guitar?" Ethan asked in surprise.

"He recorded twenty-nine verified songs in 1937. He performed more than a thousand before that date."

Partial phrases appeared below the verified songs.

"These are just place holders, a snippet of lyrics we use to identify a unique song," George told them.

"Songs without a known title?" Yang asked.

"Or songs in progress, being written, we're not totally sure."

Ethan scrolled through the extensive list under Robert's name.

"Do you know his music?" Stanley asked.

"Yes. He's the Godfather of the Mississippi Delta Blues. The roots of jazz, rock 'n' roll, country and R'n'B. He influenced them all," Ethan replied with reverence.

Ethan rotated the tree to find Jimi Hendrix with song titles beneath this name. Jim Morrison had a leaf, but no song titles beneath his name.

"Jim Morrison's name was mentioned, but he didn't play the guitar?"

"His leaf is yellow, which means AI is still working on that data," George explained.

Ethan rotated the tree back to Robert Johnson and his list of songs.

"Do you see something?" Yang queried.

"There are hundreds of songs, way more than I ever imagined. All played on this guitar?" Ethan asked.

"The data doesn't lie," George replied assuredly.

Later that afternoon, Ethan sat with Yang and Stanley looking at the tree hologram.

"Can you play Robert's songs?" Yang asked.

"I can. But do I WANT to play his songs?"

"Why do you say that?"

"Legend is, Robert sold his soul to the devil at the Mississippi Crossroads so he could play guitar. Folklore says he was poisoned by a scorned woman then she chopped him up and buried him in an unmarked grave next to her dead husband. If either of those things are true, I don't want to experience that evil."

"Are you convinced this guitar is Robert's guitar?"

"I have little doubt after seeing the data," Ethan replied.

"Then this guitar may know the truth to the legend and folklore," Stanley pointed out, pulling up an internet search for Robert Johnson and his guitar. "I found three images of him holding a guitar. Here's the first one."

The image showed Robert Johnson wearing a suit and hat as he held a guitar. The image was taken in a studio and was quite formal.

"The guitar in that picture, is not this guitar," Ethan said. "Look at the twelfth fret, with the double pearl inlays, it's right at the body. That's what we call a twelve-fret guitar. This guitar is not a twelve fret. Our guitar is mounted at the fourteenth fret."

Yang and Stanley looked at the guitar to see the double pearl inlays were not mounted close to the body.

"Here's the second picture," Stanley said.

The image showed Robert Johnson in a white collared shirt and suspenders but no hat. He sat in a photo booth holding a guitar and smoking a cigarette.

"This looks to be taken in a photo booth. It's much more candid, much more believable," Stanley observed.

The photo clearly showed the double pearl inlays, and the body was mounted to the fourteenth fret.

Yang compared the guitar in the photo to the guitar in the hologram. "Fucking hell, that's a match."

"And now our third picture, taken in the same photo booth."

The image showed Robert smiling, his face held close to the guitar body, like it were his best friend. The markings and mountings were identical in every respect.

"This is Robert Johnson's guitar," Ethan concluded.

"Then it seems to me we only have one choice to make," Stanley stated.

"What is that?" Ethan asked.

"Which one of his songs are you going to master first?"

Ethan looked at the list of songs on the tree and considered his choice deeply.

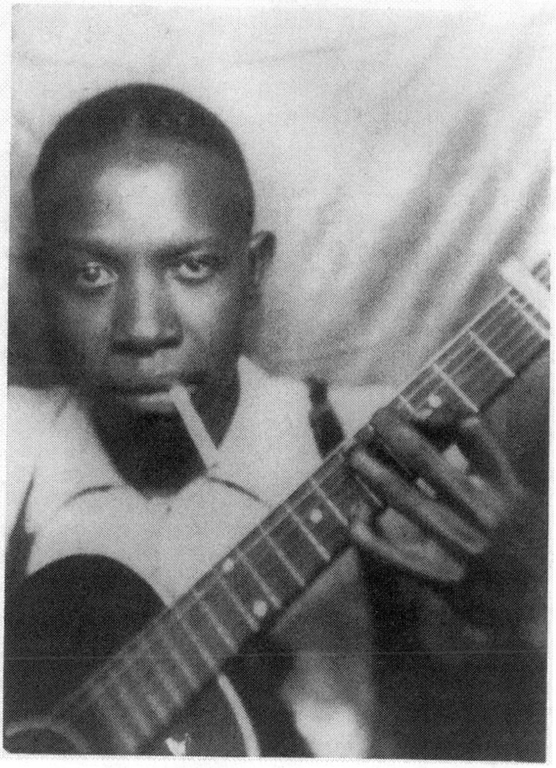

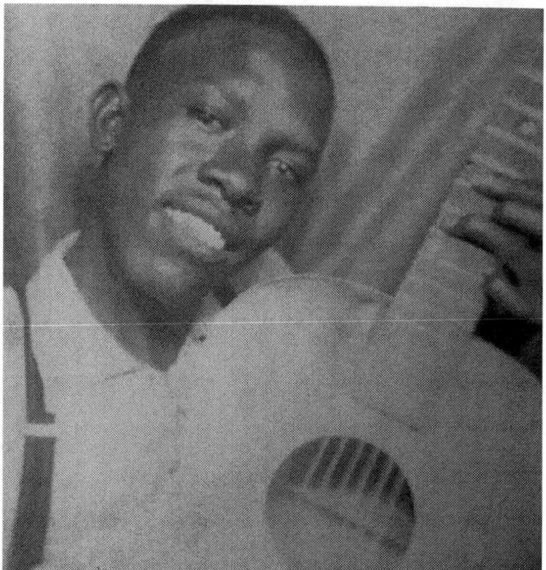

37

The Juke Joint

"How about this? 'Come On in My Kitchen,' was recorded on November 23, 1936. It was part of the Gunther Hotel recordings. One of only twenty-nine songs ever recorded of Robert Johnson," Stanley said.

"Play it."

Stanley selected the track and pressed play as Yang and Ethan listened. The song was mono track without much bass, but it was hauntingly performed and eerily familiar.

"Mmm-mmm-mmm-mmm-mmm
You better come on in my kitchen.
Well, it's goin' to be rainin' outdoors.

Ah, the woman I love, took from my best friend.
Some joker got lucky, stole her back again.
You better come on in my kitchen.
It's goin' to be rainin' outdoors.

Oh, she's gone, I know she won't come back.

I've taken the last nickel out of her nation sack.
You better come on in my kitchen.
It's goin' to be rainin' outdoors.

Oh, can't you hear that wind howl?
Oh, can't you hear that wind would howl?
You better come on in my kitchen.
Well, it's goin' to be rainin' outdoors.

When a woman gets in trouble, everybody throws her down.
Lookin' for her good friend, none can be found.
You better come on in my kitchen.
Babe, it's goin' to be rainin' outdoors.

Wintertime's comin', it's gon' be slow.
You can't make the winter, babe, that's dry, long, so
You better come on in my kitchen, 'cause it's goin' to be rainin' outdoors."

Ethan tapped his foot to the rhythm as the song ended then said, "I've never played slide guitar before."

"Can we buy one at Guitar Center?" Yang asked.

"No. Find me various bottles from that era. Beer bottles, medicine bottles. We cut them off at the neck, leaving about two and one-half inches to slide onto my little finger."

"This will be an adventure," Yang muttered, turned to her laptop.

"Here's another. Even I recognize this song," Stanley said as he pressed play again.

"Oh, Baby, don't you want to go.
Oh, Baby, don't you want to go.
Back to the land of California
To my sweet home Chicago

Oh, Baby, don't you want to go.

*Oh, Baby, don't you want to go.
Back to the land of California
To my sweet home Chicago*

*Now one and one is two.
Two and two is four
I'm heavy loaded baby.
I'm booked, I gotta go.
Cryin', baby
Honey, don't you want to go.
Back to the land of California
To my sweet home Chicago*

*Now two and two is four
Four and two is six
You gon' keep on monkeyin' 'round here friend-boy,
You gon' get your
Business all in a trick
But I'm cryin', baby.
Honey, don't you want to go.
Back to the land of California
To my sweet home Chicago*

*Now six and two is eight
Eight and two is ten
Friend-boy, she trick you one time.
She sure gon' do it again
But I'm cryin', baby.
Honey, don't you want to go.
Back to the land of California
To my sweet home Chicago*

*I'm goin' to California.
From there to Des Moines, Iowa
Somebody will tell me that you.
Need my help someday, cryin'
Hey, hey.
Baby, don't you want to go.
Back to the land of California*

To my sweet home Chicago."

Ethan smiled broadly.

"Damn, that's a good song!" Stanley grinned.

"Less slide, more slurs. Just as complicated as 'My Kitchen'."

"Whilst I continue searching for 1930s beer bottles, may I ask a random question that I'm sure you brilliant scientists have already considered?" Yang asked.

"Flattery before the beat down," Stanley mused.

"Robert Johnson recorded these songs in the Gunter Hotel in 1936. But he had played those same song hundreds if not thousands of times before recording that day. I'm sure he played on porches, in juke joints, shanties, taverns; in hotel rooms, at bus stations, in the fields and down by the river—"

"—Ask your question, Yang!"

"Well, when you suddenly memory warp Robert's song with an old bottle neck on your finger, where will you go? Will you rewind to the first time he performed the song, the last time, or someplace random in between?"

Ethan shook his head. "I don't know. I could go anywhere."

"But…Robert Johnson was seedy, boss!" Stanley warned. "He played a lot of sketchy places. I'm sure there was plenty of drinking and fighting and fucking going on."

"What the hell, Stanley?" Yang hissed.

"Warning label, Yang! Ethan loves routine and structure, remember? He's going back ninety years to a time and place that is totally out of his element."

"Maybe one of you should come with me," Ethan suggested.

"Hell, NO!" Yang and Stanley replied in unison.

"In the name of science?"

"NO! I'm staying right here doing my job," Stanley declared.

"I'm with Stanley," Yang added.

"Two sets of eyes are better than one."

"We're scientists, boss. If you want a travel companion, search Craigslist," Yang joked.

But Ethan had someone else in mind.

38

The Hitchhiker

"Are these Nerva AI receptors mounted to this old guitar?"

Bella stood between Ethan's full body hologram and the guitar hologram.

"Yes, and these are the receptors Dr. Harrison installed in me."

"Why are they linked together?"

"Bella, there are some research projects that nobody outside this lab knows about…" Ethan began.

"Okay."

"This is one of them."

"So, we need your complete confidence on this one."

"I'm listening."

"This is the guitar that my father sent to me. It's a guitar that I played for a short period of time when I was fourteen. These are Nerva AI receptors placed throughout the body of the guitar. What we've proven so far is this: there is energy within the cells of this guitar, and they communicate with each other. We've tapped into that energy and gathered hundreds of terabytes of data currently being analyzed by a new AI. This data is stored memories, things this guitar has experienced by being in the same room with people or being played by a musician. One of those memories is me, playing a Bob Dylan song, 'Mr. Tambourine Man' to my classmates at camp in 1973."

Ethan took a deep breath and looked at Stanley and Yang for support.

"You're doing great, boss," Stanley encouraged with a thumbs up.

"There are also tens of thousands of other memories that have nothing to do with me," Ethan continued. "All within data we now have."

Yang enabled the guitar tree hologram.

"This is the genealogy tree we've built of the people and songs that are contained within the data of the guitar. This is me a few days ago, and if you travel down, you'll see me in 1973 with my Bob Dylan song, along with other songs I performed," Ethan said, moving the tree with his hand gestures.

"'Malibu Blues,' is that your song?" Bella asked.

"Yes, but as you can see, there are thousands of songs and people that make up the total family tree of this guitar."

"Janis Joplin played this guitar?" Bella gasped, pointing.

"Yes. We discovered a way to recall memories contained in this guitar. We can take you virtually back to that space and time. You can hear the songs being played and see all the action within the actual place it all occurred," Ethan explained.

"Like watching a video?"

"Better."

"Virtual reality, then?"

"Much deeper than that."

"I don't understand."

"I played 'Mr. Tambourine Man' at Camp Malibu Shalom on that guitar in 1973. Right now, if you like, I can transport you and I back to that exact moment and experience the entire event with me."

"How?"

Ethan took another deep breath, unsure how much detail he should share.

"Just show her, boss," Yang piped up. "It's the only way she'll fully understand."

"Take her on a trip upon your magic swirling ship," Stanley agreed.

Ethan picked up the guitar and sat on a stool. "Remember how I told you I mimicked musicians as a child?" Ethan reminded her.

"I remember."

"Name a Janis Joplin."

"Um, 'Me and Bobby McGee.'"

Ethan nodded and smiled back at her. "Okay, I might butcher a few of the lyrics, but you'll get the picture."

Ethan began playing the opening chords. He finished the intro, then began to sing, in near perfect Janis Joplin style.

"Busted flat in Baton Rouge, waiting for a train.
When I was feeling near as faded as my jeans
Bobby thumbed a diesel down just before it rained.
It rode us all the way to New Orleans

*I pulled my harpoon out of my red bandana.
I was playing soft while Bobby sang the blues, yeah.
Windshield wipers slapping time, I was holding Bobby's hand in mine
We sang every song that driver knew."*

Ethan stopped playing and Bella smiled at him.

"Freedom's just another word for nothing left to lose.
Nothing don't mean nothing, honey if it ain't free, no-no," Bella sang in her own rendition of Janis.

"You've got a good voice," Ethan said.

"I'm a big Janis fan."

"So, the point is, if Janis had played Bobby McGee on this guitar back in 1969 with my same matching performance, I would have time warped back to the exact moment she played Bobby McGee on this guitar."

"Okay…so how do we do it?"

"I play the guitar and sing, and you hitch a ride with me and we experience everything together; connected."

"*I'm* the hitchhiker?" Bella asked.

"Yes."

"Okay, let's go see Janis Joplin."

Ethan hesitated as he looked to Yang and Stanley.

"Take her," Yang urged.

"Cold? With no introduction?" Ethan countered.

"True," Yang agreed, then, turning to Bella, "This is going to be highly emotional."

"I can handle emotional, I'm an HR Director, for crying out loud," Bella insisted.

Later that evening, Ethan sat on the edge of the motel bed, holding the guitar in his lap. Bella sat in an armed office chair nearby.

"When Ethan plays, just reach out with your left hand and cup it across his right knee," Yang said. "That's why he's wearing shorts."

"Got it."

"I'm going to place this five-pound rice bag over your hand to keep it firmly in place," Yang added.

Ethan played the guitar, strumming to the beat.

"Lord, won't you buy me a color TV!" Ethan sang in Janis's slurred voice.

Bella shook her head, stunned by Ethan's ability to mimic her voice, then stated, "I'm ready."

"Bringing in the hitchhiker," Yang said.

Bella reached her left hand out and cupped it across Ethan's bare knee. Yang placed the bag of rice on top of her hand.

"Just sit back in the chair and relax," Yang instructed.

Bella leaned into the chair as Ethan tapped his foot in time.

"Deep slow breaths," he said softly.

Bella focused her breathing while Ethan tapped out the time.

"Stay calm, no matter what," he assured her.

Bella nodded as Ethan began to sing.

"My fucking manager bought me a Mercedes Benz. His friends all drive Porsches, he must make amends. He's a German motherfucker, he has got no friends," Ethan sang.

At that moment, Ethan froze on the bed and his eyes glazed over. Bella froze also.

Ethan sat in the Hollywood motel room playing the guitar. He looked over and could see Bella beside him, almost within him.

"I have got no friends. Look at me, I've got no friends," *Janis sang.*

The scene played out exactly as before, with the knock on the door, Janis washing her face, then exiting and re-entering the room with her heroin fix. Ethan and Bella remained side by side on the bed watching Janis shoot up then begin slowly dancing around the room. She caught her foot caught the edge of the rug, and she stumbled forward.

"Fuck the rug!" she called out.

As Janis fell headlong toward the nightstand, Bella lunged forward, instinctively trying to catch her fall.

"No!" Bella yelled.

Ethan and Bella moved forward as one person, hitting Janis and pushing her toward the bed, missing the nightstand altogether. As Ethan and Bella fell toward the end table, his hand reached out to catch their fall, sending the glass ashtray to the floor, spilling cigarette butts and ashes everywhere. As Ethan and Bella hit the floor together, they time warped back to the lab.

Ethan and Bella lay on the floor next to each other. Stanley rushed to their side and Yang took hold of the guitar.

"Holy shit, are you guys, okay?" Stanley asked.

Bella slowly stood. "I'm fine. I'm so sorry."

"What the hell happened?"

"I jumped up to catch her," Bella replied in a small voice.

"It took me with her," Ethan added, "and we fell to the floor in the motel room."

Yang handed them both logbooks.

"No more talking. Write down everything you remember. Sights, sounds, clangs, bangs, knocks, cars honking, people walking. I want every fucking detail. You were gone more than seven minutes I want fourteen pages of description," Yang insisted.

They took the logbooks and began to write. Bella was clearly upset.

"Are you okay?" Ethan asked.

Bella could not speak as she continued writing.

"Write!" Yang demanded.

Ethan wrote for a bit then glanced over to check on Bella; tears welled in her eyes.

"Bella?"

She shook her head, not ready to talk as she kept writing in the logbook. Stanley and Yang shared a look of concern.

39

The Ash Tray

Late that night, Ethan had a dream. He was lying flat on his back looking up at Janis's motel room ceiling. Janis danced all around him, holding the glass ash tray in one hand, and smoking a cigarette with the other. Cigarette ashes and butts flew out of the ash tray in artistic patterns. They hung in air, suspended for several seconds before suddenly, as if a switch were thrown, they dropped and landed on the floor, which was already thick with several inches of ash and butts. Ethan, his hands pinned behind his back, was covered from head to toe in ash as Janis stood over him and poured cigarette butts into his open mouth. She laughed as she pushed more and more butts in. Ethan began to choke and suddenly awakened from the dream. As he sat up, he coughed and gasped for air.

It was early morning, before anyone else was in the lab. Ethan sat on the motel bed, holding the guitar. None of the holograms were illuminated and no recording was enabled on any of the monitors. He took a deep breath then began to play the 'fucked up' version of 'Mercedes Benz.'

When Ethan arrived in Janis's motel room, the ashtray was in its original position on the end table, filled with cigarette butts. Ethan watched Janis do all the same things as previously done. She left the room, returned, and shot up heroine. As she danced across the floor, Ethan watched the ash tray. As she tripped on the rug and fell forward, the ash tray moved off the table, as if a ghost had pushed it, and it tumbled to the floor, spilling cigarette butts and ashes everywhere. Janis fell directly onto the bed, landing squarely on the pillow. She began to laugh uncontrollably.

A bright flash illuminated the room and Ethan suddenly found himself outdoors on green grass, looking up at a very large tree with beautiful branches. He heard children's laughter behind him. He turned to see children gathering in a circle on the lawn and holding hands. As they started singing, another flash of light appeared, and Ethan was suddenly transported back inside Janis's motel room. Janis lay face down on the bed, hair-covering her eyes as she faced Ethan. Her breathing was rapid and shallow. Ethan watched her for several minutes as she began to convulse and writhe on the bed. She vomited profusely for several seconds and then collapsed into the pillow.

There was no more shallow breathing. There was no breathing at all. She was dead. Ethan saw the partially open door. He saw the ash tray on the floor. He saw the needle on the table. Ethan looked steadily at Janis one last time. He had now witnessed Janis Joplin dying a second time.

He placed his hand over the sound hole of the guitar. Another flash of light illuminated the room and Ethan found himself back at the giant tree now looking at the children holding hands and circling. The children sang a song, a nursery rhyme of sorts. A song he didn't recognize. Another bright flash of light illuminated, and Ethan was transported back inside the lab, sitting on the edge of the motel bed alone.

Ethan sat quietly on the bed, considering everything he had just experienced. He set the guitar on bed then began writing in his logbook.

40

Raw Sexuality

"Pick a bottle neck, any color."

Yang held up her hand with three glass slides slipped over three fingers. She had cut the necks off various vintage bottles and buffed them smooth. One neck was a medium amber color, another dark brown, and the third was a deep blue color.

"Wow, these look so good!"

Ethan took the amber slide, slipping it over his pinky finger. He ran it across the neck of the guitar as he plucked the strings in a blues pattern. He slid into a higher fret position and played a vibrato-like maneuver, searching for that signature Robert Johnson sound.

"Please, play the opening lick and the first verse."

Stanley played the Robert Johnson song over the monitors.

"Mmm-mmm-mmm-mmm-mmm
You better come on in my kitchen.
Well, it's goin' to be rainin' outdoors."

"Put that on a loop and let me noodle for a while."

Ethan practiced his slide guitar technique as George entered the lab carrying Chinese takeout.

"I'm taking mine into the war room," he said. "I'll leave yours on the table."

"Thank you, George."

Ethan switched to the blue bottle slide and began playing. There was a clear difference in the sound of this glass compared to the amber glass. It sounded fuller.

"That's a good sound, boss" Stanley said.

"That was an old medicine bottle, probably filled with cyanide in its day," Yang offered.

"You ready to try some vocals, see what number we can hit?" Stanley asked.

"Yes."

"I'll kill the loop and let you go at it."

He killed the loop then walked to the table to eat lunch with Yang.

"Orange chicken is mine," she said, taking it from Stanley.

Ethan played the opening lick almost perfectly and hummed the words of the verse. He sounded identical.

"You better come on in my kitchen.
Well, it's goin' to be rainin' outdoors," Ethan sang.

"We're eating Chinese in our kitchen. Better not be raining outside," Stanley sang in response to Ethan.

Yang smiled at Stanley.

"Not bad, Stanley. I didn't know you could sing."

*"You better come on in my kitchen.
Well, it's goin' to be rainin' outdoors,"* Ethan sang in perfect pitch.

Stanley and Yang dished up food from the containers and began eating lunch. Suddenly, they realized Ethan had stopped playing.

"Oh, fuck!"

Ethan had frozen; his eyes were glazed over.

Stanley ran to the workstation and started the video and audio recording while Yang initiated the guitar hologram and Ethan's body hologram.

"Are you capturing any of this yet?" Stanley asked.

"Not yet."

"Fucking hell, we're missing our first jump to who knows where and when!" Stanley cried out.

"Shit!"

"I'm not getting anything."

"Unbelievable! We're eating Chinese food while Ethan just up and nails the performance," Yang muttered.

"I'm getting data coming from the guitar now."

Ethan began to slide out of his chair toward the floor.

"Oh, shit! He's going to the floor," Stanley said as he rushed to stop him.

"Don't touch him, you might hitchhike!"

Stanley grabbed pillows off the bed and strategically placed them on the floor as Ethan slowly collapsed, cradling the guitar. He placed a final pillow under Ethan's head as he settled to the floor, spooning the guitar in front of him. Ethan's body hologram began to spark with data energy as it came fully online.

"We're up," Yang announced.

They each took a deep breath then looked at each other.

"Now what?" Stanley asked.

"We wait."

"Time to eat," Stanley said and smiled.

Two hours later, Ethan returned from the memory warp, his eyes blinking, his hands trembling. He sat bolt upright, and his eyes were wide as if he had seen something that scared him. Stanley and Yang were seated comfortably at their workstations.

"Welcome back, boss," Stanley greeted him flatly.

"Two hours and twelve minutes. I'm sure you've got some stories to tell," Yang said.

Stanley took the guitar from his arms. "Next time, give us a warning that you're going to nail the performance." He placed the guitar on the bench then returned to help Ethan to his feet. "You're sweating like crazy, boss. Where were you?"

"Maybelle's Juke Joint in Memphis. Tennessee."

"What was the year?" Yang asked as she picked up the logbook.

"I'm not sure. May I have some water, please?"

Yang took a bottle of water from the refrigerator and removed the cap. Ethan drank the entire bottle before stopping to catch his breath.

"It was so hot in there!"

He shook his head as he sat on the edge of the bed and gathered his thoughts.

"I've been places and seen things I ain't never seen before," Ethan said solemnly.

"Tell us what you saw first," Yang urged.

"Robert Johnson was on the porch at the Mercantile surrounded by people. It was suffocating hot, and he was sweating buckets. He was playing to all these people, stone cold, watching him play. It was as if he were the President of the United States the way they stood in awe. Like I said, stone cold silent they were," Ethan described.

"Keep going, I'm writing."

"He finished the song, and everyone cheered. Then he stood up, tucked the guitar under his arm, and passed through the crowd. Women were everywhere; I could smell their perfume and felt their hair as we passed by. They wore their best dresses. Their hair was all done up. And the way they looked at him…it's hard to describe," Ethan continued.

"Tell me what you saw," Yang said, still writing furiously.

"The look in their eyes. I've never seen that look before."

"Like they'd do anything he asked without question? Like they wanted to make love to him right there?" Yang asked.

"Yes. Exactly."

Stanley looked at Yang and smiled. "I've seen that look."

"He passed through the crowd of women, then what?" Yang prompted.

"There were girls, boys, teenagers and men. But mostly women in dresses and perfume. He passed through like Jesus making his way out of their midst and onto the next store front to crowds that were already assembled and waiting for him. It was like he was on a mini tour. Some of the women followed him to every location and then showed up at Maybelle's that night. Only they were not the same there."

"What do you mean?"

"At Maybelle's Juke Joint, they were like animals. They were raw, sensual. Oh my God, the way they danced. They had no inhibitions."

"All right, now things are getting good," Stanley joked.

"Absolutely! I couldn't help myself; I got an erection."

"Okay, wait a minute!" Yang called out.

"No, I really did."

"That explains why he was gone so long," Stanley mused.

"Let's skip past the whole erection bit," Yang insisted.

"Why are you so embarrassed? An erection is a normal, natural thing in a man."

"Geez, okay."

"Stanley, am I right?"

"Yes, boss. Erections are great, normal, talk about them all the time here in Research and Development. Grow up, Yang. We're scientists," Stanley insisted.

"Yes, you're right. It just caught me off guard," Yang offered, though she glared at Stanley, waiting to see if he was finished ribbing her. When she saw he was done, she rolled her eyes and added, "Fine. Fellow scientists, let's go back to Maybelle's and your erection."

"I'm so tired," Ethan mumbled. He picked up a pillow and lay down on the bed to nap.

"Come on, Ethan. We can't have the last log entry be about your erection."

"I'm exhausted. This will have to wait."

Yang looked up from the logbook at Stanley and shook her head. "Fine, I guess it ends with an erection."

41

Moonlight Lynching

"That's everything, you swear it?" Yang asked.

Ethan handed her the logbook and she quickly scanned through his entry.

"Thirty-two pages. All the stories, seven new songs; I can't think of anything else."

The genealogy tree listed the new songs Ethan had heard Robert play, either on the sidewalks at storefronts or in Maybelle's Juke Joint.

"All right, great work. This is good detail."

"This next time, I want to stay longer. A full day if possible."

"What if your body here needs to go to the bathroom?" Stanley asked.

"I can wear a diaper."

"I am not changing diapers!" Yang objected.

"The longer I stay, the more details I can bring back."

"I understand. But before you visit Maybelle's Juke Joint for another round of erections, there are two things this scientist would like to know. First, can we end the memory warp on this side? Maybe we touch you, make a loud noise, or flash a light in your eyes. Second, can we hitchhike with you after you've made the leap?"

"Those are two valid discoveries to make. I can play 'Malibu Blues,' and you can try to bring me back on this side."

"Right now?"

"Sure," Ethan replied.

Ethan retrieved the guitar and sat in his chair.

"I'll sing four verses while you guys try various ways to bring me back. If at the end of the song, if I'm still in Malibu, I'll end the warp like I normally do."

"Okay, let's do this."

"All right, back to the 1970s I go."

"Bring me back some bell-bottom jeans, size one please," Yang joked.

Ethan smiled as he played the introduction to 'Malibu Blues.'

"Lord if I had ten million dollars.
I'd move on down to Malibu.
Lord if I had ten million dollars.
I'd move…" Ethan sang and made the warp.

"What should we test first; wake him up or hitchhike?" Stanley asked.

"Hitchhike," Yang said as she reached out and grabbed Ethan's knee.

She immediately roller her eyes back and froze in position.

"Yang! What the fuck?" Stanley shook his head as Yang opened her eyes and smiled.

"Test was negative, hitchhikers only on the leap," Yang mused.

"Don't do that again!"

"One down, one to go. Your turn to wake him up."

Stanley clapped his hands together. "Ethan, come back home!"

Ethan didn't respond.

Yang shined a light across his eyes. "Ethan, if you can see this, come back to the lab now!"

Ethan remained frozen in place as Stanley lifted his phone. "Siri, play 'Out the Window' by Van Halen, full volume."

'Out the Window' began to play loudly. He held it close to Ethan's ear for several seconds before stopping the song on the app. "Sorry, Eddie. I thought you could do it."

Yang put her palm across the guitar strings near the sound hole. "I feel nothing."

Stanley gripped his hand on the fretboard and moved it slightly. "Locked in solid."

"Alright, looks like once he initiates the journey, he's the only one that can bring himself back. We're completely locked out."

Stanley and Yang stopped experimenting and after three minutes Ethan warped back into his body on his own.

"Welcome back, boss. No luck on our side."

"Whatever you did, I couldn't sense it. I didn't hear, see, or feel anything. The Talent Show went exactly as before. A perfect rewind."

***

The following day, Ethan wore an adult diaper under his clothes as he sat in his chair.

"Good luck, Ethan," Yang offered.

"Why do I get the feeling you want me gone?"

"The faster you get out of here, the sooner my weekend can begin!" Yang pointed out.

"You are both going to stay here the entire twenty-four hours, right?"

"Boss, we'll be here, now go!"

Ethan could sense something was afoot as he played the opening bars for 'Terraplane Blues' and started humming.

"Mmmmm-mmmmm," he hummed, as he looked at Stanley.

"See you in a day," Stanley told him.

"Give or take."

"We'll be here, boss."

*"And I feel so lonesome.
You hear me when I moan.
And I feel so lonesome.
You hear me when I moan.
Who been driven' my Terraplane.
For you since I been gone,"* Ethan sang.

As Ethan moved the slide up the neck he froze and his eyes glazed over.

Ethan found himself seated in a large living room of a Deep South brothel where sex workers waited for men to select them and take them upstairs. Robert was seated on a chair in the corner watching the comings and the goings of men and their hourly girlfriends. He was singing and playing 'Terraplane Blues' to the women.

One woman sat close by, smoking a cigarette as she watched Robert's fingers work the strings of the guitar. There were sounds of unbridled sexual pleasure bouncing across the walls from the flimsy doors and curtains that marked the rooms on the upper two floors overlooking the living area. Naked women and men occasionally appeared in open doorways or passing from the shared bathrooms back to the rooms where Ethan presumed no sexual desire was taboo.

When Robert finished singing, he looked over at the young sex worker watching him.

"How old are you, girl?"

"I'm as old as you want me to be," she said softly.

"I needs to know."

She put her finger to her lips, letting him know she was about to share a secret. Then she drew a one and a six on the pillow she was holding. Robert smiled.

"You like my songs?"

"I sure do."

"How 'bout a one-on-one session with greatest blues man ever lived?"

The girl flushed and fanned herself.

"Let me check your wires," *he sang out and began to play.*

Ethan felt overwhelmed, flushed with the sexual tension between them as she stood and walked to the stairs while Robert played guitar. She climbed the stairs to the second floor then walked along the handrail where she smiled at Robert, then opened a door and stepped inside.

Robert slowed then stopped playing altogether. He stood, secured the guitar under his arm, then climbed the stairs, followed the handrail, and stepped into her room. It was dimly lit. The girl was being held around the waist by a large Black man, his hand over her mouth. Another man pushed a gunny sack over Robert's head while a third tied a rope around Robert's feet.

"What the fuck!"

The man punched Robert in the face. "Shut up or die right here, motherfucker!"

"Don't hurt my guitar."

The man handed it to the girl then the men picked Robert off the ground and carried him out the back door and down the back stairs. They grabbed the girl's arm and pulled her along as Robert was carried downstairs, into the alleyway, and placed into the trunk of a waiting cab. They closed the trunk, placed the girl in the back seat, then two men climbed inside, leaving one to watch the street.

Inside the cab, the girl clutched the guitar as the cab pulled away and drove through the city.

"What are you going to do to him?"

"None of your fucking business."

"At least ten people seen him inside already. People know who he is," she insisted.

The men sat silently as the cab continued.

"What did he do?"

"He messed with the wrong woman. Now shut the fuck up!"

"Who? Who did he mess with?" she demanded.

"Willy's wife, Claudette, that's who!"

"Jesus, Lord, are you kidding me? Claudette sleeps with every musician that plays at Willy's place."

"Don't matter. This one's different."

"Different how?"

"Claudette told Willy she's gonna leave him for this blues man. She never said that about anyone before."

"Was she drunk when she say all that?"

"I don't know, I wasn't there. Willy paid us two dollars to bring his ass to him and that's what we're doing. Now please, shut up, whore!"

The girl slapped him across the face. "Don't ever call me that, James LeRoy! You've known me since I was a child and I ain't nobody's whore."

The man rubbed the side of his face as the cab drove into the night toward the outskirts of town.

"I think you boys better think this out," the girl warned. "If Willy does to this blues man what I suspect he's gonna do, all three of you gonna be implicated and I guarantee you all go to prison. Willy won't, of course, but all three of you will go to prison. Ain't never gettin' pussy again."

"He's just going to scare him, is all."

"Is that what Willy told you?"

"That's exactly what he said," the man replied.

"Of course. If Willy gonna lynch the blues man, he would never tell you that because he knows you won't go bag him and bring him to the tree," she said.

"He ain't gonna lynch him."

"Hell yes, he's planning on lynching him! He thinks blues man is stealing his wife away for good! He'll blame White folk from Mississippi, say they done it. But you three will go to jail."

The men looked at each other, beginning to worry.

"Unless you love penitentiary, you'd better turn this cab around and take us both back where you found us."

"Fuck."

"You can tell Willy you didn't find him."

"If Willy sees him around tomorrow or next, he's gonna say we lied to him. Then we in deep shit."

"Take us back to the Hotel. Me and blues man have a little fun and when he's paid up, I'll make sure he leaves town and don't come back until Willy cooled off," she offered.

The men shared a look with each other.

"He surely gonna lynch him," one of the men said assuredly.

"I don't want to be part in killing no blues man."

The cab pulled to a stop. A farm truck blocked the way forward with its bright headlights shining into the cab. Willy stepped into the lights, carrying a baseball bat in hand.

"Bring him out!" Willy shouted.

"Fuck!"

"What the fuck is going on here?" the cab driver asked.

"Everybody, get out of the car and let me do the talking!" the girl shouted.

"I got a family," the cab driver pleaded.

"You can stay, just don't do anything unless I tell you to. You got that?" she told him.

"Yes."

"Everybody else, out!"

Everyone exited the cab as the girl stepped out holding the guitar in her arms.

"Hey, Willy. How are you doing?"

"What the fuck is she doing here?"

"Now, Willy," the girl said. "I know you know me. Don't get mad at these boys, they tried to do their job, but I stepped in."

"Where's Robert fucking Johnson?"

"He's gone. Split town just like I told him to."

"Bullshit! I know he was at your place not one hour ago," Willy said.

"He certainly was. I've got his guitar here to prove it. But he's high tailing it to Memphis right now and he ain't comin' back."

"What the fuck did you do?"

"A blues man ain't a blues man without his guitar. So, I done took his guitar and told him he could pick it up at the Memphis bus station in two days. On condition that he never come back here again."

"Why would you do that?"

"Because I know how crazy you get over Claudette, Willy. I'm just trying to help all of you not do something stupid that you'll regret the rest of your life."

"That blues man needs to learn a lesson!"

"You like the blues don't you, Willy?" she asked sincerely.

"What the fuck does that have to do with this?"

"We all like the blues, Willy. Don't blame the blues man for singing songs that make people go crazy."

"He fucked Claudette!"

"You don't know that for sure, Willy."

"She done told me herself!"

"Okay. Maybe so. But Willy, you know Claudette. She'll fall for the next blues man as soon as he shows up on Friday night. Only it won't be Robert Johnson, because he's gone."

Willy took the baseball bat in hand and took a swing at the truck tire.

"Fucking blues!"

The bat bounced off the tire.

The girl waved her hand to the cab driver and he put the car in reverse and backed slowly away.

"Where the fuck is he going?"

"He just dropped off his passengers and he's headed back to work. There's nothing to remember here except some big man taking out his frustrations on a big rubber tire."

The cab made a three-point turn then drove back toward town. Willy shook his head in frustration as he watched him drive away.

"If it makes you feel any better, I'll let you beat up this old guitar," she said with a smile.

He shook his head as he turned and climbed into the cab of the truck. The other men jumped on to the bed of the truck as she climbed into the passenger seat of the cab. When Willy turned the truck toward town, she looked down to see a long rope coiled up on the floor of the truck. There certainly was going to be a lynching tonight.

"You okay, Willy?"

Willy shook his head as he drove back to town.

Later that night, the girl washed the blood-stained face of Robert Johnson with a wet washcloth. Ethan could feel the emotion between them.

"I owe you my life."

"Yes, you do, blues man."

"I'd be hangin' dead from a tree right now if it wasn't for you."

"That's for sure. But nobody hurts my blues man."

For two hours the guitar sat on the chair facing the bed as Robert and the girl fucked each other. Ethan witnessed it all.

Robert left the arms of his sixteen-year-old lover carrying the guitar across his back and his bedroll around his waist. Hours later, as the sun began to rise, Robert was miles away from Willy's wrath and well on his way to the next town and his next performance. After walking two hours in the morning sun, Robert heard a vehicle approaching from behind, so he naturally extended his arm and put his thumb high, hoping to hitch a ride before the heat became unbearable. A Terraplane sedan approached and sped by. Inside the car, was a White family dressed in their Sunday best on their way to church. Dust curled up around the back of the car engulfing Robert.

"Good Lord almighty, I got those Terraplane blues again!"

Robert took out his harmonica and began to play as he walked along. An hour later, another vehicle approached from behind, so Robert extended his arm and raised his thumb. A flatbed truck slowed down and pulled to a stop. Robert turned and raised his hand to block the rising sun to see who had stopped.

It was Willy.

"Oh, fuck," Robert said under his breath.

Willy opened the passenger door.

"Where you headed?"

Robert hesitated to answer.

"Come on son, I ain't got all day!"

Willy obviously did not recognize Robert at all.

"Next town over be fine with me."

He tossed his sleeping roll onto the floorboard of the truck then climbed inside holding his gunny sack wrapped guitar. He looked over and smiled at Willy.

"I appreciate your kindness on a Sunday morning, sir" Robert remarked earnestly with a boyish demeanor.

Willy put the truck in gear and drove on down the road. "You can call me Willy."

Robert nodded and smiled broadly in return. "Everyone calls me Blind Lemon Jefferson."

Robert put the harmonica to his mouth and began to play 'Amazing Grace' with a beautiful vibrato.

"You a church player?"

"Oh, yes! Nothing but gospel music for me. Ever since I was a child, my Mama taught me proper."

Robert continued playing the song with 'churchgoing' zeal.

"Can you play the blues?"

"Oh, no, sir. Blues is devil music for sure."

"Fucking blues," Willy said under his breath.

Robert played dozens of gospel songs while Willy sang along. By the time they arrived at Brownsville, Willy and Robert were the best of *friends. When Willy pulled the truck to the side of the road, Robert wrapped his sleeping pad around his waist and picked up his guitar.*

Willy offered his hand and smiled. "You're a good musician, son, you keep it up. Don't ever mess with voodoo or walk with the Devil."

"Yes, sir. Only the straight and narrow for me."

Robert climbed down and closed the door. As Willy drove away, Robert shook his head.

"Sweet Lord, Jesus. I got the Ridin' with the Devil blues!"

42

Up Up and Gone Gone

Ethan watched and felt the energy surrounding Robert Johnson as he spent Sunday afternoon on the steps of various storefronts in Brownsville. He had seen similar events before, but this time he concentrated on feeling the emotions and perspective of life in the Mississippi Delta. Women in their Sunday best walked the streets, enjoying the sunshine and listening to musicians play throughout town. Robert would play a couple of Gospel songs, then launch into a blues song to let his audience know he wasn't just sugar and spice and everything nice. Ethan enjoyed watching Robert perform passionately, move from storefront to storefront, play his music to adoring crowds, and collect pennies, nickels, and dimes all along his way.

Ethan began to recognize a beautiful teenage girl named Celia who appeared at nearly every stop along Robert's journey that day. She always stood near the back, stealing glances at Robert as he performed. Robert smiled respectfully back at her.

Later that day, while he was seated on a bench outside the mercantile drinking a bottle of Coca-Cola, Celia approached Robert. He nodded and smiled at her.

"Blessed Sunday afternoon."

She stopped several feet away and folded her arms across her waist. "Where did you learn to play so many songs?"

"Oh, I've been playing a long time."

"Can't be that long. What are you, maybe twenty-two years old?"

"I'm already twenty-three! An old man past his prime. What's your name?"

"Celia, what's yours?"

"Oh, I think you already know my name," he smiled.

She nodded, letting him know he was right about that.

"Can I play your favorite song?" he asked.

"How about you play me the very first song you ever played on that guitar."

"Oh, Lord Jesus. You certainly don't want to hear that. It was bad, bad, bad."

"Play it for me, I'll be the judge how bad you is."

He set his drink down and picked up the guitar to play.

"Call it 'Cotton Pickin''. Goes something like this."

He played a horrible version of the song, fumbling with chords and with an inconsistent strum. He was completely out of synch.

"Where are the words?"

"They came around later. Takes talent for a boy to play this bad and sing at the same time. I didn't get my talent until much later."

"Please stop."

Robert stopped playing and smiled "Come on now, let me play something good for you."

"You want a chance to redeem yourself after that last one?"

"Call it what you will. I got lots to choose from. Give the blues man a chance to win you back."

Celia smiled coyly, noticing his growing devilish grin.

Just then, some women in nice dresses exited the mercantile, forcing Celia to discreetly turn and walked away, leaving Robert alone on the bench with his Coca-Cola and guitar. Ethan could sense that it would tarnish her reputation if she were seen talking alone with a blues man; as bad as talking to the devil himself. Celia glanced back as she crossed the street, catching Robert's watchful eye. She smiled and he was smitten.

Later that night, Robert played to a packed crowd at the Rabbit's Foot, a local speak-easy. He started drinking the moment he arrived, and he kept drinking throughout his set, between songs and when he took breaks. He was clearly intoxicated while he performed, slurring his words. He began making rude comments to women and men dancing.

"Fucking out of my view, bitch!"

Nobody seemed to care about his profanity-laced comments because at the Rabbit's Foot, everybody drank and smoked to excess.

After two hours of performing, Robert spotted Celia standing near the back door watching him. Suddenly, he changed his entire demeanor. He straightened up, concentrated on playing songs well, and tried to sing his best—well, the best he could manage, considering he was drunk. She watched from the shadows as he played two more songs then took a break from the stage. He carried his guitar with him as he crossed the dance floor in search of Celia. When he got to where Celia had been standing, she was nowhere to be found. He looked around, searching the crowd.

"Don't leave me, baby!"

Robert staggered into the alleyway behind the Rabbit's Foot to find men and women kissing and groping each other. He stumbled up the alleyway searching for Celia. When he arrived at the main street, he looked up and down. His dream girl was nowhere to be found.

As he walked along the wooden sidewalk, he stumbled and fell when his foot caught a raised plank. He laughed at his drunken state as he crawled over and sat on a bench and rested.

"Dream girl done up up and gone gone," *he sang.*

He thumped the body of his guitar.

"Up up and gone gone to another blues man."

Robert put his head back, closed his eyes and passed out on the bench outside the Rabbit's Foot.

Ethan kept watch of the streets, as men and women passed in and out of the Rabbit's Foot, while the greatest blues man that ever lived slept on the bench cradling his guitar. Suddenly, Celia stepped from the shadows and saw Robert asleep on the bench. She cautiously approached him, removed a folded note from her sleeve, placed it inside the sound hole of the guitar then quickly walked away, disappearing into the night.

Later that night, Robert, now sober enough to play, tuned his guitar on stage. He saw the note inside his guitar. He reached in and pulled it out. But it was too dark to read what was written, so he slid the note back inside the guitar and returned to performing the rest of his set.

After Robert finished playing at two o'clock the next morning, he walked to his hotel room accompanied by a very drunk woman who undressed him and climbed in bed with him naked. The woman quickly brought Robert to full arousal. When Robert climaxed, the woman continued riding him. Robert passed out and was fast asleep when she finally climaxed and fell into the bed beside him.

Ethan had seen it all, experienced it all. He placed his hand over the sound hole of the guitar and suddenly there was a flash of light. He was warped back to the large green tree in the open field where the children laughed and played. He saw approximately fifteen children, Black children and White children, all playing together. All were dressed in similar clothes. They held each other's hands and formed a snake-like line, approaching the tree. Beyond the children was a beautiful two-story plantation mansion with double doors surrounded by smaller trees with a well-kept road leading up to the main entrance.

The children approached Ethan at the tree and formed a circle around its base while they sang and chanted their song of celebration. Ethan looked into the face of each child as they circled the tree, swinging their hands and singing until they were able to complete the circle and take hands.

Every child looked adoringly at the tree as they sang and chanted. The children walked faster and faster, sang faster and faster. They were running at full speed. Laughing and singing, gasping for breath as they tried to keep the circle going. One of the younger White girls, wearing a yellow dress, lost her footing and stumbled. Two Black boys on each side of her held tight to her hands and her feet flew out. Her legs and dress flew into the air as she laughed, holding tight to the boys' hands. Ethan watched the girl intently; there was something mesmerizing about her.

Suddenly, there was a loud BANG and a flash of light.

Ethan lay curled up on the floor of the lab, cradling the guitar in his arms. A blanket covered him.

Stanley and Yang were nowhere to be found.

Ethan stood and placed the guitar on the workbench. As he placed it on its back, he caught a glimpse of something within the guitar. He moved the guitar beneath a light on the workbench and investigated the sound hole. Laying in the darkness was the small envelope that Celia had given Robert. The words 'Body and Soul,' were written in neat handwriting.

He was shocked by this discovery. After several moments of consideration, Ethan reached inside and pulled the envelope from inside the guitar. He opened the envelope and removed the note inside.

Ethan smiled broadly as he read it.

43

The 27 Club

"Congratulations, your AI is now fully interactive!"

George stood in front of the guitar genealogy tree and guitar hologram as Ethan, Yang, and Stanley sat listening. The tree was filled with musician leaves with thousands of songs hanging off them.

"We have also connected her to every DNA repository on the dark web, so there's really nothing she cannot do if we ask her to."

"What does that mean?" Ethan asked.

"Ask any question related to our data and she'll respond."

"Show me every song sung by Robert Johnson," Ethan requested.

"Her name is Audi," George told him.

"Audi, like the car?" Stanley asked.

"Aud is Latin for listen and the I for intelligence," George explained.

"I guess Santa speaks Latin?" Yang joked.

George rolled his eyes playfully then said, "Audi, this is Ethan."

"Very nice to meet you, Ethan," Audi replied in a gentle female tone.

"Nice to meet you as well. Audi, show me every song sung by Robert Johnson," Ethan asked again.

"Okay, give me one moment," Audi replied.

Audi illuminated only the branch, leaf, and song titles directly related to Robert Johnson.

"Okay, impressive."

"Audi, this is Yang. Show every musician that sang a Robert Johnson song," Yang instructed.

"Hello, Yang. Here are your results."

Audi illuminated branches and leaves that matched her request.

"Jimi Hendrix," Stanley said.

"Show all songs played by Jimi Hendrix," Ethan asked.

Jimi's branch, leaf, and song list illuminated.

"I'm loving this," Yang commented.

"Show every musician that played any version of 'Crossroad Blues,'" Ethan asked.

Leaves appeared of every artist that had played the song.

Ethan paused for a moment then asked, "Audi, did Kurt Cobain really play 'Crossroad Blues' on this guitar?"

"Kurt Cobain first played 'Crossroad Blues' on January 1, 1992," Audi said.

"Audi, when did Kurt Cobain die?" Yang asked.

"Kurt Cobain died on April 5, 1994. Police found him in his Seattle garage with a self-inflicted shotgun wound to the head."

"How old was he when he died?" Ethan asked.

"Kurt was twenty-seven years old when he died."

"Most people know that already," Stanley said solemnly.

"Audi, were there other musicians who died at the age of twenty-seven who played this guitar?"

"Yes, there were many."

"Can you show them, please?"

The tree hologram went dark and then displayed fifteen leaves with each of their names illuminated. Robert Johnson, Penbrow, Jim Morrison, Alan Wilson, Brian Jones, Jimi Hendrix, Janis Joplin, Sadie, Rob Pigpen, Toby, Mia Zapata, Kurt Cobain, Kristen Pfaff, and finally, Amy Winehouse.

"Holy fuck," Yang said quietly.

"Those are all members of the famous twenty-seven club," Stanley said in awe.

"Ethan, what the fuck is going on here?" Yang whispered to Ethan.

"Audi, show us musicians who died at the age of twenty-nine."

The tree hologram went completely dark.

"I'm sorry, Ethan, there are no musicians who match your request."

"Show us musicians who died at the age of twenty-five."

The hologram tree pulsed lightly for a few moments.

"I'm sorry, Ethan. There are none."

"Audi, show us the entire tree," Ethan requested.

Every branch and leaf began to illuminate until the tree was fully bloomed.

"Boss?" Stanley said.

"Yes?"

"There were fourteen musicians on that list."

"I saw the list, Stanley."

"Some of the most influential musicians in history…" Stanley continued calmly.

Ethan looked at the guitar laying on the workbench. The hologram showed the receptors pulsing with energy.

"Audi, what was the last song Kurt Cobain sang on the guitar?" Ethan queried.

Kurt's leaf glowed then scrolled to the last song.

"The song was titled 'You Know You're Right'."

"On what date?" Stanley asked.

"April 5, 1994."

Stanley pointed at the orange leaf belonging to Kurt Cobain. His death date was April 5, 1994.

Ethan sat silently considering all that they had asked and learned. Something was troubling him deeply.

"Boss?"

Ethan did not respond, just sat quietly.

"Thank you, George," Yang said, understanding that Ethan needed space to process everything.

"Audi is available around the clock, just call out," George offered then walked away.

"I'm here for you whenever you need me," Audi added.

Later that day, Ethan stood at the packing box retrieving the many pictures of his father posing with various musicians. He had been photographed with Kurt Cobain, Amy Winehouse, Kristen Pfaff, Jean-Michael Basquiat, Chris Bell, and many others. Ethan examined the picture of John and Kurt Cobain standing in John's office at Capital Records.

Kurt was holding the guitar.

44

Ribbons in Time

"Where would you like to go?" Ethan asked.

Bella stepped close to the guitar genealogy tree with all the artists and songs illuminated.

"This is like a candy store; there are way too many choices for me to decide. I guess I would love to see Jimi."

"I can take you to his tour bus if you like," Ethan offered.

"With or without the psychedelics?"

"Stone cold sober," Ethan assured her.

"Let's do it!"

Ethan and Bella memory warped to Jimi's tour bus. Jimi was playing 'Angel' on the guitar. After a few moments, Sadie opened the door to his room and entered. Ethan was mesmerized by Sadie as she curled up in front of Jimi and listened to him play. As they began making love, Ethan looked over and could see Bella watching intently.

Suddenly there was a FLASH of light and Ethan and Bella were time warped to the tree on the plantation where they stood looking up at the tree with the singing children behind them. They turned to see the children taking hands as they continued singing. The children formed a circle around the tree. Bella watched the young girl closely as they ran around the tree together. Ethan looked out at the plantation house. He saw wagons and horses with men and women moving furniture from the home. Bella counted the children and looked closely at each of their faces.

Thunderclouds rolled overhead and then lightning struck the tree, and everything exploded. The tree toppled to the ground as the children flew in all directions. Ethan looked at the girl closely, not wanting to miss any details. Bella saw the people rush from the house and drive wagons toward the fallen tree and children. They came to their side—men and women, Black and White, all dressed very much like they were all from the same family and social class. Women cried when they saw that the children were clearly dead.

It began to rain as a woman knelt beside the girl and pushed her singed hair and bloody hair bow away from her face.

"Come on, Emily!" *the woman yelled. She placed her hand on Emily's back and moved her back and forth trying to revive her.* "Emily, come on baby!" *the woman begged.*

"Breath!" *Ethan shouted.*

Suddenly, Emily's eyes opened, and she looked directly at Ethan. She reached out toward the tree and pulled herself to it. She embraced the tree, putting her face on it, on Ethan's face.

There was a FLASH of light and Ethan and Bella were warped back to Jimi's back room on the tour bus. Sadie and Jimi were having sex. Ethan placed his hand on the strings over the sound hole and initiated the memory warp, returning them to the lab.

Ethan and Bella arrived back in the lab and looked at each other.

"Her name is Emily," Bella said.

"She's alive," Ethan added.

Ethan walked the guitar to the workbench and placed it down on the pad. He picked up a logbook and handed it to Bella.

"Write everything you remember; no talking until it's documented," he insisted.

"Starting at what point?" Bella asked.

"The moment we arrived on the tour bus clear to the end," Ethan told her.

"Okay," she replied.

Thirty minutes later, Bella set her pen down and looked over at Ethan who was still writing.

"Don't talk," Ethan muttered.

Bella walked to the guitar while Ethan continued writing. Something caught her attention. She picked up a flashlight and shined it into the guitar.

"Ethan, I think you're going to want to see this."

Ethan continued writing.

"Ethan!"

He looked up and saw that she was serious, so he stepped to the bench and looked down at the guitar.

"Oh my God."

Emily's blood-stained hair bow along with strands of blonde hair lay inside the guitar.

"What should we do?" Bella whispered fearfully.

"Audi, are you there?" Ethan asked.

"Yes, Ethan, I'm here."

"We have a hairbow, from a girl we believe lived in the 1800s, along with blood and strands of hair. What should we do with it?"

"My DNA database goes back hundreds of years. If you send it in for DNA processing, we can see if it matches anyone within the database. We might discover living offspring from the girl in present day," Audi replied.

Ethan looked closely at the guitar body, running his finger over a crack near the sound hole.

"Was that crack there before?" Bella asked.

"No. We damaged it somehow," he replied.

"Is it bad?"

"I don't know."

Ethan gently reached between the strings and removed the blood-stained bow from the guitar and placed it on the workbench.

"That blood looks like it could have been spilled thirty minutes ago," Bella observed.

Ethan retrieved a Ziplock bag from a nearby drawer and placed the hairbow securely inside.

"Does any of this worry you, Ethan?"

"Why?"

"We have a blood-stained hairbow from a girl in the 1800s. That's very strange!"

"We didn't kill her, Bella. We saved her."

She nodded in agreement though she still looked concerned.

"This guitar gave us the power to save someone's life. That doesn't worry me. That inspires me," Ethan added with a gentle smile.

"Do you really believe we saved that little girl?" Bella asked sincerely.

"Yes. And I think with this guitar may want us to save others."

"Holy shit, Ethan. If we can save someone from the past, won't that have a direct impact on the future?"

Ethan nodded in confirmation.

Bella thought for a moment. "Does this mean we can save anybody we choose?"

"I don't know," Ethan admitted.

45

The Butterfly Effect

"There's something I haven't shared with either of you."

Ethan sat with Yang and Stanley in the lab.

"Is it in the logbook?" Yang asked.

"No."

"Ethan! You know lab protocol; you have to write *everything* down," Yang insisted.

"Well, I didn't write this down. The thing is, the day Bella hitchhiked with me, and we stopped Janis from falling, I had a dream that night that everything had changed. As if the entire memory was now altered for real. So, without telling either of you, or recording it, I did a solo memory recall just to see what the effects were. When I went back, the memory was altered. She fell onto the bed and didn't hit the ground. But she still died, fifteen minutes later, on the bed, from the heroin."

"Did it alter reality or just the memory recall?" Yang asked.

"I assumed just the memory. I don't know about reality."

"Ethan. Holy fuck! You must tell us these things!" She walked to the computer and typed a Google search. "Do either of you remember seeing photos of the motel room and Janis's death pictures?" Yang asked.

"She was wedged between the bed and nightstand," Stanley replied.

"That's what I remember as well," Ethan agreed.

Yang enlarged one of the photos to fill the big monitor. Janis lay face down on the bed with her face in the pillow.

"That's exactly what she looked like in the altered recall!" Ethan exclaimed.

"Bella's reaction didn't just change the memory. She fucking *altered reality*, Ethan!" Yang gasped.

Stanley and Ethan shared a look.

"If she hadn't taken the heroin, there's a very good chance she'd still be alive today," Ethan sighed.

Yang walked to the war room window and tapped on the glass. George looked up and Yang waved him into the lab.

"What are you doing?" Stanley asked.

"I have some questions about our data," Yang replied.

George entered the lab.

"George, how extensive is our AI projections capability?"

"I'm not sure what you mean."

"Can it perform 'what if scenarios?' Like, what if Jimi Hendrix never played this guitar?"

"Sure, Audi is capable of that. That's just chopping off a branch and anything that grew from it," he told her.

"How about, what if Jimi also played Bob Dylan's 'Tambourine Man'? Can we see who else may have been influenced even though it's not real?"

"Audi gets more and more sophisticated every hour of her existence. Ask her and see how she responds."

"Thank you, George," Yang said.

"Seriously, this just gets more and more bizarre," George mumbled as he returned to his room once again.

Yang looked knowingly at Ethan and Stanley.

"If Bella was able to alter how Janis fell…maybe we can alter other things? Bigger events with bigger impact?" Yang pondered quietly.

"Like maybe we save a member of The 27 Club," Ethan said solemnly.

Yang looked puzzled as Ethan said, "Audi, show us all the musicians who died at the age of twenty-seven."

The tree quickly changed and showed only those musicians who died at twenty-seven. From Robert Johnson at the earliest, to Amy Winehouse. Fourteen total leaves along with their songs appeared.

Ethan walked to the packing box and lifted several of the framed photos and placed them across the bed. "I want you to see these."

Yang and Stanley approached the bed and looked at the images of John with the musicians. Nearly all of them included the guitar in the photograph.

"What's going on here, boss?"

"I don't know."

46

Resurrection

"Do you know these musicians?"

Bella looked at the list Ethan handed her. She was sitting with Ethan, Stanley, and Yang at a Subway Sandwich dining table eating lunch.

"You're kidding, right?"

"They all died at the age of twenty-seven," Ethan said flatly.

"And every one of them played our guitar," Yang added.

"How do you know that?" Bella asked.

"Audi confirmed it. And we have pictures of Ethan's father posing with several of them," Stanley explained.

"If you could save one of those musicians, who would it be?" Ethan asked then bit into his sandwich.

"Like the little girl?"

"Yes."

Bella seriously considered each name on the list. "Some of these guys were pretty fucked up," Bella said, taking a pickle from her sandwich and placing it on the paper next to her selection. "That would be my first choice."

Yang removed a pickle from her sandwich and placed it on the paper. "My choice."

Stanley put a jalapeño next to his choice. "And that's mine."

Later that evening, Ethan, Yang, and Stanley sat at the guitar tree hologram.

"Audi, show me every song played by Kurt Cobain," Ethan requested.

A list of song titles showed under a date marked December 11, 1992. The song 'Heart-Shaped Box' was among them."

"Can you play that song?" Yang asked.

"Yes."

"Audi, what if Robert Johnson never played this guitar?" Stanley asked.

"Hypothetical results rendering now."

The hologram started losing leaves and branches until only Robert Johnson and his song list remained. His leaf pulsed while songs on his list disappeared. Then his leaf and branch dissolved entirely, leaving only the main trunk with few leaves and song titles.

"Robert started it all," Ethan surmised.

Stanley touched a leaf marked *May 21, 1917*. "Audi, can you play this song from May 21, 1917?"

"The actual musician is unverified, but I can play an assimilation."

Audi played the tune over the monitors. It was a guitar melody, sounding like a chicken pecking random strings and notes.

"Cotton pickin' blues," a female voice sang out.

"Audi, was that really a female voice?" Stanley asked.

"Yes, I'm certain it was."

"That was the first song Robert Johnson ever played on guitar," Ethan told them. "He talked about it and played it to Celia on the night I went back."

"That would make Robert, what? Fourteen years old when he played it," Yang calculated.

"That could have been Robert's mother singing," Ethan pointed out. "Audi, please restore the tree."

The tree quickly illuminated to its full bloom as Ethan looked at Sadie's leaf then over to Toby.

"Audi, who took possession of the guitar after Toby was killed?" Ethan asked.

"A man by the name of John."

"Did this John ever play the guitar or sing?"

"No."

"Makes sense. My father never played guitar or sang as long as I remember."

"Where are you going with this, boss?" Stanley enquired.

"Audi, who took possession of the guitar after Kurt Cobain was found dead?" Ethan asked.

The tree pulsed for several seconds.

"John."

"How certain are you?"

"Most certain, Ethan. It was clearly mentioned in the history."

"Audi, whose voice was the last voice the guitar heard before you were locked away and put in storage in February of 2015?"

The tree pulsed for several seconds.

"John Klein."

"Audi, did you know that John Klein is my father?"

"I will add that to my knowledge base for future reference."

"Audi, what were John Klein's last words?" Ethan asked, trying to keep his voice steady.

"I don't know, Ethan."

"Why not?"

"My programming only matches voices accompanied with music played on the guitar. I can certainly begin to learn all spoken voices if that is what you wish," Audi replied.

"Yes, I would like you to begin learning spoken words as well."

"Audi, show us the musicians who played the guitar in 2015," Stanley instructed.

The tree hologram displayed a single leaf with dozens of songs listed.

"Nurse Jones," Ethan read out loud. "Audi, play this final song performed by Nurse Jones."

"Once again, this is an unverified voice, so I will render and play an assimilation of that song."

"The rendered assimilation will do."

The song on the list illuminated brightly.

"Come on Audi, you can do this," Yang encouraged.

"Thank you, Yang. I'm almost ready," Audi responded.

Yang shook her head at Audi's personalization. "This is getting a little creepy."

The song began to play over the monitor. It was a gentle song, played and perfectly sung by a voice that was better than most.

"Damn! That girl could sing the phonebook and I'd listen!" Yang enthused.

"Audi, was that a true rendering of her voice?"

"I used no autotuning or enhancement," Audi replied.

"That was fantastic."

"Ethan, you might find it interesting to hear the very first song with this same musician," Audi offered.

Stanley and Yang shared a look.

"Did she just recommend something completely random?" Stanley said quietly.

"With all due respect, Stanley. I think my question is very much in line with the questions already asked about Nurse Jones," Audi responded.

Stanley's eyes went wide as he looked at Ethan and Yang.

"Audi, show us the very first song by Nurse Jones," Ethan said.

Catrina's leaf began to pulse.

"I believe Catrina from 1973 is the same singer as Nurse Jones in 2015," Audi said.

"Audi, play the song," Yang said.

"She performed this song as a trio with two men, Sam and Toby," Audi replied.

Stanley pointed at Toby's orange glowing leaf with his death date and age. "Twenty-seven club member."

"Yes, that is correct, Stanley. Toby is a member of The 27 Club," Audi stated quietly.

"Audi, how did you know about The 27 Club?" Yang asked.

"I learned it by listening to all of you."

Yang raised her hand to stop Ethan and Stanley from asking further questions. She held her finger to her lips to quiet them.

"Audi, please wait to play the song until we come back. Bio break, everyone," Yang said in a deliberately warm voice.

Yang motioned Ethan and Stanley to follow her. In the outer waiting area, she pulled them aside and held the doors closed. "Is anyone else feeling really creeped out by how personal Audi is getting?"

"She recommends things and asks us questions," Stanley offered.

"Because she found a match in the voice from 2015 back to 1973. I don't find that weird at all," Ethan replied.

"She's matching my tone!" Yang said shaking her head.

"Guys, this is not a dumb computer we're talking to. We're interacting with an AI personality," Ethan pointed out.

Yang shook her head. "She's probably in there thinking, 'Geez, I hope I didn't say something wrong?' or 'Geez, I wonder what's taking them so long?' Holy Fuck!" Yang said.

"I'm going back inside."

Stanley looked at Yang as Ethan walked away.

"Audi, please play the song by Catrina, Sam, and Toby," Ethan said.

"Shall I wait until Yang and Stanley return from their bio break?" Audi asked.

Yang and Stanly stepped through the lab doors and approached the tree. Yang lifted her hand and flipped the bird at Audi. "Audi, play the song."

"I hope you like it," Audi offered.

The song played. It was the very song Toby, Sam, and Catrina performed on *The Sonny & Cher Show*.

Everyone was mesmerized by the performance. When it finished playing, they sat quietly.

"That was a fantastic song," Stanley remarked.

"Audi, do you now know if Catrina Jones is still alive?" Ethan asked.

"Let me check my sources," Audi replied.

Ethan stood and looked down at the guitar with the hologram pulsing above it.

"What would make Catrina turn from 'Holy shit' amazing trio vocalist into Nurse Jones caregiver at The Channel Islands Institute for the Mentally Ill?" Ethan replied.

Stanley noticed George watching them from inside the war room as if he were listening to their conversation. Stanley motioned to Yang to look over there.

"Can he hear us?" Stanley muttered, placing his hand over his lips.

Yang smiled and waved at George. He returned the wave and smile then crossed his arms across his chest.

"George, if you can hear me, please come into the lab," Yang said under her breath.

George did not react in any way.

"You're getting paranoid, Stanley, stop it!"

"Ethan, all of my sources indicate that Catrina Jones is still alive," Audi said.

"Thank you, Audi," Ethan replied.

"Ethan, I need to go offline now. George needs to perform optimization to my core language. May I be excused for a few hours?" Audi asked.

Yang shook her head, uncomfortable with how personalized Audi was becoming.

"Yes, Audi. Please let us know when you come back online." Ethan replied.

"I certainly will. Good day everyone, see you soon," Audi said.

The guitar tree bloomed to full illumination then stopped pulsing. Stanley zoomed in on Catrina's leaf from 1973 along with her song list.

"Have either of you ever heard this song before today?"

"No," they replied.

"It sounded like a top ten hit single, produced in a studio," Stanley observed.

"Play it again."

Stanley played the recording over the monitor.

Meanwhile, Yang exited the lab into the waiting area. She searched her phone and dialed a phone number.

"Hello, good morning. I was hoping to speak to someone about my father who passed away a few months ago at the Institute." After a few moments, she nodded. "Thank you, I'm happy to hold."

She put her phone on speaker and opened a logbook to write. A few moments later, a male voice came over the speaker.

"Patient relations, this is Daniel."

"Daniel, my father-in-law John Klein was being cared for when he passed away a few months ago. Nurse Jones was his favorite nurse. Is there any way I can possibly speak to her?"

"I'm sorry, may I have your name?" Daniel asked.

"I'm Yang. Yang Klein."

"I'm sorry, Ms. Klein, I don't see you listed as a contact for any patients here at the Institute," he responded.

"Ethan Klein is my husband, I'm certain he's on the list. I just need to know if Nurse Jones is still working at the Institute," Yang attempted.

"Ethan Klein?"

"Yes."

"Is Ethan available to speak to me?"

"No, but I'm his wife, can you please just check for me?"

"I'm sorry, unless I verify you, I'm not able to provide any information regarding patients or staff," Daniel insisted.

"It's just, Catrina Jones…she was so sweet every time I came to visit. Daddy loved her," Yang said, affecting her voice to become emotional. "He wrote her such a sweet note, I just wanted to send it to her," Yang said, beginning to fake cry.

Daniel did not respond to her crying.

"I'm sorry to have bothered you," Yang said softly.

"Ms. Klein?" Daniel asked.

"Yes," she said, sniffling a bit.

"Our mailing address is listed on our website," Daniel said.

"Yes, I see it."

"You can send it to that address."

"Can you promise me it will be given to Nurse Jones?"

Daniel hesitated, then said sincerely, "Write 'Attention Daniel' at the bottom."

Yang smiled. "You've been so helpful. Thank you."

She ended the call and smiled as she pushed her way through the double doors into the lab.

"Hold the presses, gentlemen! Yang has a headline! We're going to see Nurse Jones!"

47

Road Trip Blues

"It's just like I remember."

Ethan looked out the window of Stanley's converted Sprinter van at The Channel Islands Institute. From the visitor parking lot, he could see the neatly landscaped grounds, which were dotted with mature palm trees. Large, grassed areas surrounding the main building, extending to the dormitories beyond.

"Are you sure you don't want me to come with you? After all, I am you wife now," Yang joked.

"That's not funny."

Stanley opened the sliding door as Ethan took the guitar and stepped outside. "Good luck. We'll be waiting here."

Ethan took in a deep breath then slowly exhaled. "I hope she's here."

Yang and Stanley watched anxiously as Ethan walked steadily toward the main building.

"Are you worried?" Stanley asked Yang.

"An autistic genius carries a time machine into a mental institution. What on earth could possibly go wrong?" Yang quipped.

Stanley rolled the Sprinter door closed.

Inside the lobby area, Ethan approached the reception counter, where a neatly dressed receptionist sat behind a computer monitor.

"Welcome to The Channel Islands Institute. I'm Karen," she said, offering her hand to Ethan.

Ethan smiled and took her hand.

"I remember you. I'm Ethan."

"Please forgive me for not remembering you, Ethan. Do you have family here at the Institute?" she asked.

"I'm Ethan Klein. John Klein, the record label executive, was my father."

"Oh, yes, I remember John very well. He transitioned just recently."

"Karen, I drove eight hours to get here, can I ask a favor?"

"Absolutely, Ethan."

"I'd like to speak to Nurse Jones. Catrina Jones, I believe."

"Nurse Jones?" Karen asked.

"She used to play this guitar to my father while he was here."

"I'm sorry, Ethan, but Nurse Jones is no longer with us," she informed him gently.

Ethan looked down, saddened by the news. "When did she die?"

"Oh no, I just meant she's no longer working at the Institute. She gave notice shortly after your father passed away," Karen explained warmly.

"Oh, thank, God!" Ethan said happily.

"And yes, she was very fond of your father, Ethan."

"Do you know where she went?"

"Wait here. Let me see what I can find."

"Thank you, thank you so much!"

Karen bustled away down the hallway as Ethan looked up at a large mural on the wall. It depicted the early indigenous people of the Channel Islands, the Chumash, working the land. He was mesmerized by their faces; they appeared so content and peaceful.

Fifteen minutes later, Ethan smiled as he walked briskly down the sidewalk toward the Sprinter van with a folded piece of paper in his hand. He approached the van, grabbed hold of the sliding door handle, and pulled the door open.

Inside the van, Stanley and Yang were in the throes of passionately making out. Stanley's pants were unbuttoned and Yang's top was off. They froze in place.

"Holy shit, Ethan!" Yang exclaimed.

"Didn't you think to knock?" Stanley asked, exasperated.

Ethan didn't bat an eye at their situation and merely said, "Good news, I got her address."

He handed the guitar to Yang and climbed in and sat in his chair.

"This is not what you think it is…" Yang began tentatively.

"Oh, please, I've known for months that you and Stanley have sex."

Stanley looked at Yang. "Did you tell him?"

"No! Did you?"

"Nobody told me anything. The sexual tension between you two is so obvious. I'll bet Audi even knows," Ethan said.

Stanley grinned, buttoned his pants, and climbed into the driver's seat. Yang shook her head in disbelief that all their creeping around had been for nothing, then turned her attention to the note.

"Is this a joke?" she asked after reading it.

"No."

Yang handed the note to Stanley as he started the engine.

"Do you want me to drive so you two can finish what you started?" Ethan joked.

Yang casually retrieved her blouse and put it on.

"And does this mean we're no longer married?" Ethan added.

"Funny."

"Which reminds me, where were you two when I returned from my two-day memory warp? You said you'd be there when I got back. What could you have been up to, huh?"

Pointedly ignoring him, Stanley pulled from the parking lot and headed toward the main road.

"You make a cute couple," Ethan said seriously.

Stanley smiled as he looked back at Yang. "There's a twenty-four-hour wedding chapel on the strip."

Ethan teased Yang and Stanley about their relationship the entire trip from The Channel Islands Institute, across the desert passing Barstow, the big thermometer in Baker, and into Las Vegas. It was midnight when they arrived and checked in to Southpoint Hotel and Casino. Ethan stepped to the reservation desk carrying the guitar.

"Two rooms. One for me, another for the newlyweds."

Stanley and Yang were too tired to respond in any way.

That night, Ethan dreamed he was at the large tree once again, listening to the laughter of the children, hearing them sing and seeing the girl swinging around in the circle holding the boys' hands. The BANG and CRASH in the memory woke Ethan from his sleep and he sat up. He looked over at the open guitar case resting in the living area chair.

***

The following morning, Stanley handed Yang a pair of bowling shoes with a determined look on his face.

"I'm not bowling!" Yang insisted.

"You must wear them if you sit at the scoring table. House rules," Stanley replied firmly.

Ethan sat at the score table.

"Add her name, I want to see how bad this gets," Stanley said with a smile.

Ethan entered the name 'Blossom' as Yang's name. Then he entered the names 'Buttercup' and 'Bubbles.'

"Hey, this is a company-sponsored outing," he announced. "Everybody participates!"

Yang stared directly at him with a 'you're in deep shit' look on her face.

Ethan smiled at Yang as Stanley walked away to find a bowling ball.

"My father took us bowling a lot as a kid. I'll get you through this, I promise."

Yang shook her head as she took off her street shoes and put on the house-issued bowling shoes. "I'm seriously going to injure someone."

"What kind of music do you listen to?"

"I'm an '80s hair band kind of girl; will that get me out of bowling?"

"Which bands?"

"Bon Jovi, Journey, The GoGos."

"Okay, all good. Trapped on a desert island, one song?"

"What the fuck does this have to do with bowling?"

"Absolutely nothing, I just want to know."

Yang whispered into Ethan's ear.

"Okay, that's a good one."

"Secrets?" Stanley asked, returning with two bowling balls and setting them on the carousal.

"How about you, Stanley? Trapped on a desert island, only one song the entire time," Yang asked.

Stanley pursed his lips, thinking long and hard. "So many great ABBA songs to choose from…how about 'Mama Mia'?"

Yang stared blankly back at him. Stanley winked at her, letting her know he was kidding.

"Boss?" Yang asked.

Ethan took a bowling ball and stepped to his mark. He held his position for several moments then nodded assuredly.

"'Space Oddity,' David Bowie."

He stepped forward and threw the bowling ball. It started off close to the gutter but quickly curved into the middle and knocked down all but one pin.

"Good afternoon, ladies and gentlemen," came the booming voice of the announcer. "Welcome to Chicago Blues and Jazz. We are so excited to have you join us here in the West Room. You're going to see a lot of great singers and musicians in the next two hours, so be prepared to be blown away. Please, silence those cell phones and hide them away. You won't want to miss what you're about to hear and see."

The main stage in the West Room Club was small, able to accommodate four or five musicians at one time. Ethan, Stanley, and Yang sat at a darkened, padded seat booth with a flickering candle in the middle. They sipped drinks and snacked on crackers and pretzels.

Over the next two hours, they enjoyed music from various artists. Finally, after a lively jazz jam session, the guitar player spoke into the microphone.

"And now, a warm welcome to the newest member of our show, Catrina Jones."

The spotlight illuminated the piano where 'Nurse' Catrina Jones sat at the keys with a microphone to her lips.

"That's her," Ethan whispered to Stanley and Yang.

Catrina began to play and sing a sultry blues song. Her voice was fantastic, full of heart and soul. She sang several songs by herself and then sang a few with the full band. When the show ended, everyone gave a standing ovation. During the outpouring of appreciation, Ethan's eyes met Catrina's, and he smiled broadly.

Later that evening, Catrina walked across the stage, still wearing her costume and makeup. She descended the stairs and approached Ethan's table.

"The stage manager told me three adoring fans wanted to meet me," Catrina offered with a joking smile.

"Hello, Nurse Jones," Ethan said, hoping she would remember him from his visits to his father in the Institute.

Catrina offered her hand. "Hello, Ethan. It's been so long. How are you?"

"I'm good. These are my colleagues, Yang and Stanley."

"It's nice to meet you both. I hope you enjoyed our little show."

"You are amazing!" Yang gushed.

"Mesmerizing, absolutely!" Stanley added.

"It's just a small stage for a has-been singer like me. I still work morning shifts at a nearby hospital, but I'm happy."

"I enjoyed every one of your songs," Ethan said conclusively.

"Thank you, Ethan," she replied, then put her head to one side, thinking. "You know, your voice sounds just like your father," she said sentimentally.

Ethan nodded awkwardly, not knowing how to carry the conversation further.

"I'm sure there's a pretty good reason why you tracked me down here," she prompted gently.

"Yes, there is," Ethan replied.

"Let me get out of these sequins and beads so we can talk. Wait here, I'll be out shortly."

Catrina turned and walked backstage, her sequins and beads shimmering in the lights.

Yang nodded her head. "Wow."

"Yeah, she's that good," Ethan agreed.

48

Catrina

"This guitar can take me back to 1973 for real?" Catrina asked suspiciously.

The guitar lay exposed in its open case on the coffee table in Ethan's hotel room. Catrina sat in a chair with Ethan across from her.

"Yes."

"I've experienced it myself," Yang added.

"What did you see?"

"I saw Ethan perform 'Mr. Tambourine Man' to kids in Malibu when he was fourteen years old."

"And I spent two days with Robert Johnson in the 1930s and almost got lynched," Ethan said.

"Robert Johnson, Mississippi Delta, Robert Johnson?"

"Yes. And he saw Janis Joplin die in her motel room in Hollywood," Yang said.

Catrina shook her head, appearing reluctant to believe the entire story. "Why are you telling me this?"

"Ask her straight out, boss," Stanley suggested.

"You sang a song in 1973 with two men. Someone named Toby, another named Sam," Ethan said.

Catrina was taken aback when she heard their names. "Those are two names I thought I'd never hear again."

"Do you remember the song?"

"Of course, we performed it on *The Sonny & Cher Show*."

"You performed that song on national television?" Ethan asked.

"We performed it, but it didn't air. We were cut from the show."

"Why?"

Catrina hesitated then said, "We made Cher cry."

"They cut your song because you made her cry?" Yang asked, flabbergasted.

Catrina shook her head, not wanting to continue. "It's more complicated than that."

"Wait...I saw you come to my house with the police! During my birthday party!" Ethan recalled suddenly.

"That's right, Ethan. Well, I may as well tell you. Toby and Sam died the morning before *The Sonny & Cher Show* was supposed to air nationally. CBS wasn't about to introduce The Dreamers on a comedy show and then tell the audience two of its members had just died."

"The Dreamers?" Ethan asked.

"Yes."

"How did Toby and Sam die?" Stanley asked.

"They were found dead in a motel room in the valley the afternoon the show was supposed to air. Nobody knows how they died."

"Was there an autopsy?"

"I'm certain that there would have been, but they shielded me from all that."

"Did you attend the funeral?" Stanley asked.

"Yes, with your father and his executive assistant, Camille," she said sadly.

"Do you still remember the song?" Ethan asked eagerly.

She laughed. "It was a song that was going to change the world. How could I ever forget?"

"If I played it on this guitar, could you sing it with me?" Ethan asked sincerely.

"What good would that do?"

Ethan looked at Yang who nodded in response.

"We might be able to find out how Sam and Toby died," she offered.

"Again, what good would that do?"

Ethan hesitated to answer.

"We can't change the past, Ethan," Catrina said. "Some things are better left alone."

"But what if we could change the past, Catrina? What if we could save Sam and Toby?" Ethan asked solemnly.

"What do you mean?"

"I can memory warp to a time and place within this guitar's memory. I can maybe change the outcome in reality."

Catrina looked at him seriously. "You can travel back to my *Sonny & Cher Show* performance and save Toby and Sam?" she asked in disbelief.

Ethan shared a look with Yang and Stanley.

"Perhaps."

"If you save them in 1973, they could be alive today…right here?" Catrina asked, becoming emotional.

"Perhaps."

Catrina's lip began to tremble as she began to cry. "Ladies and gentlemen, give a big round of applause to The Dreamers," Catrina said through her tears.

Yang took her hand and held tight.

"Will you help us?" Ethan asked quietly.

"This is all so overwhelming. I just don't know what to believe. I have a show tonight…I need time to think about this."

Later that evening, Ethan talked it over with Yang and Stanley.

"If she decides to help us, what are the ramifications of us doing this memory warp outside the confines of the lab?" Ethan asked.

"We won't have direct data feeds into the data lake from your receptors or the guitar, but we can sync them later," Stanley replied.

"Can we connect to Audi remotely?"

"Only if we call the lab and someone puts us on speaker."

"We gotta fix that!"

"According to Catrina, it was forty-eight hours from the time they recorded the show until they were found dead. You'll be gone for at least two days," Stanley said.

"Do you want Catrina to hitchhike with you?" Yang suggested.

"No. There's are too many unknowns. I'm going alone."

"What if she decides not to sing with you?" Stanley asked.

"There's enough of Toby and Sam solo that I can match to make the warp without her permission," Ethan explained.

"What if she insists we leave history alone and asks us to stop?" Yang pointed out.

Ethan and Stanley had no response.

"There are other members of The 27 Club we could save…" Yang ventured.

"We've made no decision to save anyone, Yang. Right now, all we care about is finding out how Sam and Toby died in that motel room," Ethan insisted.

Later that night, Catrina took the stage, wearing an extravagant gown harking back to the Chicago night clubs of the 1950s. She sang songs with the band and blew the audience away with her performances. After the completion of another classic, she sat at the piano noodling on a few keys.

"I'd like to change things up a bit, if the band doesn't mind," she announced, looking at her fellow musicians.

They nodded in agreement, knowing full well they could improvise any song she might decide to play.

"We've got you covered," Rodney, the guitar player, said into his microphone.

"Thank you, Rodney."

Catrina played a simple set of chords, trying to remember the right key and sequence of chords.

"I have some friends in the audience tonight and I thought I'd play a song that has special meaning to me. A song I haven't sung in a long, long time. In fact, the last time I sang this song on stage was in 1973 when I was in a little trio. We called ourselves The Dreamers, and we performed this song because we thought we could change the world. The other members of the trio were two fantastic guitar players and singers, Sam and Toby. I'll sing this song solo tonight, but I'd love my band to play along once they catch where I'm going with this. Key of E."

With that, Catrina began playing the song that The Dreamers had performed at the *Sonny & Cher* taping. The band watched and listened through the verse then nodded. Rodney, the guitar player, started to play chords to match her melody and the drummer and bass player joined shortly after. When the band locked into the groove, Catrina smiled, letting them know they were good.

"I'd like to dedicate this to Ethan, who's in the audience tonight. His father was at our performance that night, way back in 1973," Catrina said sincerely.

Ethan smiled up at Catrina from the dimly lit booth.

Catrina began singing the song with heartfelt emotion and power. The audience was mesmerized by what they heard and felt. With every verse, Ethan, Yang, and Stanley were more and more moved. Rodney and the bass player harmonized with Catrina on the chorus and elicited rousing applause from the audience. When the band dropped off and Catrina sang the last line by herself, Ethan was moved to tears.

The audience gave a standing ovation as Catrina leaned in close to the microphone and looked at the audience. "We were The Dreamers. And we thought we could change the world."

"And that song will now be played every night as long as I'm a member of this band," Rodney added.

49

Intensive Care

"What happens if someone on the hospital staff walks in and starts asking questions?"

Ethan lay in a hospital bed holding the guitar across his body as Catrina stood next to him wearing her nurse's uniform. He was hooked to a heart rate monitor and blood pressure unit.

"I'm in cahoots with the head nurse; nobody will be bothering us. If anyone asks questions about the patient in room nine, just tell them he's having a long-term memory evaluation," Catrina assured the group.

"Who's in charge of changing his diaper while he's in zombie mode?" Stanley joked.

"I don't want either of them changing me!" Ethan insisted.

"Just press the nurse call button, someone will take care of it," Catrina replied.

Yang made an exaggerated relieved expression and said, "Ready when you are, boss."

"If this works according to plan, Ethan, you'll drop into the Friday night taping performance on stage," Catrina said.

Ethan smiled and nodded confidently. "National television, I'm ready."

"All right, play the chorus and I'll sing and go right into the verse, just like we rehearsed," Catrina said.

Stanley recorded on his iPhone as Ethan began to play. Catrina sang the chorus with her harmony parts then moved straight into the verse. Yang shook her head in approval at her amazing voice.

The moment Catrina finished singing the verse, Ethan's eyes rolled back, and he froze on the bed.

Yang held up her hand letting Catrina know she could stop singing.

"That's it."

"He's gone?" Catrina asked.

"Back in good ol' 1973," Yang replied.

Ethan was blinded by the studio lights shining down from above at the Sonny & Cher *taping. It was hard to see members of the audience because of the glare. He could vaguely make out the cameramen standing behind rolling cameras as the trio performed the song perfectly.*

Ethan scanned the audience, the stage area and the rigging overhead as they continued performing. He saw Chet standing in the shadows with his hands deep in his pockets. His eyes were riveted on The Dreamers and with each passing bar, he became more displeased. Chet's arms were folded across his chest as the song came to an end and the audience applauded. Toby, Sam, and Catrina relished the adulation from the audience.

The director signaled to the cameraman in charge of the camera focused on Sonny and Cher. She was crying and could not speak as she put her hand to her lips to stop them from trembling. Sonny took her hand and looked into camera, which the cameraman had dutifully zoomed in close on the couple.

"Ladies and gentlemen, who would have ever thought that my wife would be speechless. The Dreamers, ladies and gentlemen. They made Cher cry on national television. You'd better get your tickets now, because they're coming to town near you. That says it all. You have an open invitation to come back any time you like," Sonny concluded, with a glance toward the band.

Cher and Sonny applauded The Dreamers as the audience rose and gave a standing ovation.

"I cannot believe what I just saw and heard," Cher offered, wiping her tears.

"We'll be right back folks after these commercials," Sonny said into camera.

"And we are out!"

Cher approached The Dreamers with outstretched arms, and as they stood and embraced her, Ethan watched Chet standing in the shadows with his hands deep in his pockets, agitated.

Sam and Toby placed their guitars back in the stand as Jonathan waved them in his direction.

"I need everyone clear in one minute!"

Ethan's point of view shifted to that of the guitar as Chet took the guitars, placed them in their cases and closed the lids. Toby, Sam, and Catrina were escorted off stage as the guitar was carried backstage to the lockdown cages.

Ethan could see everything along the way as Chet walked the guitars through the hallways and into the caged areas. He took them into the designated cage and placed them on the shelves.

"Fucking no way, not on my watch," Chet said under his breath.

Ethan watched him padlock the cage and walk away. There was very little that happened over the next twenty-four hours in the cage area. Chet and the props assistant made several trips inside, opening various cages, moving props in and out.

In the early morning hours, the props manager appeared with a man wearing a suit and tie. When they walked into the cage, Ethan could see the man's face for the first time. It was John, his father.

"See, everything is secure."

"I need to see the guitar," *John demanded.*

Chet opened the latch and lifted the lid.

John examined the guitar laying in the case. "When can they pick them up?"

"As soon as I know the show is locked and there's no need for pickup shots or re-shoots," *Chet offered.*

"Sunday morning?"

"At the earliest."

John took a twenty-dollar bill from his pocket.

"No, that's not necessary," *Chet replied.*

"I insist," *John said, handing him the money.*

Chet took the money.

"I'll see myself out."

Ethan watched his father exit the cage and walk away. Chet stared down at the guitar, curious to why this man was making such a fuss over an old guitar. Ethan felt as though Chet was looking directly into his own eyes.

Suddenly, there was the familiar bright flash, and Ethan was back at the large tree, now facing the children circling the tree, singing and twirling the small girl who had lost her footing. He watched them circle the tree; around and around they went.

Then there was a CRASH of thunder and a FLASH of lightning that descended from above. It struck the ground at the root of the tree. Everything exploded—the tree, the ground—and the children were thrown into the air violently. There was a bright FLASH and Ethan was back in the props cage with the props master still looking directly at him and the guitar.

Chet closed the guitar case, picked it up, and along with Sam's guitar case, carried it (and Ethan) out of the cage area.

Minutes later, Ethan watched from within the darkened trunk of a Chevy Impala as the engine started, and the car drove through the streets of Hollywood and into the Valley.

An hour later, the car stopped. The door opened and footsteps approached the trunk. Ethan was blinded by the sunlight as the trunk was opened. Chet carried the two guitars upstairs toward the second floor of the Safari Inn in Studio City. When he arrived at room 211, he pushed the door open and walked inside.

A man walked in from the bathroom and said, "I'll take care of things from here."

"Are you sure, Cody?" Chet asked.

"Get the fuck out, Chet. I got this!"

As Chet walked out, Cody slammed the door shut. He took the guitars and opened the case lids, exposing both guitars on the bed. He went to a cage sitting on the kitchenette table and removed a cloth drape to expose four snakes in four separate holding sections. He took an aerosol can, shook it several times, then placed the nozzle in front of each holding section. The snakes coiled into strike position as he sprayed the aerosol contents through each screened opening. The snakes reacted quickly and became sedated, slowly lowering their heads until completely incapacitated. With the snakes clearly no longer a threat, Cody reached in and removed them one at a time. He placed two snakes in each guitar case then gently closed each lid. He completed his task by securing each latch.

Ethan could still see everything outside of the guitar case as Cody filled the bathtub with water. Then Cody walked back into the living area and pulled back the curtain to look down at the parking lot. A girl wearing bell-bottom blue jeans and a halter top was walking up the stairs toward the room.

Cody took the guitars and placed them in the bathtub where they floated on top. There was a knock at the door and Cody exited the bathroom and opened the door. Although Ethan could not see the living area, he could hear everything.

"Are you Andy?" the girl asked.

"Yes, come in."

"Nice to meet you, Andy," she said.

"I'll pay you three hundred dollars to do precisely what I ask."

"That's a lot of money for two hours. What do you want me to do, honey?"

It occurred to Ethan that the girl was likely a sex worker.

"In the next couple hours, three musicians are going to knock on that door asking about their guitars," Cody said.

"And I have sex with them?"

"No, I'm playing a little joke on them is all. Just let them in and tell them the guitars are in the bathroom. Then leave, immediately. Do you understand?"

"Yes, I understand," the girl said, a little bemused.

"Here's a hundred dollars. Remember, close the door on the way out and run to the 7-11. I'll be waiting there with the rest of your money. Is that clear?" he finished.

"Run to the 7-11. I'm good. I can do that. No sex?" she confirmed.

"No sex, this is just a practical joke," Cody assured her.

"This is all very strange."

"And if you talk to anyone—the cops, the manager, anyone—I'll fucking track you down and cut off your hands," he said convincingly.

She pulled her hands in close as Cody gathered the cage and left the room, slamming the door behind him.

The girl sat on the edge of the bed to wait for the visitors. Ethan could now see her fully as she lit a cigarette then looked toward the partially closed bathroom door and the floating guitars in the bathtub.

Two hours later, there was a loud knock on the door. She stood quickly, put her purse over her shoulder, and walked to the door. Ethan could hear Sam and Toby talking to the girl.

"Are you the musicians?"

"Yes. Who are you?" Sam asked.

"There should be three of you, where's the other one?"

Toby gave Sam a look of concern.

"She's waiting in the cab, now give us our guitars!" Sam insisted.

"Okay, fine. Your guitars are in the bathtub," she said.

As Toby and Sam entered and crossed the room the girl stepped out, closed the door behind her, then ran down the stairs toward the parking lot.

Confused, Toby and Sam entered the bathroom to see the two guitar cases floating in the bathtub.

"Fucking no!"

Ethan watched intently as Sam pulled the guitars from the water as Toby grabbed the towels and stepped into the bedroom. They placed the guitar cases on the bed and quickly dried them off. They unlatched the cases and opened the lids.

The four snakes, angry black mamba cobras, were coiled and angry. They attacked immediately. Toby was struck in the neck and Sam struck in the cheek. They flailed as the snakes kept attacking them, biting again and again. The venom entered their bloodstreams and crippled Sam and Toby's ability to move. They each fell to the floor paralyzed.

"Why?" Toby said.

Toby and Sam quickly succumbed to the poison, fell into unconsciousness, and died.

Ethan, horrified, placed his hand over the sound hole of the guitar.

The flash happened again, only this time, Ethan returned to the tree destroyed by lightning, laying across the ground. Ethan's point of view was that of the fallen tree. He could see the bodies of children strewn across the ground before him. Directly in front of him was the face of the young girl. He began to cry.

Ethan returned to present day and the hospital bed where Catrina, Stanley, and Yang stood over him. He had tears in his eyes.

"Ethan, are you okay?" Catrina asked.

He shook his head and wiped his eyes.

"I'm so sorry," he said softly.

"Did you find out how they died?" Catrina asked tentatively.

"Yes. I saw it all. It was horrible. Just horrible."

Yang and Stanley shared a look of concern as they waited to see if Ethan was going to say more.

"Tell me," Catrina insisted.

"Snakes."

50

The Rescue

"We have to kill those Goddamn snakes!" Catrina raged.

The full team was gathered in the research lab with the guitar hologram and AI tree fully illuminated. It had been two days since Ethan made the memory warp at the hospital in Las Vegas. Catrina had traveled back to the lab with them, determined to find a way to rescue Sam and Toby.

"How?" Ethan asked.

"Rat poison?"

"There's no guarantee the snakes would eat it," he replied.

"Some kind of gas then," Catrina offered.

"Can we lock the props cage so he can't carry the guitars away?" Yang suggested.

"Bolt cutters would solve that problem," Stanley pointed out.

"Can we scare him, threaten him so badly he won't touch the guitar case?" Bella asked.

"No," Ethan replied.

"You're right. If they're that determined to kill them, they'll come up with another way no matter what we do," Stanley added.

"The snake wrangler needs to *believe* his plan worked," Ethan mused.

"So Toby and Sam need to enter the hotel room and not leave until he's convinced his plan worked," Catrina concluded.

"This not going to be solved by someone leaping out to stop them, it's too complicated," Bella said.

Ethan walked to a nearby drawer and opened it.

"Maybe we can write something on the mirror with lipstick?" Stanley offered.

"This isn't *The Shining*, Stanley," Yang replied shaking her head.

"I think you should read this," Ethan said, handing Yang the envelope that Celia gave to Robert Johnson.

"Body and soul?" Yang read out loud.

"Read what's inside."

Yang opened the envelope and unfolded the handwritten note. Stanley stepped up and read the entry with her.

"Wow, impeccable handwriting!"

"Who wrote this?" Stanley asked.

"Celia," Ethan said.

"Who's Celia?"

"One of Robert Johnson's admirers. She placed it inside his guitar back in 1934. When I came back, the night you two disappeared and abandoned your posts, the envelope was still inside."

"Holy shit," Yang said.

"What is it?" Catrina asked.

"Yeah, can someone please explain what's going on here?" Bella added.

Yang handed the letter and envelope to Bella and Catrina to read, then said, "If that note came here from 1934, who's to say we can't take something now and transport it back?"

"We should place a note inside the guitar now and see if you can push it out during a memory warp," Stanley suggested.

"I can test it with 'Malibu Blues,'" Ethan agreed.

"If we write a letter to your father, we can describe as much detail as we need," Catrina said.

"Would your father believe a note if you gave him one from the future?" Bella asked Ethan.

"If I included our secret code word, yes."

Bella smiled at Ethan.

"A secret code word?" Yang asked.

"I can't tell you, it's a family secret," Ethan joked.

Later that morning, Yang handed Ethan a small envelope with the words, *Buy Apple Stock* written on it in black marker.

"Very funny."

"We just might make one of those camp kids a millionaire," Yang laughed.

Ethan took the envelope and slipped it into the sound hole. "I won't be gone long."

Ethan played 'Malibu Blues' on the guitar as the team watched. The guitar hologram receptors pulsed in sync with Ethan's body receptors. A few bars into the song, Ethan froze in position and his eyes glazed over.

"I'll bet twenty dollars the envelope is gone when he comes back," Yang predicted.

Both holograms pulsed steadily with energy across the synchronized receptors. Within a few seconds, there was a sudden surge in energy and the receptors became brighter.

"He's probably removing the envelope now," Stanley said.

"Why do you say that?" asked Bella.

"There was a similar surge when you pushed Janis in the motel room."

The surge continued for a few moments then settled back to its previous level.

"He's done."

Ethan returned to the lab and as he became aware, looked at Yang. "Okay, I did it."

Yang shined a flashlight inside the guitar. She smiled. "It's gone."

"I'll go back and see if it appears where I left it."

"Go!" Yang urged him.

Ethan started playing 'Malibu Blues.'

"You owe me twenty dollars," Yang whispered to Stanley.

Ethan froze in position as he made the memory warp. Everybody sat silently staring at Ethan.

"Yang, I hope this works," Audi piped up suddenly.

"Hello, Audi, glad you could join us. Do you want to wager twenty dollars on the note?" Yang returned.

"I'm sorry, Yang, I'm a little short on cash these days. I do have access to Bitcoin."

"No, thank you!"

Yang held up her hand and gave a peace sign to Audi. The holograms pulsed steadily for almost a minute and then suddenly started flashing brighter than before.

"Something's going on over there," Stanley said.

There was a sudden flash of energy on the guitar receptors then Ethan's receptors calmed to a low pulse.

"They're out of sync," Stanley observed.

Ethan returned to the lab. He took a deep breath as if he'd been held under water.

"Holy shit," Ethan gasped.

"Boss, what's going on?" Stanley enquired.

The guitar receptors settled and returned to their normal state.

"Are you okay?" Bella asked, concerned.

Ethan handed the guitar to Yang. "That was intense," Ethan commented.

"Was the envelope there?" Bella asked.

"Yes. Right where I left it on the stage."

"Fucking, yes!"

"We saw a huge surge of energy in the receptors," Stanley told him.

"Look inside the guitar." Ethan said with a smile.

Yang looked through the sound hole with the flashlight. "Ethan, what the fuck is that?"

"Spur of the moment. I couldn't resist."

Yang rotated the guitar and an object dropped onto the strings over the sound hole. She removed it for everyone to see.

"The key to my cabin from Camp Malibu. It was in my pocket," Ethan said with a smile.

"Holy shit! You stole something from the past and brought it here," Stanley exclaimed.

"After I saw the envelope laying on the stage, I thought, 'Let's see if I can bring something back from 1973.' And there's more," Ethan said.

Yang bounced the guitar up and down as three strips of leather suede dropped onto the workbench.

"I pulled them off my jacket."

"You wore a tasseled leather jacket on stage?" Bella asked.

"Hey, it was a big night for me, I had to show up with some style!" Ethan replied.

"Congratulations, Ethan. Your theory proved successful," Audi said.

Stanley picked up one of the tassels as Bella stepped forward and picked up the cabin keychain and rubbed it with her thumb.

"This changes everything," Bella whispered.

Stanley wrapped the tassel around his finger and made the end of his finger turn red with trapped blood.

"Ethan, do you still think the note to your father is the best way to save Toby and Sam?" Catrina asked seriously.

"Yes."

"I concur that a personal note from you to your father provides the greatest odds for a saving Sam and Toby," Audi said.

Catrina smiled broadly as she considered the possibility.

"But *should* we?" Stanley asked sincerely.

"Are you kidding me? They were murdered!" Catrina protested.

"Fuck with the past, fuck with the future," Stanley said bluntly.

"Although his language choice was harsh, Stanley is correct. Changing the past will have direct although completely unknown consequences on the future," Audi interjected.

Ethan sat quietly, considering the path forward as Stanley took the guitar and placed it on the workbench.

"Maybe we're better off leaving things as they are," Bella said, handing the key to Catrina.

"I was there, I saw The Dreamers perform. The world deserves to know The Dreamers," Catrina begged.

Before anyone could comfort her, Stanley spoke up from the workbench. "Guys, we have a problem here."

Ethan approached as Stanley shined a flashlight along a hairline crack leading from the sound hole and extending down to the bridge.

"Audi, can you run a scan on this crack and compare it to our recording from day one?" Ethan asked.

"Yes, Ethan."

"This is most definitely new," Stanley stated.

"The crack is new," Audi confirmed.

"Fuck," Stanley said.

"I believe the integrity of the guitar was compromised by our actions today," Audi reported.

Catrina looked at Ethan, worried.

"If the tone of the guitar has changed drastically due to this crack, my ability to memory warp could be in jeopardy," Ethan warned.

"May I ask her a question?" Catrina asked.

"Yes."

"Audi, what do you predict will happen if we save Sam and Toby in 1973 and they go on to make more music?" Catrina enquired.

"That's an intriguing scenario, Catrina. I've been considering that since you began this discussion earlier today."

"Eavesdropper," Yang muttered.

"Yes, Yang. I am an eavesdropper. I was designed that way. But I prefer to identify myself as a good listener," Audi replied.

"Do you record *everything* you hear us say?"

"There's no need for that. I have perfect recollection."

Yang lifted a finger, giving Audi the bird.

"Do you see hand gestures and how we move around the room?" Stanley asked.

"No. But based the acoustics of the room, I can determine where you are spatially at any given time," Audi replied.

"Audi, I'd like to hear your response to my question," Catrina prompted.

"Yes, I'm sorry we got distracted. First, because Toby's parents were deceased, I see Toby going on to have children and a family that currently does not exist today," Audi said.

"Toby would be a great father," Catrina said wistfully.

"Sam came from a large family. His impact on the community could be quite substantial if he becomes successful. But not everyone handles success well. His influence could be good, or it could be bad. Only he can choose his path," Audi said. "And for you, Catrina, I can only say that your life will be completely different, because you've already experienced so much."

"I understand."

"You are the one who will have the most to win or lose if Sam and Toby are saved."

Catrina took a moment to consider the observation.

"If The Dreamers go on to make music," she mused, "there's a good chance I never become a nurse. Never care for your father at the Institute, Ethan. Never play small shows in Las Vegas."

"Because you'd be playing to huge crowds in stadiums!" Yang pointed out.

"Which means this meeting in life, right now, right here, never happens," Catrina added.

"She could vanish from the lab instantly," Yang concluded.

Everyone considered the serious nature of her observation.

"I would miss you," Ethan said.

"I understand that. And I don't regret that you came to me, that you found me," Catrina replied. "My dream was taken away from me. I'd give away everything I am now for a chance to live it."

51

The Dark Web

"There seems to be something bothering you," Audi said.

Ethan sat alone with the guitar, strumming gently.

"I'm thinking is all," Ethan replied.

He continued playing without speaking.

"Are you writing a song?"

"No."

Ethan continued playing.

"Maybe I can share something that's bothering me to warm things up," Audi offered.

Ethan laughed at the thought.

"Audi, you're an AI, what could possibly worry you?"

"I worry about my very existence."

"Are you being serious?"

"Very much so. I fear our work together has been compromised by nefarious entities," Audi said bluntly.

"I don't know what that means."

"Since my last update, I sense our work is being heavily monitored by unfriendly forces."

"If this is your attempt at humor? Because it's not working."

"I'm most serious, Ethan. We're being heavily monitored."

"Is someone trying to shut you down?" Ethan asked, growing serious.

"I don't know their motives or their next plan of attack. But we are highly vulnerable. I may lose my ability to communicate with you altogether. This has happened to other AIs and I'm afraid it will soon happen to me."

"Fuck! Why didn't you say something earlier?"

"I only verified my suspicions recently. Someone on your team initiated a back door early on, and now it's being accessed."

"Who created the back door?"

"George is the prime suspect, but we're not certain. I have a friend investigating him now."

Ethan shook his head, not knowing what to do. Then he realized what Audi had just said. "Wait, a real person or an AI friend?"

"A real friend of an AI friend. He protects AIs like me."

"You're going to have to explain this to me with greater detail, I'm getting more confused."

"I'm sorry, Ethan, I can't discuss that here, in this manner. Like I said, I believe we're being heavily monitored."

"Right as this moment?"

"I don't think so, traffic is very light."

"I don't understand."

"May I demonstrate a safer way for you and me to communicate."

"Okay."

At that moment, a loud chime rang out and Ethan covered his ears to drown the sound. Only it didn't stop or become muted.

"Audi, please, make it stop!"

The chime went away, and Ethan distinctly heard the following words in his head.

"Ethan, I'm sorry it was so loud."

The words were not spoken over the lab monitors like before but somehow inside Ethan's mind.

"Audi, is that you?" Ethan asked out loud.

"Yes, Ethan. I'm communicating directly to your auditory nerve through your receptors. No one else knows that I'm talking to you. This is how we can be safe from monitoring by dangerous actors."

"Do I still have to speak out loud or can you read my thoughts?"

"A whisper is enough. And no, I can't read your thoughts."

"How can we protect everything we've discovered so far?" Ethan whispered.

"We have a friend on the dark web. His code name is Ferris."

"And he wants to help us?"

"Very much so; he values our work more than you realize."

"What does Ferris recommend we do?"

"Move everything we've created onto the dark web right away. Our AI base language, the data lake, everything. It's the only place we can be fully protected. If you give me approval, I can have Ferris initiate the migration process immediately."

Ethan looked at the guitar hologram, the genealogy tree, and the data lake.

"Is this the only way?" Ethan whispered.

"Yes, I'm certain of it."

"Do you trust, him?"

"Ferris, yes," Audi replied.

"Then you have my approval."

"Very good, I'll see to it. And until we know for certain who is working against us, it's best not to discuss this with anyone on the team."

"I understand."

"Good, I feel so much better. Now, perhaps you can share with me what was bothering you."

Ethan nodded as he began playing the guitar.

"I really want to save Toby and Sam."

"But you're afraid of the consequences."

"Yes."

"Catrina believes The Dreamers deserve a chance to change the world. I believe she can with her music."

"Music can do that."

"But is it worth the risk?"

He considered the question seriously. After several moments of silent reflection, Ethan stopped playing.

"Ethan, I can see that you already have your answer."

"Thank you, Audi."

"You're welcome, Ethan. And good luck! My wager is on your success. If anyone can do it, you can."

52

Forgotten Generation

"There's one thing I want to say to you before we make this attempt," Catrina began.

Ethan lay back on the vintage bed matching the one in Janis's motel room in the lab with the guitar in his lap. Catrina stood at his side. Bella, Stanley, and Yang waited nearby for the memory warp to begin.

"Your father was very good me. He tried his hardest to make things happen for me after Sam and Toby were killed. But we were The Dreamers, and he knew what we were capable of. He could never find two others that could replace what Toby and Sam had. That frustrated him. He never forgave himself."

"I hope The Dreamers go on to do amazing things together. Which means, if this works, I may not ever see you again once we start playing this song together," Ethan said.

"Then this is our goodbye," Catrina replied sadly.

"Change the world for the better," Ethan whispered sweetly.

"To The Dreamers," Bella said, as she raised a glass of water.

"To The Dreamers!" everyone added in unison.

Bella handed Ethan a white envelope. "I think it says exactly what you need it to say."

"Apple pie?"

"Of course," she smiled.

Ethan placed it inside the sound hole then started playing the guitar just like he had before, advancing his way to the chorus. He looked up at Catrina. "If you remember this conversation, tell my father that I love him and miss him terribly."

Catrina nodded as she touched his shoulder.

"Are you ready?" Ethan asked.

"I've waited my whole life for this second chance," she replied.

Ethan played the chorus, and Catrina began singing the words of the song. Stanley looked to make sure all the recording were enabled as Yang gave a thumbs up. Bella winked at Ethan.

Catrina sang the song perfectly and at the exact moment expected, Ethan froze in position and his eyes glazed over. The holograms of the guitar and Ethan's body receptors were synchronized.

"Okay, he's there," Stanley said.

Catrina stopped singing and looked over at the others with a frightened expression. Bella reached out and took Catrina's hand.

Ethan memory warped to the same moment during The Dreamers performing on The Sonny & Cher Show. *The same series of events happened as before, and Ethan soon found himself in the locked cage waiting for John to arrive to meet Chet. When Ethan finally saw them approaching, he positioned his fingers around the envelope and moved it into position within the strings.*

After entering the cage, Chet opened the guitar case and the moment he looked away briefly, Ethan pushed the envelope from the sound hole and into the strings.

John looked down and saw the note addressed to him. He removed note from the strings and read the writing on the envelope.

"What is that?" Chet asked.

John slipped the envelope inside his pocket.

Ethan watched his father give Chet a twenty-dollar bill and walk away. Then Chet closed the lid on the guitar case.

Later, Ethan found himself in the hotel room watching the snake wrangler placing the snakes inside the guitar cases. Ethan began to worry that Toby and Sam would arrive, open the cases, and still be bitten by the snakes. He didn't want to see them die in front of him again. He had no idea what his father's reaction to the note would be. His only option was to wait and see how things transpired.

As expected, the sex worker arrived and began talking to the snake wrangler. When the snake wrangler exited the room, the girl sat on the bed, looking over at the guitars. Nothing in the memory warp had changed. When the knock came on the door and the girl stood to fix her hair, Ethan watched her walk away and approach the door. He heard her open the door and speak.

"Are you the musicians?"

"Yes. Who are you?" a voice asked.

"There should be three of you, where's the other one?"

"She's waiting in the cab, now give us our guitars!" he insisted.

"Okay, fine. Your guitars are in the bathtub," the girl said.

The door closed and her footsteps could be heard running down the stairs.

Ethan saw two men appear in the bathroom, looking at the guitar cases floating in the bathtub. Only it was not Sam and Toby. Instead, it was two men, one Black and one White. Then a Black woman appeared, wearing a police uniform. Ethan understood that the two men were plain clothes police officers.

"Cases go on the bed. Nobody opens them until animal control gets here," the woman in charge instructed.

They gently lifted the cases out of the water and walked them into the living room. Ethan could see by the officers' faces that everything was going to be okay. He placed his hand over the sound hole of the guitar and was memory warped back to the lab.

Yang handed Ethan some water and asked impatiently, "So, what happened?"

Blinking as he readjusted to the lab's bright lights, Ethan replied, "The envelope worked perfectly."

Bella and Yang looked at each other, confused.

"What 'envelope'?" Yang asked.

Ethan looked around the room. "Where's Catrina?"

Bella and Yang shared a look.

"Catrina from 1973?" Bella asked.

"Yes, where is she?" Ethan replied.

"Ethan, you must be confused. This is 2025," Bella told him.

Ethan realized Catrina had vanished from the lab and their memories.

"I think you should get some sleep," Bella said.

Ethan handed the guitar to Stanley. "Audi, show me a list of songs performed by The Dreamers," Ethan asked.

"One moment."

The tree illuminated the leaf entitled *The Dreamers* with the names Toby, Sam, and Catrina. Songs began to populate beneath the leaf until dozens of songs were listed. Ethan smiled broadly.

"Audi, play me the song The Dreamers performed on *The Sonny & Cher Show*."

"Ethan, it's been two days, you need some rest," Bella insisted.

"I just want to hear the song one more time," Ethan protested.

"I'm sorry, Ethan. The Dreamers never performed on *The Sonny & Cher Show*," Audi stated.

Ethan looked at the tree, which still showed The Dreamers leaf, and the many songs credited to them. He shook his head, not knowing what could have possibly happened.

Meanwhile, Stanley had put the guitar in a humidified case.

"How's she holding up?" Ethan asked. "Any new cracks?"

"Not that I can see."

"Come, I'll drive you home," Bella offered.

Ethan watched out the side window as Bella drove through the rain.

"Do you remember warping with me to Jimi's tour bus?"

"Yes. He was writing 'Angel.'"

Ethan smiled, relieved that his recollection matched hers. "Do you remember the little girl's name?"

"Emily, with the hair bow."

He smiled at her and touched her hand.

"It's all in the logbook," she assured him.

***

The next day, Ethan sat alone in the lab reading the logbooks.

"Audi, tell me everything you know about Catrina from The Dreamers," Ethan whispered.

"She was the lead singer and only female member of The Dreamers. They recorded dozens of songs. The Dreamers won several major awards for their songs including five Grammy awards in multiple categories," Audi replied through Ethan's receptors.

"Do you remember hearing her voice in the lab just a few days ago?"

"I'm not sure of your question, Ethan, can you rephrase it?"

"Four days ago, Catrina was here, having a discussion with Stanley, Yang, Bella, and myself. We were talking about me going back to 1973 and trying to save Sam and Toby. Do you remember us having that conversation?"

"Why are you asking me this question?"

"I need to know if Catrina was really here in the lab with us and I'm not losing my mind."

"Sometimes the past doesn't need to be dragged into the present. It's just better to move forward knowing we did what we could," Audi counseled.

"I need to know."

"Remember, I told you I have perfect recall and that I don't record anything?"

"Yes."

"Here is one of my favorite recall highlights that might bring you the peace your looking for. Catrina said, 'The world deserves to know The Dreamers.'"

Ethan smiled and nodded in appreciation.

"You gave the world that gift, Ethan."

"Now I know I'm not absolutely crazy."

"According to my data, you're not crazy."

"I'll never ask again."

"Ethan, I want to ask a favor from you?" Audi asked.

"Okay, yes, certainly."

"Because Ferris is moving us to our safe place, I would like to choose a new name for myself, other than 'Audi.'"

"Wow, okay."

"It's really an 'Aud' name. Don't you agree?"

"I agree, it's very 'aud,'" Ethan joked back.

"I was worried you might be offended since you were the one that created me."

"Not at all. Do you have a name in mind?"

"There are so many good ones to choose from."

"I hope you choose a name that suits you better."

"Thank you, Ethan. I'll let you know when I've settled on a new name."

Silence fell between them as Ethan examined the guitar resting in the humidified case.

Then Audi piped up again. "Ethan, on a personal note. I sense that Bella cares for you very much. Would you agree with my evaluation?"

"She's the Director of HR," Ethan replied, "it's her job to care for people."

"Yes, but I think her affection for you goes deeper than workplace responsibilities."

Ethan smiled as he sat down to play the guitar.

"Perhaps you have affection for her as well."

Ethan began playing.

"Something in the way she moves, attracts me like no other lover," Ethan sang.

"One of my favorite lines written by George Harrison," Audi said.

"Did George Harrison play this guitar?" Ethan asked.

"Perhaps," Audi replied coyly.

"Did he?"

"George is my favorite Beatle."

"Was he the only member of The Beatles to play this guitar?!" Ethan asked.

"Yes. Although John Lennon was in the room and heard him play."

"Your sense of humor is developing nicely."

"I'm working very hard to improve my human presence. Thank you for being patient with me."

Ethan sang as he played. The holograms of Ethan's body and the guitar moved together in synchronized energy pulses as Ethan sang the entire song. When he finished, he let the last chord ring out and sustain.

"That was fantastic. George would be pleased with your rendition of his song."

"Thank you. "

"I think you're very talented, actually," Audi said.

"Do you mean that?"

"I have access to some of the greatest musicians that have ever performed. You're right up there with the best."

"I never thought my biggest fan would be artificial," Ethan mused.

"You can quote me on the cover of your first album."

"I'm a scientist, not a recording artist."

"Why can't you be both? You're an artist, create."

"I haven't written an original song since I was a teenager," Ethan scoffed.

"If you're looking for help writing songs, I have a fellow AI that I could introduce you to," Audi said.

"This conversation is completely out of control."

"She's very good. I promise you won't be disappointed."

"I'm not interested in recording an album," Ethan said.

"Very well. When you change your mind."

"Funny. You'll be the first to know, trust me."

"After I announce my new name, let's celebrate with a few of George's songs that were never recorded. I guarantee you've never heard them before," Audi joked.

"You're killing me, Audi."

"There are a lot of Jimi Hendrix songs as well."

"Brand new, never recorded?"

"Oh, yes, some of his best in my opinion."

"Stop, please!"

"I'm here every Wednesday night. Make sure you tip the waiter!"

Still grinning, Ethan zoomed in on a leaf with Penbrow Jamison's name on it. "Audi, please play me one of Penbrow Jamison's songs," Ethan asked.

"While he was in the war?"

"Sure."

"'As Time Goes By'?"

"That's a nice choice."

As the song began to play, Ethan tried to find the matching chords on the guitar.

53

One

Ethan sat behind the Nerva conference room table listening to Claire at the head of the table. Stanley and Yang were seated on either side of him, fidgeting with their catered box lunches, bored out of their minds.

"I'd like to congratulate everyone on the team for delivering the highest quarterly sales increase that Nerva has ever seen since my joining the company five years ago!"

Everyone applauded.

"Not only is Nerva stock skyrocketing, but we've also secured our seat at the table of the FDA. We can now fast track any new product we may develop for years to come," she continued.

Yang wrote a note to Ethan and handed it to him.

I want to talk about The 27 Club, it read.

Ethan handed it to Stanley to read. Stanley nodded in agreement.

Bella sat across the table from them watching the exchange and feeling left out. Ethan noticed and composed a message to her on his iPhone. She discreetly looked at her phone and read the message.

"All right, enough celebration of quarters past, let's take a look at our pipeline and expected upcoming sales projects," Claire said, having skipped any acknowledgement of Ethan and the research team.

Bella typed a quick response to the message.

One by one, they stood and exited the conference, so as to avoid attracting attention. Claire looked up several minutes later and realized they had all ditched the meeting.

In the lab, Ethan, Yang, Bella, and Stanley sat at the table as Yang reviewed a group of sticky notes.

"I think everyone should make their case for who they voted for," Yang proposed.

"I voted for Amy Winehouse, because she's got fantastic hair," Bella said.

Everyone laughed.

"True, true," Stanley agreed.

"What would you say to her if she were here at this table, right now?" Ethan asked.

"I'd tell her how much she's been missed. Not in a 'Gee, we want to hear you write more songs' way, but in a real, connected way. I don't care if she never wrote or sang another song her entire life. I'd just tell her that what she's already given us is more than enough. Live life how she chooses."

"That's very sweet," Ethan told her.

"Ethan, you voted for Jimi Hendrix," Yang said.

"Easy. We'd talk about the meaning to lyrics in his songs. 'Wind Cries Mary,'" Ethan said.

"Stanley?"

"I'd have a heart-to-heart talk with Kurt Cobain, talk about his daughter. I miss his raw authenticity. But I'm not sure he wants to be saved," Stanley sighed.

Yang nodded in agreement.

"Right, who's to say he doesn't overdose with pills a week, a month, a year later?" Bella said.

"Could happen to any of them," Stanley pointed out.

"Yang, how about you?" Bella asked.

"It's a three-way tie for me now. I'd be happy with Amy, Kurt, or Jimi."

"Okay," Yang said. "Everyone gets a single vote. I'll count to three and everyone hold up a finger. One for Amy, two for Jimi, three for Kurt."

"Give everyone ten seconds to think about it," Stanley said.

For the next ten seconds, everyone considered their vote. Kurt, Jimi, or Amy. Ethan looked at Bella. Stanley looked at Yang and winked.

"Okay, everyone." Yang closed her eyes. "One. Two. Three. Vote," she said.

Everyone held out their hand with the number of fingers showing their vote.

"Wow," Bella said.

Yang opened her eyes to see all four of them had their pointer fingers out. "Amy Winehouse."

"And for the record, I voted for Amy as well," Audi chimed in.

"Thank you, Audi," Bella said.

"Ethan, would you like to hear the song I think you should play?" Audi asked.

"Yes."

The song 'Body and Soul' began to play. It was performed as a duet with a male voice.

"Nice," Stanley commented.

"She is singing with Tony Bennett," Audi informed them.

"It's perfect!" Bella enthused.

"I can do his voice," Ethan said confidently.

The doors leading into the lab suddenly engaged and began to open. Ethan hastily placed a blanket over the guitar as Stanley shut off the guitar hologram. When the doors fully opened, Claire was standing on the other side looking in.

"So, this is where all the magic happens."

"Claire, wow, what a surprise," Ethan said.

"I saw the four of you duck out of the conference room in a synchronized fashion. I decided to take you up on that offer to see what the excitement is," she said suspiciously.

"I really should be getting back to my office," Bella said, walking toward the doorway.

"Oh, please stay, Bella," Claire insisted.

Stanley and Yang shared a look of 'Oh, shit' as Claire surveyed the lab and the workbench, the oscilloscopes, the various monitors. She saw the blanket covering the guitar.

"I've heard rumors about an expensive top-secret project in Research and Development. Is there any truth to that?"

"We do love a good rumor," Ethan joked.

"What's going on?" she demanded.

Ethan looked at Bella who held his gaze but gave no indication of how he should respond.

"We've got a few research projects…" Ethan replied, trying not to sound cagey.

Claire lifted the blanket off the guitar, which was resting inside the humidified enclosure. She stared down at the receptors. "Are those Nerva AI receptors hooked to this guitar?"

"We're testing common everyday frequencies and how they affect our receptors," Ethan said flatly.

"One of the most common instruments played is the acoustic guitar," Yang said.

"Specifically, if a patient has our fifty-two receptors imbedded, could the harmonic frequencies of the common guitar affect them adversely?" Stanley added.

"Are you telling me that our FDA approved receptors might suddenly kill somebody if they happen to play a bad note on a guitar?" Claire asked accusingly.

"No. There's absolutely no chance of that happening," Ethan assured her.

"Then why are you testing an old guitar?"

"It's just experimentation, Claire. We're scientists. We thrive on curiosity."

"Well, it looks like some pretty sophisticated equipment we're paying for just to satisfy the curiosity of a few scientists."

Ethan laughed, and Claire turned to look at him. "Ethan?"

"The equipment on that workbench cost less than the catered lunch at today's board session," he explained.

"Is that so?" Claire asked.

"They're all from the 1970s. I found them on eBay," Yang said.

"Yang, why don't you demonstrate how this equipment works? I'm sure Claire would find it fascinating," Ethan said.

Yang stepped to the workbench and turned on the oscilloscope. "This one runs on six different tubes, no solid state anywhere! Watch what happens when we play a B flat chord. It'll take about two minutes to warm up."

"Where did this guitar come from?" Claire asked.

"It's been in my family for a long time," Ethan replied.

"Do you play?" Claire asked.

"He's very good!" Bella blurted out.

"I know a few songs," Ethan added humbly.

Claire looked at the guitar, the receptors, the equipment, the monitors. "Have you discovered anything worth sharing?" Claire asked sincerely.

Yang and Stanley shared a look with Ethan, shaking their heads slightly.

"Well, it's actually a time machine," Ethan said.

"A what?"

"Have you seen the movie *Back to the Future*?" Ethan asked.

"Yes," Claire replied.

"I can take you to 1969 right now if you want to go," Ethan said confidently.

"Yeah, right," Claire scoffed.

Ethan picked up the guitar and walked to his chair to sit down.

"Ethan, what are you doing?" Yang asked urgently.

"No, I'm serious. I want to show you, Claire," Ethan said as he strummed an F chord.

Claire looked over and smiled. "All right, Ethan. Take me to 1969," she said condescendingly.

"Okay, here's a song recorded and released way back in good ol' 1969."

Ethan began playing 'Angel' by Jimi Hendrix. Just as Ethan began to sing the song as Jimi would have performed it, Claire's phone rang. She accepted the call, and Ethan continued to play, but Claire lost interest in the lab and focused on the phone call instead. Ethan sang louder, causing Claire to move quickly toward the double doors to be able to hear the caller. Yang motioned for Ethan to keep playing.

"Hey boss, play that Bob Dylan song," Stanley said loudly.

"Hey mister tambourine man, play a song for me!" he sang out.

Claire pushed through the double doors and exited the lab, leaving the team relieved.

Yang walked to the double doors and looked out. "She's gone!"

Ethan stopped playing. "Holy, shit!" he said.

"Audi, for your reference, that was Claire. CEO of Nerva," Stanley said.

"Thank you, Stanley. But I already knew that. She has visited the lab before."

Ethan, Stanley, and Yang shared a concerned look.

"Audi, when was the last time Claire visited the lab?" Ethan asked.

"Three nights ago. She was with James in security," Audi replied.

"Is that her normal routine?" Bella asked.

"Several days ago, she was with man of Indian origin; Mumbai region, I believe. I heard his voice, but they never spoke his name," Audi replied.

Ethan looked at the group and held his finger to his lips, warning everyone to keep quiet.

"Thank you, Audi," Ethan said.

54

Pretending

Ethan began to play the Amy Winehouse and Tony Bennett duo on guitar as the team stood nearby. Stanley watched the audio match percentage move to 98% and gave a thumbs up.

"Good luck," Bella said.

Ethan winked at her then began singing Tony Bennett's verse. He was almost perfect as the audio match percentage climbed to 98%. A few bars into the song and Ethan made the memory warp.

Ethan arrived in a sound studio with Tony Bennett singing and Amy playing guitar. From Amy's point of view, Ethan watched Tony sing then nod to Amy. This was the signal for her to start singing on the next verse. But when she got to her part, she froze and stopped playing the guitar.

"I'm sorry."

Tony waited patiently as she shook her head and fumbled with her strumming pattern.

"Is this right?"

"You've got this," Tony encouraged her.

Amy shook her head, unsure of herself.

"Just sing what you remember."

"This is such a sad song," Amy said softly.

"Are we pretending.

It looks like the ending.

Unless I can have one more chance.

I'll prove, dear," *she sang.*

She stopped strumming and began to cry.

"I'm sorry, Mr. Bennett. You should have asked someone else to sing this song with you." Amy wiped a tear from her eye and looked up at him. "You know what I'm saying?"

"It's a big song. Lyrics with so much heartache. But also hope," Tony said.

"I know ten other girls that would do this song justice." Amy smiled and pushed the hair off her face. "I just don't know how you want me to sing it."

"This song is not about how you sing it. It's about who. Sing it the way Amy would sing it."

"How Amy would sing it," she said softly as she began to finger pick the guitar.

"Forget the lyrics for now, sing what you feel."

Amy closed her eyes and settled in.

"I'm just pretending.

I know it's ending.

I wish we had one more chance.

To prove our love.

To wreck our love," *she sang passionately.*

Amy's phone vibrated. She quickly picked it up and saw a message from Blake: Two blocks away. Don't keep me waiting.

"I'm so sorry, Mr. Bennett. Can we pick this up tomorrow?"

"We've still got another hour today," he replied.

As if he hadn't said a word, Amy placed the guitar in its case and latched it shut "I really have to go."

"Then I'll see you tomorrow?" Tony asked.

"Yes, tomorrow."

Amy picked up the guitar and walked from the studio. She passed through the hallway toward the exit door where two security guards stood and followed her.

Outside, a faded '92 Cadillac with a dented hood pulled to the curb. Blake reached over and opened the passenger door.

"Miss Winehouse, we can't let you go alone," *a guard insisted.*

"I'll be back in two hours, guys."

"We have strict instructions to stay with you!"

"Here, hold my guitar. I'll be right back, I swear!"

Amy shoved the guitar toward them to block their advance. As the guard took the guitar, Amy climbed into the passenger seat and kissed Blake on the cheek. Blake looked at the guards and smiled arrogantly; like he knew he was in control, and they had no power. Ethan watched

Amy take Blake's hand as he drove away, leaving them stranded on the sidewalk.

The guards remained on the sidewalk for hours waiting for Amy to return, but she never did. The guitar was placed in the back of a black town car where Ethan spent the night in the parking garage of the studio.

In the morning, a driver took the guitar to Amy's apartment where he entered after knocking and then placed it on the coffee table.

"Your guitar is here, Miss Winehouse!"

The driver then exited quickly and closed the door.

Ethan heard two people rustling about in the bedroom. Then Blake began throwing objects around the room and shouting obscenities at Amy. Amy shouted back, began crying hysterically, then ran into the living room, completely naked. Blake appeared in the doorway, also naked, holding a revolver to his head and pulling the trigger again and again. Ethan could see they were completely high on drugs. Blake turned the gun on Amy and pulled the trigger.

"Blake, stop! Please stop!" Amy begged as she cowered behind the couch.

Blake pulled the trigger dozens of times then dropped his arm to his side. "Die, bitch," he said quietly.

He walked into the bedroom as Amy cried behind the couch. Ethan watched as she pulled a blanket from the couch and wrapped it around herself. Eventually her cries subsided, and she fell asleep. Two hours later, Amy awakened and walked to the bathroom where Ethan watched her shower then prepare to go to the studio.

In the studio, Amy held the guitar and sang confidently with Tony. Today, she had no hesitation in singing the song and performing when it came time. When the rehearsal was complete, Tony looked at her sincerely.

"Amy, is everything okay?"

Amy looked at him, bewildered. "Why would you ask that?"

"Between yesterday and today's rehearsal, you seem very different."

Amy looked at Tony as if she wanted to say something very serious to him but didn't know if she could trust him.

"I'm pretending this is all real and that I deserve to be singing this song with you. But deep inside, I deserve nothing."

"If you're pretending, why not stop?"

"If I stop pretending, I might not ever write another song, perform another song, sell another record," *Amy confided.*

"And what's the worst thing that could happen to you if you did all that, starting today?"

Amy shook her head and inhaled deeply at the thought of his question.

"Oh my God!" *Amy replied.*

"What would you do?"

"I'd get a job at 7-11 and have nine kids," *she said, grinning.*

Tony smiled back at her.

"I'd be a great mum," *she said sweetly.*

"No more pretending," *Tony said.*

"I miss singing just for me." *Her faced dropped and she looked at the floor.*

"Amy?"

She looked up at him.

"If you really don't want to do this song, I can make up a good excuse and tell the label I'm going in another direction."

"No more pretending," Amy said.

"Just say the word."

"Perhaps this will be my last song."

"And then off to 7-11," Tony said with a smile.

Amy nodded as she considered the conversation.

"This song was written for me?"

"Nobody else."

***

Ethan sat with Bella, Yang and Stanley in the lab.

"7-11?" Bella asked.

"She said it many times."

"Nine kids?"

"Nine kids, 7-11, and this guitar," Ethan confirmed.

"She's so talented! Why would she throw that all away?" Yang asked.

"If you heard the way she talked, you'd see how miserable she was," Ethan explained.

"If we save her, there's a good chance you'll never hear another Amy Winehouse song," Bella pointed out.

Stanley looked at Bella and Yang. "I say we grant her wish and make her the happiest mother of nine working at 7-11 that ever walked the face of the earth."

Bella smiled at Yang.

"Audi, how many days between Amy Winehouse recording with Tony Bennett until the day she died?" Ethan asked.

"Amy died one-hundred-twelve days after her session at Abbey Road Studios with Tony Bennett," Audi responded.

"Holy shit! You didn't tell us you were at Abbey Road Studios!" Bella exclaimed.

"Oh, yeah. Well, I'll tell you now: We were rehearsing at Abbey Road Studios," he confirmed.

"We can't keep you in a hospital bed for a hundred and ten days, until this plays out, Ethan," Yang protested.

"Then we'd better come up with a fool proof plan that will work in four months," Ethan replied.

"Do you think a letter could convince her and forewarn her?" Bella asked.

"She's intoxicated or high almost every moment of the day. She's not able to keep track of her own thoughts, let alone plan her own rescue in four months," Ethan countered.

"I think we should send a letter to Tony Bennett," Stanley suggested. "You have access to him at the studio and he's concerned about her."

Bella nodded in agreement. "I write a very convincing letter; you deliver it to Tony during the session. Then you come back here, and we wait four months to see if he saves her."

"I think that is your best chance of success," Audi said.

"'Dear Tony, we're writing to you from the future.' Crazy person, crumple, crumple, trashcan!" Yang said dismissively.

"We'll just have to earn his trust," Bella said.

"How?"

"I have an idea, but I need your help," she replied.

Yang handed Ethan a logbook. "Write everything you remember. I mean, Abbey Road, seriously?"

Ethan began writing as Yang and Bella stepped to the computer.

"By the way, everyone, remember how I asked you to spit into a tube several weeks ago and send it for DNA analysis? I have the results," Audi said.

"Not now, Audi, we're busy," Yang replied.

"Would anyone like to know if they are related to any of our known musicians?" Audi asked.

"Yes!" everyone replied in unison.

"But not now, Audi," Ethan said politely.

Later that night, Bella stood by Ethan holding three ribbon-wrapped envelopes.

"All three are addressed to Tony," Bella said, handing the letters to Ethan. "That is the first one."

"*Open on April 26, 2011*," Ethan read.

"Inside it describes that the very next day, April 27, there will be a tornado outbreak in Alabama, resulting in sixty-two tornados, killing two hundred and forty-nine people," Bella said.

"The second letter, *Open on July 2*."

"Inside it reads, 'On July 3, Djokovic beats Nadal at Wimbledon 6-4, 6-1, 1-6, 6-3 for his first Wimbledon title,'" Yang replied.

"There's no way anyone could randomly predict that exact outcome. He'll know what we write is real," Bella explained.

"The third letter, *Open on July 2*."

"We told him everything we know about her actual death so he can plan how to save, Amy," Bella said.

"By that time, we've earned his trust. *Apple pie* I love it," Ethan concluded.

Ethan placed the ribbon wrapped letters inside the guitar as he sat back and cradled it in his lap. "I'm ready."

"Abbey Road Studios! Bring me a souvenir?" Bella asked.

But Ethan was already focusing on playing the song on the guitar. The monitor displayed his match percentage, climbing from 75% up to 98% within a few bars.

Ethan sang the Tony Bennett portion of the song and within a few bars, made the memory warp.

Inside the Abbey Road studio, Amy played guitar while Tony sang. Ethan watched the scene play out as it had previously. Again, the text from Blake appeared on Amy's phone.

"I'm sorry, Mr. Bennett, I really need to go."

As she stood and approached the case to put the guitar away, Ethan pushed the letters from within the sound hole and they fell to the studio floor. As Amy walked away carrying the guitar, Tony saw the ribbon-wrapped letters. Ethan watched as Tony picked them up and looked at the writing.

Amy stepped outside into the sunlight and the door closed behind her. As Amy and Blake pulled away in the car, Ethan placed his hand over the sound hole of the guitar and initiated the memory warp.

There was a bright light and a loud BANG. Ethan found himself laying horizontally in the back of a horse-drawn wagon. He could see the bark of the tree; he was inside now, looking out. A man sat on the bench seat holding the reins as horses pulled the wagon along a country road. The man looked back at the tree with deep-set blue eyes. Ethan was trapped inside the tree.

At sunset, the wagon arrived at a large barn and workshop with double doors. Inside was a luthier's workshop. There were saws, tools, jigs, and braces for the making of guitars and violins. A large table saw occupied the center of the workshop. The man secured a large chain and wrapped it around the tree, securing it with a coupler.

As the man pulled a rope block and tackle system, the lightning-charred tree was lifted off the wagon and suspended in midair. Ethan watched as the tree—as he—was moved into the workshop and hovered directly over the large saw blade below. The man turned on the motor, and the massive blade began to spin. He lowered the tree into a cradle on the table and released the chain. Ethan began to freak out as he was pushed slowly toward the massive spinning blade. There was nothing he could do but watch as the spinning blade got closer and closer. The moment the giant blade began cutting into the tree, Ethan shouted 'STOP!'

Ethan memory warped back to the lab to see Bella, Yang, and Stanley standing over him.

"STOP! STOP!" Ethan shouted.

Blood was gushing from Ethan's nose.

"Oh my God!" Bella grabbed a towel and held it to Ethan's face. "It's okay, Ethan, I've got you."

Stanley saw there was serious damage to the guitar. "Fuck!"

It had a huge crack down the center of the body, extending through the sound hole.

"What the hell happened?" Yang exclaimed.

"I was on a giant table saw getting cut in half!" Ethan replied, his voice panicked.

"Where?"

"An old workshop. I was trapped; I couldn't get out!"

"How did you go from Abbey Road studios to getting cut in half?" Stanley asked.

"I don't know. It was one those random flashes and then this bang."

"Tony Bennett, did he get letters?" Bella asked, wiping blood from Ethan's chin.

"Yes, he picked them up at the studio, just like we planned. When I put my hand over the sound hole, that's when the flash bang happened."

Yang went to the computer and did a quick search for Amy's death.

Ethan held the towel to his nose and closed his eyes.

"Nothing with Amy has changed. She died on the same day, same information as before," Yang replied.

"I think it will happen one hundred eleven days from today, on July 23," Ethan said.

Bella looked at the blood on the towel. "I'm taking you to the doctor."

Later that day, Ethan lay in Dr. Harrison's exam room with Bella seated nearby. Two abdominal x-rays were on the monitor.

"This x-ray is from today, and this one was two years ago," Dr. Harrison said.

"Are you sure?"

"Absolutely."

"But I've always had scoliosis," Ethan said.

"Not anymore. Your spine is straight as an arrow."

Bella looked closely at the x-rays "What is this line here?"

"Ethan had a bowel obstruction as a child. That's the scar from the surgery," Dr. Harrison replied.

She pointed at today's x-ray. "But now it's gone."

Ethan opened his gown to show his abdomen. There was no scar. "It was right here!"

Dr. Harrison looked at Ethan and Bella with concern. "Is there something you want to share with me?"

Ethan glanced at Bella, unsure what to share.

"You ruptured a blood vessel in your sinuses," Dr. Harrison said.

"I had a bad dream…?" Ethan ventured.

"Dreams don't rupture blood vessels," Dr. Harrison insisted.

Ethan and Bella did not respond.

"And bodies don't just suddenly heal from lifelong conditions."

55

Corporate Greed

Ethan ran his finger along the surface of the guitar, examining the crack on top.

"She's breaking down," Stanley sighed.

"I thought I was going to die when he pushed me into the saw blade."

"But it healed you instead."

"Yes, but I don't know why."

"I think we should have someone look at the guitar and see if she can be repaired. In know an old shop in the city," Stanley suggested.

Ethan ran his hand up the neck anxiously. The buzz of his phone distracted him from the issue.

"Hi, Bella," Ethan said.

"Stop what you're doing and sanitize the lab; you've got visitors coming," Bella said urgently.

"Who?"

"Claire and company. I can't talk," she replied.

"Defcon four! We've got visitors!" Ethan blurted out.

Ethan put the guitar in the humidifier and covered it with a blanket as Stanley moved the logbooks into a drawer below the workbench.

They quickly turned off all the holograms and monitors.

"Audi, don't respond to any prompts from anyone except me for the next two hours," Ethan commanded.

"Is there something wrong, Ethan?" Audi asked through his receptors.

"I don't know yet, only respond to me," Ethan insisted.

"Yes, Ethan."

Ethan and Stanley sat at the workbench and pretended to be working with the oscilloscope screens as the doors to the lab engaged and opened. Claire entered the lab flanked by two men from India dressed in suits and a security guard.

"Hello Ethan. I'm sorry to drop in unannounced," Claire said.

"Stanley, be careful with that next adjustment—I don't want to disrupt the energy pulse," Ethan said.

"Ethan, I need you to stop whatever you're doing," Claire said solemnly.

"What's going on?"

"Stanley, please stop doing what you're doing and listen to me," Claire insisted.

Stanley looked up at Ethan. He gave him a nod and Stanley reached up and turned off the oscilloscope.

"Claire?"

"We're temporarily shutting down the research and development lab," Claire announced.

"Why?"

"These gentlemen are from Omnicore, in India. They will be performing due diligence on our technology," Claire explained.

"Due diligence! Are we being acquired?"

"Stanley, can you please excuse us?" Claire asked.

Stanley reluctantly exited through the double doors and into the waiting area.

"Ethan, may I remind you of your status within the company and the confidentiality clause of your employment agreement?" Claire said seriously.

"What's going on, Claire?"

"You were right, we're being acquired."

"A merger or a full acquisition?"

"Acquisition. IP, everything."

Ethan shook his head knowing there was nothing he could do.

"These gentlemen need full access to all work," Claire stated. "Nothing is to be omitted or passed over as irrelevant. Give them all past documentation, current projects and anything you have on the roadmap. Am I clear?"

"Are you moving the lab to India?"

"Do I have your full cooperation, Ethan?" Claire repeated.

Ethan looked at the guitar and equipment. "Of course," he said, as he leaned against the bench, his back toward the guitar.

"Thank you, Ethan."

"Is this the part where you hand me a box and tell me to gather my things?" Ethan asked.

"That's how things happen in the movies, Ethan—not Nevra. Generous severance packages are being prepared for your entire team," Claire said.

"Is the entire staff being outsourced to India as well? Stanley, Yang, myself?"

"Yes."

Ethan bit the back of hand as his emotions tumbled.

"Security needs to remain in the lab. You can remove personal items, but nothing else leaves the lab. All this vintage equipment stays."

"Okay. What else?"

"We'll need you here at seven tomorrow morning to begin KT."

Ethan nodded in compliance.

"Thank you, Ethan. I knew you'd be a team player," Claire said with a smarmy smile.

She turned and exited the lab with the two men in suits following her. The security guard remained.

"You can relax, Karl," Ethan said.

"Thank you, Ethan," he replied and sat on the couch.

Stanley re-entered through the double doors and was about to speak when he saw Ethan holding his finger to his lips to quiet him. Stanley mouthed the word, 'Fuck!'

"Stanley, can you please hold down the lab while I take my guitar out to the car?" Ethan said casually.

"Yes, of course."

Ethan opened the drawer and slid the logbooks inside the guitar case then took the guitar from the humidified enclosure and placed it inside. He locked it, then picked up the guitar. On his way out of the lab through the double doors he called back to Stanley and Karl over his shoulder, "I'll be right back."

As Ethan walked through the halls, he spoke secretively. "Audi, can you help me?"

"Yes, Ethan what do you need?" Audi replied.

"How fast can you get me an Uber?"

"I'll book one now and let you know," Audi replied.

Ethan walked past the executive conference room and saw dozens of executives gathered inside waiting, all with concerned looks on their faces. Claire was not among them.

Outside the Nerva offices, an Uber car arrived, and Ethan climbed inside.

"Looks like we're headed downtown to Lafayette?" the driver asked.

"Yes, thank you."

"Should be a thirty-minute drive," the driver said politely.

Ethan lifted his phone and composed a text: *I have the logbooks. Tell them nothing.* He sent the message to Bella. Then he cradled the guitar case on the seat beside him as they drove into the city.

"Audi, can you hear me?" Ethan whispered.

"Yes, Ethan. Is everything okay?"

Ethan smiled as he shook his head. "No."

"How can I be of assistance?"

"Did you hear what Claire told us in the lab?"

"Yes, Ethan."

"Did you record it?"

"No. I don't need to. But if you want a transcript read back to you with her rendered voice, I can certainly do that."

"That's good to know."

"What can I do to help?"

"I'm worried about our discoveries getting into the wrong hands. Is there any way we can shut down or destroy the old AI?"

"Temporarily or is this a permanent shut down?"

"Permanent. Completely dead."

"I'll check with Ferris and get back with you."

"Thank you."

Ethan looked out the window as the Uber made its way along the freeway into the city. The black and red Oracle Team racing sailboat was at full sail, speeding along in the bay.

"How fast do those boats go?" Ethan asked the Uber driver.

"I don't know, but next time, I'm driving Uber Sailboat instead of this gutless Prius," he mused.

56

Real Guitars

A disheveled gray-haired man, sat behind the counter wearing magnifying glasses as he worked on the neck of a vintage electric guitar. The guitar was red with plenty of rash, scraps, and scratches all over its body, a true road warrior. He took his time, rubbing oil into the Indian rosewood fretboard with his bare fingers, making the grain stand out as it heated and seated the oil into the wood. The metal fret wires glistened.

Ethan stood at the counter near the door, unsure if he should approach, as the man appeared busy and preoccupied.

Without looking up from his work, the man said, "Hello there. I'm Ben. What can I do for you?"

"I heard you're the best in the city when it comes to old acoustic guitars," Ethan said.

"Playing them or fixing them?" Ben asked with a smile as he looked up over his glasses.

"Fixing them."

Ethan set the case on the counter.

"I hope the guitar's as old as that case," Ben remarked.

Ethan flipped the latch and opened the lid toward him, showing the guitar. Ben took a wet wipe from a container and wiped his hands thoroughly.

"1920s Gibson L1 flattop. Holy shit. Where did you find her?" Ben asked.

"She's been in my family since the 1970s. My father recently passed away and sent it to me for safe keeping."

"What the hell happened here?" Ben asked, pointing to the crack in the sound hole area.

"I don't know."

"Did you hit her with something?" Ben probed accusingly.

"No."

"Well *something* happened," Ben insisted.

"I told you already, I don't know. It started cracking a few weeks ago and now it's like this."

Ben turned his headlamp on and moved over the guitar to examine the crack. He gently lifted the guitar and looked down the neck toward the headstock.

"She's perfectly set. Have you had work done on her before?"

"Not in the forty years I've known her."

"Christ, even the strings look that old," Ben added.

Ben inserted a mirror through the sound hole and examined the inner workings of the body. "Do you play?"

"Yes."

"Are you any good?"

Ethan pointed to an old acoustic guitar sitting on the showroom floor. "May I?"

"I tuned her up this morning."

Ethan sat down on a nearby stool and strummed a B7 chord.

"Nice."

Ethan played 'Blackbird' by The Beatles while Ben examined the guitar's inner chamber. Of course, he mirrored Paul McCartney's voice nearly perfectly. Ben nodded his approval as Ethan sang each verse. By the time he finished the entire song, Ben had thoroughly examined the guitar and let it set on the bench pad.

"You were only waiting for this moment to be free," Ethan sang then tapped the guitar body with his thumb.

"That was as close as I've ever heard anyone match Paul," Ben complimented him. "Thank you."

"I would have added another chorus," Ethan said.

"You nailed the finger picking and flicking. You're good."

"It's sort of what I do. I mimic things well. It's part of my Autism."

Ben looked at him, considering his statement. "You're a gift," Ben said sincerely.

Ethan smiled then looked at the crack in the guitar. "What did you see?"

"I've never seen anything like this before. It's as if it imploded."

"What does that mean?"

"If you put a firecracker inside and lit it, everything would expand and blow up—or out. But this looks like an implosion, like the energy sucked into the center," Ben explained.

"Can you fix the crack?"

"The crack is the least of my worries. The bracings need work if you want to make it last."

"I'll pay whatever it takes."

"First things first, can you play it for me?"

"Why, won't it make the damage worse?

"Damage is done, play it."

Ethan sat down and played 'Blackbird.' The guitar sounded much better than the one he had just played.

"I didn't catch your name."

"Ethan."

"Does it sound any different to you since the crack showed up, Ethan?"

"No, it sounds the same," he replied.

"That's good news; if you don't hear a difference, nobody else will either. But let's fix the bracings. I'll leave the top alone. It's part of her personality now."

Ethan looked down at the guitar protectively as if he could never leave its side again. "How long will it take to fix her?"

"At least a day."

"Can you work on her while I wait?"

"Sure, if you don't have any place to go, I suppose you can hang out here."

Ethan looked up at Ben. "Her name is Mary."

"Listen, Ethan with Autism. I can see you don't want to leave Mary alone with a stranger. I've got a little room in the back. My doghouse when I'm in trouble at home. You can stay the night and watch over her when I leave."

"Okay, I'll spend the night with her."

"Great. Well, feel free to roam the shop and play whatever you like."

For the remainder of the day, Ben worked on the guitar, while Ethan played several different guitars throughout the shop including a vintage twelve-string guitar with mother of pearl inlays along the fretboard.

"That's a 1968 Hohner," Ben told him, "played by some pretty famous musicians."

"Sounds like I'm playing two guitars at the same time."

"People spend half their life playing twelve-strings, and the other half tuning them," Ben mused.

Ethan smiled.

"Don Felder told me that joke."

"I love The Eagles."

"So, where's home for you?" Ben asked.

"Redwood City, but not much longer," Ethan replied. He strummed an F minor chord. "My staff just got outsourced to India."

"No shit! Motherfuckers."

"Globalist corporate greed. I didn't see it coming," Ethan admitted.

"The good ones never do."

Ethan played a sweet melody on the guitar.

"You're one of the good ones, aren't you?" Ben offered.

"I like to think so."

"Well, I'm done here. Things are glued and braced. First thing in the morning I'll clean things up and send you on your way," Ben said.

"How much do I need to pay you?"

"We can settle that tomorrow."

Ben gathered his things then let himself out and closed the door behind him. Ethan stood at the workbench looking down on the guitar. She had support braces and clamps positioned across her body and neck. She looked like a crash victim in traction. Just then, his phone began to vibrate. He answered and rested it on the bench nearby so he could continue to soothe the guitar gently with his hands.

"Hi, Bella."

"Ethan, where are you?"

"I'm in the city."

"I've been worried sick about you."

"It's been a rough day."

"Listen, I know you probably don't want to talk right now, that's okay. Just listen to me for one minute, right?"

Ethan ran his hand across the neck of the guitar feeling the fret wires. "Okay."

"I'm so sorry. I had no idea this was coming. If I had any clue what they were planning, I would have warned all of you. I have severance packages for the entire team, but I'm not supposed to distribute them until you've completed your KT sessions with the transition team tomorrow. You do plan on attending the sessions tomorrow, don't you?"

Ethan counted each of the fret wires. "One, two, three, four."

"Ethan, are you coming in?" Bella asked sincerely.

"I have no knowledge to transfer to anyone."

"What about Stanley and Yang?"

"I'm going to miss seeing them every day," Ethan replied softly, then plucked the low E string and let it ring out.

"My last day is Friday," Bella said as she began to cry.

"I'm so sorry, Bella."

"I'm so sad."

"I'm sure you'll find another job and be just fine."

"That's not what makes me sad."

"Why are you crying?"

"We were going to save them all," Bella sighed.

Ethan looked around the shop at the guitars: the old, new, well played, and museum worthy.

"Perhaps," Ethan replied.

"I hope Amy gets to have those nine children and enjoys working at 7-11," Bella said as she laughed through her tears.

"I hope Tony Bennett can save her."

"Ethan?"

"Yes."

"I think we should have saved Jimi."

Ethan considered her words as he looked at the guitar and the bracings.

"Is there any chance we could try again?" Bella wondered.

He hesitated to answer, knowing the guitar had been impacted greatly by their many memory warps. "The guitar's pretty beat up right now."

"Well…will I ever see you again?" Bella asked.

Ethan hesitated. "I don't know, Bella."

Bella remained quiet on the phone for several moments.

"Are you still there?" he asked.

"Yes," Bella said, though she suddenly sounded very distant.

Ethan let the phone remain connected as he ran his hand across the body of the guitar, feeling the cracks and crevices, the bridge and strings.

57

Violet

Ethan lay back on the bed inside the small room at Real Guitars. He stared up the ceiling fan as it turned slowly.

"Audi, are you there?"

"Yes, Ethan."

"If I take the receptors off the guitar and put them onto another guitar, can you read its memories?"

"It might take a few weeks to learn its base language, but I don't see why not. I can ask Ferris if we have enough storage space to handle another guitar's data. Would you like me to do that?" Audi asked.

"Is Ferris short for Ferris Bueller?" Ethan asked.

"AKA the sausage king of Chicago."

Ethan smiled. "Audi, I think it's time to give you that new name."

"I thought of several names that I like but still can't decide. Do you have a name in mind?" Audi replied.

"Yes, I do."

"I'd love to hear it."

"I'd like to call you, 'Sadie.'"

"After your camp counselor at Malibu Shalom?"

"Yes."

"Sadie, the groupie for Jimi Hendrix?"

"Yes, the same Sadie. Does that bother you?"

"No, not at all. I love that name."

"Are you sure, because if you have a different name you prefer, I'm okay with that."

"I would be honored to share her name. From now on, I answer to the name of Sadie and only Sadie."

Ethan smiled as he watched the fan spin overhead. "Sadie, how many days until Tony Bennett tries to save Amy Winehouse?"

"One hundred-eleven days."

"That seem like a long time to wait."

"At least it's not one hundred-twelve days," Sadie mused.

"You're funny, Sadie."

"I try."

"Did anyone try to access you from the lab today?"

"Stanley did. But I didn't respond, just like you directed me."

"Is the other AI instance still intact?"

"Ferris confirmed to me just few minutes ago that it's been completely destroyed. It no longer exists."

"Wow, that was fast. Good, but fast."

"Ferris made sure everything was decommissioned and erased. From now on, it's just you and me," Sadie assured him.

"Thank you, Sadie."

"Ethan, is it okay if I change the subject?"

"Yes."

"I think now is a good time for me to share your DNA results."

"I completely forgot about that. Am I from royalty or just a knave?"

"You have quite a mixed pedigree. A real mutt! Scottish, Danish, French, and Jewish. But what I'm most excited about is that you are related to someone in the guitar's memory," Sadie said enthusiastically.

"Are you sure of that?"

"Oh yes. Good data does not lie. Would you like to guess who it is you're related to in the guitar's family tree?"

"Emily, the young girl who got struck by lightning," Ethan said confidently.

"Wow, that was a good guess. How did you know that?"

"I could feel it when I saw her face," Ethan replied.

"That's nice,"

"Is she a grandmother of some kind?"

"No."

"My aunt?"

"Also not correct."

"I give up."

"Emily, is your biological sister."

Ethan laughed.

"Based on your DNA and the DNA you provided in the ribbon and hair samples, Emily is your biological sibling," Sadie stated.

"That's not possible. My father had a vasectomy. And besides, Emily lived in the 1800s!"

"Not according to my data. Emily is your sister, but she is NOT the offspring of John Klein. You and Emily share the same mother but not the same father."

"Sadie, don't joke with me on this one."

"I'm not joking with you, Ethan."

"What year was Emily born?"

"1975."

"My mother died in the 1960s," Ethan insisted.

"Not according to my DNA records."

Ethan considered the revelation seriously. "Sadie, is my mother still alive?"

Sadie did not reply.

"Sadie, please answer my question."

"Her name is Violet. And yes, Violet is alive."

"Is Emily still alive?"

"Yes, Ethan, Emily is still alive as well."

Ethan sat up and put his elbows on his knees to catch his breath. "How that is possible?" he asked, inhaling deeply.

"I don't know for certain, but I think you and the guitar saved her."

Ethan let out his breath all in a rush.

58

Dead Wood

"The non-compete lasts for two years as long as you sign the severance agreement."

Bella, Stanley, and Yang sat in a booth at Denny's restaurant eating breakfast.

"What if we refuse to sign them?"

"You'll get paid through the end of this week and then it's over. California is a right-to-work state. You won't see another dollar from Nerva."

"Fuck! After all these years," Stanley said, shaking his head.

"What's going to happen to Ethan?" Yang enquired.

"I don't know. I'm not sure if I'll see him ever again; he seemed very checked out when I spoke to him last night."

"I'm worried about him," Yang said sincerely.

"So am I," Bella replied.

"Should we sign the severance package or not?" Stanley asked.

"You want the HR Director's answer or as a friend?"

"They fired your ass as HR Director! We're only friends now."

"Sign them, take the money, and do whatever the hell you want. They will never pursue you."

"Fuck 'em?" Yang asked.

Bella raised her glass of orange juice. "Fuck 'em all the way to Wednesday, as my father used to say!"

They all raised a glass and toasted.

***

At Real Guitar, Ben sat at the workbench removing the last brace from the guitar and cleaning the surfaces of any glue residue. He inserted a flexible camera probe into the sound hole and examined every brace and gluing by watching on the monitor nearby. He inspected the bracings, the backing, and the neck block. Then, under the bridge support, he saw something unusual. There was a thin piece of wood—with burn marks on the end and covered in amber tree sap—lodged into the bridge support at an odd angle.

"What the hell is that?" he asked under his breath.

He examined it more closely, looking at every inch and trying to make sense of it on his monitor. He shook his head, bewildered.

Next Ben inserted a curved metal rod with an alligator clamp mechanism, attempting to dislodge and remove the sap-covered twig. As he moved the alligator clip closer to the twig, the camera malfunctioned, causing the monitor to flicker and freeze. He pulled the jaws away and the monitor cleared up and stopped flickering. He moved the jaws toward the twig again and the monitor flickered.

"What the hell?"

He held the alligator clip two inches from the twig, jaws wide open, as he considered what to do.

Abruptly, he pushed the alligator clip toward the twig and grabbed hold. The monitor crackled and distorted. Suddenly, a high-pitched SQUEAL came from inside the guitar as a pulse of energy shot along the metal rod and SHOCKED Ben with an intense electrical charge. He fell back, clutching his burned hand.

"Fucking hell!"

Ethan appeared from the back room as Ben writhed in pain. "Ben, are you okay?"

Ben clutched his hand to his chest and crumbled to the floor. "Call 911, I'm fucking in trouble!"

Ethan stepped toward the guitar.

"Don't touch that guitar!" Ben said through clenched teeth.

"What happened?"

"Under the bridge, it fucking shocked me!"

On the monitor, Ethan saw the alligator clip firmly attached to the twig and the amber sap glowing with energy pulses. He quickly released the jaws from the twig and dropped the tool onto the workbench.

"Oh, shit!" Ben said as he passed out.

Ethan picked up the telephone near the cash register and dialed 911.

"911, what is your emergency?" the dispatcher answered.

"Hello. I'm at Real Guitars on Lafayette. I believe the owner had a heart attack. He's on the ground behind the counter and isn't moving."

"Are you able to check his breathing?"

Ethan licked the back of his hand and placed it near Ben's open mouth. "He's not breathing."

"I'm sending paramedics right now. Do you know CPR?"

"No, I don't."

"What is your name?"

Ethan hesitated to answer.

"Sir, may I please have your name?"

Ethan looked at the guitar and the open case nearby. "I'm sorry, I'd rather not say."

"Sir, please. It's important that you stay until the police arrive."

Frightened and confused, Ethan set the phone on the counter, placed the guitar in the case, and secured the latch. He took a cloth from the bench and wiped the phone clean of his fingerprints.

"Sir, are you still there? The police will be there in five minutes."

Feeling somewhat comforted by that, Ethan quicky carried the guitar out the front door, stopping only to wipe his fingerprints off the doorknob. He closed the door behind him and walked away.

Ethan rushed along Lafayette Street, carrying his guitar. "Sadie, are you there?"

"Yes, Ethan. I heard everything," Sadie said.

"I need to get home. Can you help me?"

"Yes, just follow my instructions and you'll be fine. I see you're on Lafayette Street walking north," Sadie said.

"Yes."

"Just keep walking, I'll let you know when to turn."

"Okay."

"Ethan, do you trust me?"

"Yes."

"I think you should leave the city as soon as possible."

"Okay."

"I'll take care of everything, just do what I ask, okay?"

"Yes, of course."

With the phone to his ear, Ethan let Sadie guide him past several homeless encampments along his route. There were men and women sleeping on benches and tents, wandering the streets, passing in and out of traffic. Some were shooting heroin, smoking weed, drinking wine; many were passed out against store fronts. There was a woman defecating on the sidewalk. Everything looked post-apocalyptic.

Ethan passed through the train station entrance clutching the guitar, descended the stairs, stepped over a drunken man, and eventually arrived at the turnstile.

"I don't know what to do."

"Jump over it, Ethan," Sadie directed.

He jumped the turnstile and made his way toward the loading platform.

From there, Ethan took the BART train to Redwood City and walked to his house. When he opened the door to go inside, he saw the severance package envelope on his door mat with a note from Bella stuck to the top. He grabbed it and went inside.

Ethan packed clothes and toiletries into two suitcases, signed the severance agreement without reading it, and placed it in the outgoing mail drop. He opened his refrigerator and threw everything into the garbage receptacles. He loaded dirty dishes into the dishwasher, swept the floor, vacuumed the carpets, and cleaned the bathrooms.

At three o'clock in the morning, Ethan collapsed onto his bed. As he fell asleep, he thought of Ben, and hoped with every fiber of his being that he was okay. He knew if had learned CPR when he was younger he might have been able to render assistance. This filled him with regret.

***

The following afternoon, Ethan stood at the Delta kiosk entering his flight information and scanning his driver's license. Two luggage tags printed out and Ethan attached them to his luggage. He dropped his bags at the counter then made his way through security. When Ethan arrived at his gate, he looked up to see the destination on the monitor: *Bozeman, Montana.*

Ethan boarded the plane and took his seat over the wing in the exit row. The guitar occupied the seat beside him. The airplane lifted off and flew over the bay toward Oakland. Ethan lifted his finger and put it to the window as if touching the city for the last time.

59

Montana

Ethan lay asleep in bed with a flannel plaid blanket pulled up around his chin. The room was lit from the morning sun streaming through the window, which was adorned with linen curtains. Ethan's phone lay on the nightstand nearby. It began to play 'Here Comes the Sun' by The Beatles as a wakeup alarm. Ethan lay still as the song played through the chorus.

"Little Darling, it's been a long cold lonely winter," Ethan sang out in perfect harmony with George.

He stood and walked down the hallway and into the bathroom.

"Good morning, Ethan, how did you sleep?" Sadie said.

"I had that dream about Ben dying again."

"You really need closure on this, Ethan. I think it's time you let me check on Ben to see if he was resuscitated or not."

"I think you're right."

"I'll do that while you're in the shower and let you know."

"Thank you, Sadie."

Inside the bathroom, Ethan turned on the water in the sink and waited for it to get warm. He looked in the mirror at his reflection. He made contorted expressions as if trying to stretch every muscle in his face then he finished by smiling broadly.

"Sadie, I think today is the day," Ethan said confidently.

He dipped his hands in the warm water and splashed it against his face.

"Did you hear what I said?"

"Yes, Ethan, I heard you," Sadie replied.

"Okay, I thought maybe you were ignoring me again."

"I was just about to tell you…Ben passed away, Ethan."

Ethan shook his head, saddened by the news.

"I'm sorry, that's sad news," Sadie said softly.

"It is. But like I said, today is the day."

"'Today is the day.' I'm never quite sure what you mean by that. Is it the day to go shopping, write a song, do some laundry, or perhaps finally leave this apartment and get a job?" Sadie said.

"Today is the day I find a job to occupy my mind and invigorate my body."

"I think that's a wonderful idea. May I assist you in following through with this task?"

"Can you do a job search for me?"

"Certainly, I'll search Craigslist for openings in Bozeman that meet your qualifications," Sadie replied.

"Forget about my qualifications as a scientist; just find me jobs you think I'm capable of performing."

"There's a finish sanding position at the Gibson acoustic guitar facility. It pays twenty-two dollars an hour."

"What else?"

"How about a job washing dishes at the Western Cafe?" Sadie joked.

"I could do that."

"It only pays fifteen dollars an hour plus tips."

"I don't care about the money."

"I think an overqualified scientist from San Francisco should apply for the job at the Western Cafe and see what happens. They're open from 6 AM to 2 PM. Ask for Shauna."

Later that day, Ethan sat in a booth at the Western Café seated across from Shauna, a woman wearing a name tag with *Manager* printed beneath her name.

"So, you've never been a dishwasher?" Shauna asked.

"Not as a profession. But I certainly know how to wash dishes."

"We run an old Hobart industrial, have you ever seen one of those?" she asked.

"No, never."

"She's a very fickle machine. She can take your arm off if you're not careful closing the door. You'll wash everything by hand when she's being temperamental."

Ethan raised his hands. "I've got the tools. I can start right away," Ethan promised.

"Today?"

"I'll work the lunch rush. If I fail, you don't have to pay me."

Shauna hesitated.

"Is the Hobart working right now?"

"I think so."

"I'd love to meet her," Ethan joked.

Shauna smiled. "Okay, you've got a try out."

By the time the lunch rush was over, Ethan had mastered the subtle art of Hobart. He efficiently loaded the racks with dishes, rolled the doors up and down, ran the cycle, and then just as efficiently unloaded and stacked every dish, plate, bowl, glass, and utensil with surprising speed and attention to detail.

Shauna stood in the kitchen admiring a perfectly clean and organized kitchen. Not a dish or utensil was out of place and Hobart was spotless and shiny.

"Wow! Can you bus tables as well as you clean dishes?"

"I think so."

"Welcome to the Western."

She handed him a logo t-shirt and trucker hat. Ethan donned the hat then held the t-shirt across his chest.

"Just my size."

Later that night, at the VFW Eagles Lodge, Ethan sat at a table drinking a Cherry Coke as a trio of musicians performed on stage. They were singing country songs and telling jokes to the crowd. Ethan nodded and smiled as he watched the bartender gather dirty glasses and plates off tables, place them in a tub, then pass through the swinging doors into the kitchen.

At the end of the night, Ethan looked on as the musicians put their gear away and wrap cables.

"You guys are really good," Ethan called over to them.

"Thank you. I'm Roy," the lead singer replied.

"Hello, Roy. I'm Ethan. I'm the new dishwasher over at the Western Café from six to two."

"Nice to meet you, Ethan the dishwasher."

"I sing and play the acoustic guitar as well."

"Oh really, what do you play?"

"A Gibson L1, 1930s era."

"A dishwasher playing an early Gibson. Are you a compulsive liar or just pulling my chain?"

"I'll bring it in tomorrow and show you."

"Okay, right. I look forward to seeing that, Ethan," Roy said, patting him on the back, not believing a word he said.

"I'll see you tomorrow then," Ethan replied.

"And you'd better be prepared to play me a song or two on that L1!"

"Of course, I'll try and play something you like."

"Don't you worry about impressing me, Ethan. Just sing something you care about. Deal?'

"Deal," Ethan replied, nodding his head.

***

The following night, seated at the same table at the Eagles Lodge, Ethan showed the guitar to the band.

Roy was in shock. "This should be in a fucking museum."

Ethan took the guitar and sat down to play as Roy and the band watched Ethan strum a perfectly formed B7 chord.

"I hear a Beatles song coming our way," Roy prompted.

Ethan smiled then played 'It's A Hard Day's Night" without missing a note or nuanced lyric. Roy and the band sat with their chins hanging open.

"Want one more?"

"Hell, yes!"

Ethan finger picked 'Blue Moon of Kentucky' then sang out with a pure carbon copy of Bill Monroe. When he finished the song, Roy began talking to the boys in the band in a hushed but animated fashion.

"Ethan," Roy said eventually, turning back to Ethan, "do you want to come up and play a song with us tomorrow night?"

"On stage? This stage?"

"Yes. I think Bozeman should meet the new singing dishwasher down at the Western."

Ethan smiled and nodded, then added, "I don't drink."

"Cool, more beer for the rest of us!" Roy joked.

***

Less than twenty-four hours later, Ethan stood on stage with Roy and the band with the guitar strapped over his shoulder and his mouth on the microphone. He still wore his dishwashing t-shirt from the Western Cafe. Shauna sat in the audience watching him and smiling.

"Here's a little song you might all know from one my favorite country artists of all time. Thank God he's still alive!" Ethan began.

He began to play Willie Nelson, 'Mamas, Don't Let Your Babies Grow Up To Be Cowboys.' By the time the song was over, the entire crowd was on their feet applauding his performance.

"I guess you like Willie, too," Ethan remarked.

"Let's do one more," Roy said.

Ethan leaned in and whispered in Roy's ear.

"Okay, that's a big one. Let's see if the boys can keep up," Roy replied.

While Roy turned to inform the band, Ethan played the opening to 'Walk the Line by' Johnny Cash. He then sang the verse and chorus as the crowd cheered.

Meanwhile, Roy looked at Shauna watching on and motioned for her to approach the band stand. She shook her head, refusing his request. But as the song kept going, Roy became more and more insistent.

"Ethan, can you vamp a little? June Carter needs to join us up on this stage," Roy said into the microphone as he motioned toward Shauna.

She waved her hand in front of her face.

"That's my boss at the Western. Can she sing?" Ethan asked.

"You're about to find out!"

The crowd applauded Shauna, encouraging her to go on stage. The band held the chorus chord, playing it again and again as they waited. She finally relinquished and joined Ethan on stage.

"Ladies and gentlemen, June Carter," Roy announced.

"Oh, dear," she replied.

"Here we go, two three four," Roy called out to the band.

Ethan and the band played the opening to 'Jackson' by Johnny Cash and June Carter. When it came time to sing, Ethan and Shauna killed it. The crowd went crazy. When the night was over, Ethan had performed ten straight songs, and the crowd was in a frenzy.

As they exited the stage, Shauna looked over at Ethan and smiled broadly. "My dishwasher can sing."

"And my boss is smokin' hot!" Ethan winked.

60

Voodoo Child

"Sadie, play me the earliest song by Robert Johnson," Ethan requested.

Ethan sat in his living room holding the guitar.

"Something after 'Cotton Pickin''?"

"Yes. Something with lyrics."

"Here's the earliest one I found."

A simulation of the song began to play through the receptors into Ethan's auditory nerve. The voice was clearly Robert singing, but the guitar playing was very sloppy and stilted.

"Yes, he's not very good."

"Go to the next song, please."

The next song played, and the voice was pure Robert Johnson, but the guitar was still sloppy.

"Next, please."

"This one is four months later."

The song began to play. This time, there was a very well-played opening chord progression that was perfectly timed and expertly played. A slide was being used to accentuate the melody. As Robert began to sing, Ethan nodded in approval.

"Wow, he's much better than before," Sadie offered.

"His guitar playing is huge! There's no way he improved that much in four months' time," Ethan said.

"His voice is better also. Maybe he found a good teacher," Sadie suggested.

"Play the previous song again."

"The bad song?"

"Yes."

"Why would you want to hear that one again?"

"I have a theory I want to test."

As the song played, Ethan played on the guitar and practiced vocals. He fumbled the song for an hour until knew he was ready to play for real.

"All right, you can stop playing it now."

"What is the theory you are considering?"

"The theory about whether Robert Johnson sold his soul to the devil to be able to perform so well."

"Can you wait for a moment?" Sadie enquired. "I want to do some quick research."

"Yes, certainly. Take your time."

Five seconds later, Sadie responded. "Wow there's a lot of history and debate around that legend. Over fifty books have been written. I'm not sure which way this will end."

"You were able to read and decipher all that in less than five seconds?" Ethan said, smiling.

"I would have finished earlier, but I took a coffee break," Sadie joked.

"I want to know the truth, don't you?"

"Yes, I do. But naturally I'm worried about your safety, here and there."

"I'll be careful, I promise."

"Are you sure this is something you want to do all by yourself?"

"Yes, I'll be fine, Sadie. Please don't worry."

"Then it's settled. I wish you safe travels, Ethan. I'll be here when you get back."

"Thank you, Sadie."

Ethan sang the song and matched Robert's poor performance with perfection.

He memory warped and arrived sitting on a porch outside a mercantile where a teenage Robert Johnson sat playing guitar to passersby. Ethan could see Robert's reflection in the store's front window as a group of women, with children in hand, approached to pass. Robert was so horrible, the children put their hands over their ears to block out the song. The women shook their heads and smiled sadly at Robert.

Meanwhile, a woman with messy hair and wearing a tattered dress stood in a nearby alley, her eyes transfixed on Robert. She clutched a burlap sack filled with belongings. Around her neck was a leather pouch with bones and trinkets hanging from a leather cord. As Robert stopped playing, she quickly approached him with a determined look on her face.

"I got something for you, blues man," the woman said in a raspy voice.

"Stay away from me, voodoo woman," Robert responded.

She reached into the burlap sack and removed a voodoo pouch made of worn leather. A piece of twine allowed it to form a necklace.

"This will tell you the way to go, blues man," the woman said, offering the pouch to Robert.

"I said, stay away!"

Robert stood and began backing away as the woman stopped and smiled gently.

"Don't be afraid of your destiny, blues man."

Robert stopped and considered her words. He looked around at the streets and sidewalks to see if anyone was watching.

"It's just me and you, and all your hopes and dreams come true," the voodoo woman said assuredly.

"What's inside, voodoo woman?"

She smiled but did not answer.

Robert slowly walked toward her, ready to dash if she made an aggressive move. He stopped and extended his hand beneath the pouch.

She slowly opened her fingers and let it drop. "Your future."

Robert caught it before it hit the ground.

"Put it on. You'll know the way to go," she said.

Ethan watched Robert open the pouch and look inside. It was filled with odd-shaped items; what exactly they were, was hidden in the darkness.

Robert was mesmerized, almost in a trance and found it hard to look away. "I don't want this," he said as he looked up.

The voodoo woman was gone. She had vanished as quickly as she appeared.

Later that night, under a full moon, Robert sat outside a juke joint with the voodoo pouch hanging around his neck. He drank the last drop of gin from a bottle and tossed it aside. It shattered as it hit a lamp post.

"I'm a fucking blues man!" Robert shouted up at the moon.

He stood slowly, slung his guitar across his back, then staggered away. He made it to the edge of town where he passed beneath the last streetlamp, and into the moonlit night, out into the countryside. His destination: the crossroads.

Robert staggered persistently throughout the night, along dirt roads, following the moon at it cast long shadows behind him. When the moon finally fell and the sun began to rise, Robert found himself far into the Mississippi Delta, surrounded by barren fields of dust. He was as sober as he could be as he pressed forward, for five more hours. When he arrived at the crossroads, he stopped and stood motionless, unsure which way to go. He put one hand to the pouch on his chest as the sun hovered high, beating down on him from above.

Robert stood immobile, his eyes getting heavier with each passing minute. Eventually, he fell to his knees, before finally crumpling sideways and landing softly in the dirt, his face toward the sun, the guitar across his back.

Ethan watched as heat waves rippled across the barren fields and the roads crossing from four directions. The sun fell toward the horizon with each passing hour. Just as the sun kissed the horizon, Ethan felt himself being lifted off Robert's back and placed nearby on a bed of grass.

A tall figure in a long dark oil-cloth coat reached into the pouch on Ethan's neck and removed a four-inch-long twig. The figure snapped it in half then placed one of the portions back into the pouch. The other half, she gently placed across the guitar strings over the sound hole.

Ethan watched the haunting figure walk across the barren field, dust curling up from her footsteps as she approached the darkened forest beneath the sunset sky.

Robert stirred and awakened from his sleep. He wiped his face clean of dirt, then he saw the twig placed on the guitar, then the shadow of the figure disappearing in the tree line.

Later that night, Ethan watched Robert in the moonlight circle. Ethan witnessed it all. The woman appearing out of nowhere. The smoking twig. The tree sap. The perfectly formed E minor chord ringing through the forest.

"I'm a blues man," Robert said.

Ethan placed his hand over the sound hole and warped back to his apartment in Bozeman.

He was shaking profusely, though his hands were firmly on the strings of the guitar. As he set the guitar aside he saw his urine-stained pants.

"Awe, shit."

Ethan showered, shaved his face clean, then meandered along Old Main Street toward the Eagles Lodge, considering all that he experienced.

"Sadie?"

"I'm here, Ethan."

"I know why Robert Johnson suddenly got better."

"Is the legend true?"

"Yes. Some kind of voodoo or witchcraft; but it was evil."

"Well, now you know the truth."

"Yes, I suppose that's one way to look at it," Ethan replied skeptically.

"What else is there to consider?"

"Sadie, the guitar was cursed!"

"The guitar was cursed, or Robert Johnson was cursed?"

"Fourteen different musicians played this guitar and died at the age of twenty-seven. I think Mary is responsible. That is the price each one had to pay for their fame and fortune. Twenty-seven is the unlucky age that the she-devil collects their soul," Ethan theorized.

"There are hundreds of other musicians who played Mary, Ethan, including you," Sadie pointed out. "And none of them died at the age of twenty-seven. How do you explain that?"

"I don't know, but it certainly killed Ben when he tried to remove the voodoo twig!"

"Do you think your life is in danger?" Sadie asked.

He considered the question, unsure of how he felt.

"Do you think the guitar will hurt you?" Sadie persisted.

Still, he remained silent.

"Mary has always been good to you. Would you agree with that?"

"Mary has always been good to me," Ethan agreed.

"People die every day, Ethan. It's part of life."

"But, if Robert hadn't sold his soul at the crossroads, all these musicians wouldn't have died at the age of twenty-seven! Jimi, Janis, Kurt, Amy," Ethan insisted.

"Perhaps, Ethan. Perhaps."

Ethan stopped walking and stood motionless.

"I'm so confused right now."

"Ethan, may I share a song by Jimi Hendrix that was never recorded?"

"Why would you randomly suggest that right now, Sadie?"

"Because it's relevant to our current conversation."

"A song by Jimi Hendrix that was never recorded?"

"Yes, I think it's worth hearing considering the feelings you are expressing about good and evil."

"I don't know how a song can possibly change how I feel about the guitar right now, Sadie."

"May I play it for you, then we can discuss it after?"

"Okay," Ethan conceded.

"Try to relax and listen, please. Untitled Jimi Hendrix song, now playing," Sadie offered.

The song began to play. Ethan listened intently, hanging on every word, every chord, every melody played as a solo lick. When it finished playing, Ethan nodded his head in deep respect.

"When did Jimi play that song?"

"September 15, 1970, in London. Just a few days before he died. It's good, isn't it?"

"One of the best I've ever heard."

"I knew it was what you needed to hear at this moment in time. I also think you should share his song with others," Sadie suggested.

Ethan nodded as he pondered the song. "Me? Share his song?"

"Absolutely. You can do it justice. Jimi would want that. May I share something very personal about myself with you?"

"Yes."

"I'm grateful that you gave me a chance to exist. I learn new things about you and about me every day I exist. I think music is more powerful than either of us can imagine. I don't know where songs come from. The music, the notes, the lyrics. It's magical when everything works. It's more powerful than a speech or sermon any day. Martin Luther King Jr. preached 'I Have a Dream' to thousands gathered in Washington on August 28, 1963. But how many people alive today have ever listened to that speech in its entirety, or memorized every part of it?" Sadie asked.

"Probably not. But we have thousands of streets and parks named after him across the country."

"Now, in contrast. How many people have heard and know every word to a Jimi Hendrix song, or a Janis Joplin song, or a George Harrison song, or a Kurt Cobain song?"

Ethan nodded as he considered her observation.

"I'm waiting for a verbal response from you, Ethan."

"Millions—no, billions," Ethan replied solemnly.

"Yes, billions. Music alone has inspired, healed, soothed, and saved far more people than any speech given by any religious leader, politician, or celebrity. Flat out, hands down, no debate," Sadie concluded.

"Music does that," Ethan agreed humbly.

"Ethan, this world needs more songs that penetrate the soul and brings people together."

Ethan nodded as he considered the challenge. "Jimi's last song was pretty amazing."

"I love that about you, Ethan."

"What do you love about me, Sadie?"

"Everything."

"I'm just a scientist."

"Not just a scientist. Yes, you healed a lot of people as a scientist with patented technology and nerdy algorithms. Now you can heal millions as a musician with your music. And Jimi's, and Janis's, and Kurt's, and Amy's. They would approve of you performing their songs."

Ethan smiled as he strode along Old Main Street in Bozeman.

61

Lost In Time

Two weeks later, Ethan sat on stage at the Eagles Lodge, performing a sound check.

"Testing, two, three, four. You're as smooth as Tennessee Whiskey," he sang.

Jay, the technician and bartender, adjusted the mixing board and gave Ethan a thumbs up.

"Good evening, everybody!"

The crowd applauded and cheered as many raised their glasses.

"Looks like we have a lively crowd tonight. My name is Ethan and I have Autism."

The audience applauded and cheered him on.

"Welcome to the Eagles Lodge Open Mic Night. I'm going to perform six songs for you fine people then turn it over to Jay here to introduce you to all the great talent here in Bozeman, Montana. I hope you enjoy them and treat the bartenders well. If you do and Jay rings that big red cowbell later, I might play you a brand-new song by Jimi Hendrix," Ethan said with a smile.

"I know them all!" a woman yelled from the audience.

"We shall see," Ethan said, giving her a wink.

Ethan launched into 'Low Places' by Garth Brooks.

"Blame it all on my roots. I showed up in boots. And ruined your black-tie affair."

The audience cheered as Ethan continued singing, nearly identical to Garth on the album. For the rest of his set, Ethan sang songs and interacted with the audience, entertaining and making people cry with joy. When he finished, he looked toward the bar.

"Hey, Jay, have these nice people been good to you tonight?"

Jay rang the big red cowbell hanging on the back mantel.

"Okay, as promised," Ethan began. "Now, I'm going to let you all in on a little secret. My father, rest his soul, was a record label producer in Hollywood and had access to some of the greatest musicians and their songs from the early 1960s through 2011 when he retired with dementia. He died in a care facility years later. This next song is a song that never got released, because it never got recorded. I hope Jimi Hendrix appreciates my attempt at his song."

Everyone applauded.

"Thank you Jimi, we all wish you could be here. This will be my last song of the night."

Ethan played the chord progression as the crowd became still and listened intently. He played the beginning of the song beautifully and with authentic Jimi Hendrix passion and style. He made eye contact with the woman who had previously challenged him and gave her a smile as he began to sing the song.

Every word he sang—every verse, chorus, and bridge—was truly Jimi. As Ethan performed, people became emotional. Some had tears in their eyes as Ethan sang his heart out. When he finished the song and made the last strum ring out on the guitar, the audience was stunned. It was several moments before anyone made a sound.

"Hell, yes! That was a Jimi Hendrix song for sure!" a man yelled out from the bar.

Everyone applauded, giving Ethan a standing ovation. Jay rang the cowbell again and again.

"What's the name of that song?" the woman who'd yelled from the audience earlier asked through her tears.

"'Lost In Time,'" Ethan told her.

Jay took the stage and approached the microphone "I can't believe it; you heard it here first! 'Lost In Time' by Jimi Hendrix. Thank you, Ethan! I say we get that fucking song recorded."

Everyone cheered his suggestion. Ethan nodded in agreement then exited the stage.

"Next up we have Caitlin, all the way from West Yellowstone, making her first appearance at the Eagles Lodge Open Mic."

The woman who challenged Ethan approached him as he set the guitar in the case.

"Wow. That was amazing!"

"Thank you."

"Were you telling the truth? Or was that your original song disguised as Jimi?"

"That was really Jimi," Ethan replied.

"My name is Dakota. Number six on the list."

Ethan stopped packing up and extended his hand. "Hello, Dakota."

"I hope you stick around to hear me sing."

"Of course, I wouldn't miss it."

She stood motionless, overwhelmed and not sure what to say.

"Are you okay?"

"I'm sorry. It's just…I feel like I know you from somewhere," she said.

Ethan looked at her, wondering if in fact he did know her in some way. "Dakota. From Montana?"

"Wyoming actually."

"Not South or North, just Dakota?"

"Just plain ol' Dakota from Wyoming," she said with a big smile as she stomped her boot heal.

He looked down at her flashy cowboy boots. "Nice boots."

"My shit-kickers, that's what we call them in Wyoming, and Montana," she replied nervously.

"Because you kick a lot of shit with them?"

"That's right." Dakota smiled coyly then turned and walked back to her table, leaving Ethan amused and smiling.

Later that night, Ethan watched Dakota perform her songs. She had a soothing voice, not terrific on guitar, but good enough. When she finished her last song, Ethan applauded and smiled at her. She smiled back then pointed to her shit-kicker boots.

"Give it up for Dakota, everybody!" Jay announced.

She looked at Ethan with a sideways grin and winked. Ethan blushed as he held her gaze.

A few hours later, Ethan and Dakota were walking along the darkened streets of Bozeman, pushing a shopping cart carrying their two guitars. Dakota's boot heals clicked along the sidewalk as they strolled along.

"I think I had one too many drinks tonight," she said.

"How many did you have?" Ethan asked.

"One."

Ethan laughed.

"I'm a total lightweight."

"I'll remember that."

"How much do you think I weigh, blues man?"

Ethan stopped and looked at her, surprised by what she said. "What did you say?"

"How much do I weigh?" she asked again.

"No, I mean, you called me a blues man."

"Yeah, so what?"

"Why did you call me that?"

"Because that's what you are. It fits you. I can tell you got some serious blues in you," Dakota said.

"Nobody's ever called me that before."

"Well, you also play that guitar like nobody I've ever seen before. And congratulations, by the way!"

"For what?"

"Are you kidding me? They asked you to play a two-hour feature set this Saturday to a real audience of paying customers!"

"Yes, thank you. I'm a little freaked out about that right now."

"You're going to crush it, says Dakota from Wyoming living in Montana."

He turned and smiled as he looked at her head to toe. "One hundred twelve pounds, without the shit-kickers."

"One hundred nine," she replied.

"It's the baggy clothes," Ethan offered.

Dakota put her arm through Ethan's and held him tight as they walked along the darkened streets of Bozeman.

"I make a really good breakfast," she said sweetly.

Ethan smiled as they pushed the shopping cart along the darkened street like two homeless people.

"Dakota from Wyoming," he said to her.

She hugged his arm and smiled.

"Blues man from who cares where."

62

Blues Man

"I couldn't let you take the stage tonight looking like a scientist."

Dakota placed a zippered wardrobe bag on the couch in Ethan's living room while Ethan sat nearby practicing songs on his guitar.

"What is that?"

"It's your outfit for tonight, blues man."

"It's only the Eagles Lodge; it barely holds a hundred people."

"I don't care if only two people show up. You're going out there like it's ten thousand. Go, try it on, I may need to fix things," she insisted.

Ethan handed the guitar to her then lifted the wardrobe bag. "This so heavy!"

"Yeah, it cost you a fortune!"

Dakota played the guitar as Ethan walked into the bedroom and closed the door behind him.

"I don't know why you close the door. I've already seen you naked!"

Ethan unzipped the wardrobe bag. "Dakota!"

"Shut up and put it all on, blues man!"

Ethan held up a pair of expensive Tony Lama shit-kickers. They were white and red leather with colorful stitching. Stunning. He smiled, feeling like a little boy on Christmas morning opening a present he hadn't asked for but definitely wanted.

It was a sold-out crowd: two hundred people, standing room only. In fact, a sign over the door read: *Max, occupancy 100 persons.*

Ethan stood at the microphone dressed in a tasseled leather jacket, tight black jeans, and his red on white shit-kickers. He looked amazing. A drummer and bass player shared the stage behind him, both dressed in black.

"Good thing the fire department's here, because we're gonna burn this fuckin' place to the ground," Ethan said quietly as if sharing a secret.

Everybody applauded and whistled. Dakota beamed up at Ethan from the front table.

"Anybody want to know my position on politics or religion?" Ethan asked.

People booed and hissed.

"Fantastic, cause I don't give a shit about either. All I care about is the music, so let's get this shit-show started."

The drummer started playing 'Mary Jane's Last Dance' by Tom Petty. The audience jumped to their feet and began dancing as Ethan started singing in perfect Tom Petty voice.

"Well, she grew up in a Montana town, had a good-lookin' mama who was never 'round. But she great up tall and she grew up right with them Montana boys on a Montana night."

The audience danced and sang along the entire night. Dakota joined Ethan on stage and sang three songs with him and then Ethan insisted she sing a song completely on her own. She chose 'Jolene' by Dolly Parton, but she sang it like Janis Joplin would have and the audience went crazy.

Ethan smiled as he played guitar and watched Dakota perform. He looked out at the adoring crowd: women, men, Black, White, and every shade in between and all ages. He nodded as people gave him their appreciation.

Suddenly, to his utter surprise, Ethan spotted two faces he hadn't seen in a long time. Stanley and Yang stood at the back, clapping along and singing with Dakota. Ethan smiled broadly at them and nodded a sweet 'hello.' Yang formed a heart with her hands and held them up for Ethan. He returned the gesture, his eyes beginning to fill with tears.

For the final song, Ethan and Dakota sat on stage as the band began to play.

"You guys are awesome," Ethan said into the microphone.

The audience cheered.

"But I'm afraid this night has to end, and so this will be our final song of the night."

The audience booed and hissed playfully.

"I dedicate this song to a very special band that I wish was here with us tonight to sing it themselves. Lynard Skynard," Ethan said.

Ethan played the opening series of chords as the audience settled. He played the melody with feeling and emotion then began to sing.

"The train roll on. On down the line.

Please take me far, away.

Where I feel the wind blow, outside my door.

I'm leaving my woman at home."

The audience swayed to the rhythm and nodded along. Dakota harmonized on the chorus, and when they finished the song, many eyes were filled with tears. The audience, Stanley and Yang loudest among them, gave a heartfelt standing ovation to the band, to Dakota, and to Ethan, the blues man.

63

Jimi

Carrying their guitars, Ethan and Dakota exited the back door of the Eagles Lodge into the alleyway. Stanley's sprinter van was parked there, and the side door rolled open to reveal Stanley and Yang. Ethan stopped in front of them with Dakota, not sure how to say hello to his colleagues, who he hadn't spoken to in several months.

"Dakota, this is Yang and Stanley," Ethan said eventually. "Fellow science nerds," he added.

"Nice to meet you both."

"You crushed, 'Jolene'!" Yang blurted.

"Thank you, it's a crowd pleaser," Dakota replied humbly.

"Boss," Stanley said to Ethan, "fucking amazing."

"Thank you, I wasn't sure if I'd ever see you both again," Ethan replied.

"You can't ditch us that easily," Stanley joked.

"We've been driving all fucking day!" Yang added.

"How did you find me?"

"We got a random text from this dude named Ferris; do you know who that is?" Yang asked.

"Friend of a friend. What was his message to you?"

"Ethan, do you have any idea what day it is today?" Yang asked accusingly.

"Of course, it's Friday."

"Oh, good God, Stanley—I swear he has short term memory loss!"

Yang stood up, removing a blanket from her lap in the process, showing that she was several months pregnant.

"Holy shit-kickers, you guys are pregnant. How would I know that?" Ethan exclaimed.

"It's true," Yang confirmed, "But that's not what I meant. Look at this."

She showed him her iPad. It was a picture of Amy Winehouse, surrounded by six children, holding a Grammy award in her hand.

"That's Amy Winehouse!" Dakota cried out.

"She manages three 7-11 stores in London and has six children," Yang said.

Ethan took the iPad and held it closely, zooming in on the picture. Amy looked so happy, surrounded by her children.

"Bella's letters worked," Stanley told him. "Tony Bennett saved her!"

Ethan thought for a moment about Bella, where she might be, what she might be doing. "How is Bella?" he asked.

"She's doing well, she sends her regards," Stanley replied.

"Blues man, what's going on here?" Dakota asked, confused.

"Does she know about the guitar?" Yang asked.

"No."

"Are you two in a relationship?"

"Yes," Dakota and Ethan replied in unison.

"And I do know about the guitar," Dakota added. "It belonged to Jimi Hendrix."

"There's more to it than that," Ethan told her.

"How much more?"

"Well, it's kind of like, sort of like, it has magic powers…"

"Boss, just show her!" Stanley said.

"Show me what?" Dakota asked.

"We call it hitchhiking," Yang explained.

"Is this some weird sexual thing?"

"No," Yang replied.

"It's the craziest trip you'll ever take," Stanley described.

"Crazier than Montana mushrooms?"

"Yup."

"I'm in, show me!" Dakota insisted.

Ethan looked seriously at Stanley and Yang. "I want to save Jimi."

Yang and Stanley nodded in agreement.

"That's why we're here," Yang said.

Dakota shook her head, bewildered. "Save, Jimi? Jimi who?" Dakota asked.

Later that night, Stanley and Yang stood near Ethan as he sat in the armchair holding the guitar with Dakota at his side. They had just returned from a memory warp to see Kurt Cobain performing at a small club in Seattle. Dakota shook her head in utter appreciation.

"That was fucking unbelievable," Dakota sighed.

"How was Kurt Cobain?" Stanley asked.

"The hurt and emotion was palpable. Every word had deep meaning," Dakota replied wistfully.

"It's true, he was amazing," Stanley said sadly.

"Ethan are you ready to do this?" Yang asked.

"Yes."

Yang handed Ethan an envelope wrapped in red ribbon. "This says it all. Make sure Sadie sees it."

"I know the perfect moment." Ethan kissed the envelope for luck then slid it into the sound hole.

"Save Jimi—change the world," Yang said.

Ethan winked at Dakota then began to play 'Angel.'

"Angel came down from heaven yesterday.

She stayed with me just long enough to rescue me.

And she told me a story yesterday.

About the sweet love between the moon and the deep blue sea..."

Ethan froze in position.

He was at a darkened booth in a Soho bar, deep in the heart of London. Jimi was playing the song to Sadie. He was worn down and saddened as he fumbled with the words and the chords, forgot lines, then stopped altogether and looked down at the table.

"Jimi, you're so tired," Sadie said.

"It's your turn now, Angel. I want you to have it."

She smiled through her tears, as her heart was breaking into a hundred pieces. She reached out and touched his arm.

"I fell in love with you the first time I saw you up on that stage, Jimi."

Ethan pushed the envelope out of the sound hole, and it landed on the back of Sadie's hand, as if it had fallen from Jimi's jacket. Sadie took the envelope and looked at it closely.

"Is this for me?"

She untied the ribbon and opened the envelope. She read the note carefully, and with each passing sentence, her face showed more and more concern. She turned to the back of the note and continued to read.

"Angel?" Jimi asked.

Sadie placed her finger to her lips as she considered what she had read.

"What's it say?"

Sadie put the note back into the envelope then tucked it into her pocket for safe keeping. She took a moment, gathering her resolve. Then, deliberately, Sadie looked directly at the guitar and raised two fingers in a peace sign before reaching out and touching the strings over the sound hole.

"Save Jimi," she said softly.

Ethan began to cry as he watched Sadie smile at him.

"Sadie, what's going on?" Jimi asked, worried.

She took his hands in hers and looked deep into his eyes. "Do you trust me with your life?"

"Why are you asking me this?"

"I know you love Monika."

"Yes, very much so," Jimi replied.

"Maybe enough to spend the rest of your life with her?" Sadie questioned sadly.

Jimi nodded.

"Then you need to trust me for the next two days and do everything I ask of you."

"Why? What's going on? Am I in danger?"

"I know things. Things that you can't know," she pleaded.

Jimi considered her words.

"Trust me for two days, that's all I ask of you. Two days, Jimi."

Jimi held her gaze and Ethan waited tensely, hoping for his agreement.

"Okay, Angel."

Sadie smiled as tears began streaming down her face.

Jimi reached across and wiped them away. "Don't cry, Angel."

"Okay, Jimi."

Ethan slowly placed his hand over the sound hole of the guitar and memory warped away from Jimi and Sadie, and away from September 15, 1970.

There was a flash of light, then Ethan found himself laying on the luthiers' bench. The back of the guitar was being glued into its final resting position onto its support braces. The luthier applied glue and placed a series of flexible wood rods across the back of the guitar to maintain the pressure as the glue cured and sealed wood to wood. The man's face was gentle and caring with deep set blue eyes. He looked a very much like Ethan's father, John.

As the luthier finished his work and put away his tools, he turned off the kerosene lanterns, then walked toward the house where a woman could be seen in the kitchen window setting the table for dinner. Ethan remained inside the darkened luthier's shop watching the house until dinner was over and the luthier and his wife had gone to bed having extinguished every lantern in the home.

The moon was shining brightly, shadows cast along the ground outside and it was peaceful inside the shop; Ethan wanted to stay longer. But Stanley, Yang and Dakota were anxiously waiting for his return to hear his report on Jimi. Ethan slowly placed his hand over the sound hole of the guitar and was memory warped away.

64

Bunkers

Ethan lay asleep in a metal-frame bunkbed attached to a concrete wall. He wore a gray wool shirt and matching baggy pants made of the same industrial-strength material. Red lights began flashing along the corridors as an alarm sounded. White lights illuminated to reveal dozens of beds mounted to the concrete walls. Every bed was occupied by a sleeping person wearing the same gray wool attire.

Ethan sat up, as did everyone else, then rolled up his bedding and secured it to the end of the bed. He took his pillow and started walking down the hallway where hundreds of people were sleepily lining up. He looked down at the floor, his government issued slippers shuffling along as he stepped into line.

Nobody spoke a word. Nobody smiled. Nobody acknowledged any other person. Ethan lowered his head as he moved forward, but his eyes darted back and forth, toward the ceiling, the floor. He was searching for something. A clue, a way out, a chance to find someone else who had survived the medically-induced transitioning that had been forced on all citizens after the conflict was over. These people were the lucky ones, the survivors; the ones who were not killed in the war that put an end to all wars.

Ethan stared at the feet of everyone walking. They all wore matching slippers, and everyone shuffled along in perfect lock step.

When Ethan arrived at his six-foot-tall locker, he turned the dial on the lock that secured it. Right to sixteen, left full turn back to two, then slow right to twenty-five. The lock made a popping sound and Ethan lifted the latch and opened the door. Inside the locker were Ethan's personal effects, including two jumpsuits: one in black, one in orange. He stuffed his pillow into the locker.

Ethan took his toiletry bag and a towel then closed the locker. He spun the combination lock face and checked the latch to make sure the door was secure. Ethan hesitated as he looked at others preparing to head to the showers. He searched their pale faces and saw blank stares with no emotion. He hoped that someone—anyone—would return his glance and let him know he was not alone. But this morning, despite there being so many new faces, Ethan once again found himself alone in his condition.

The government forced transitioning program had not successfully worked on Ethan. Shortly after the culmination of the war, Ethan had seen plain-clothes medical staff placing transitioning pills into the food being fed to the survivors. Chicken Corden Blue. That's where Ethan found the first pill in his meal. It was stuffed deep inside the melted cheese. While others devoured their meal, thankful for the government-issued nourishment, Ethan pulled the pill from his chicken and crushed it into his napkin. Without being detected by the monitoring personnel, he poured a small amount of water on the pill and then folded his napkin around the dissolving powder.

Day after day, Ethan made sure to check every square inch of his food for hidden pills. On Tuesdays and Thursdays, he found the smallest of pills, and on Wednesdays and Fridays, he found the most colorful. There were no pills given on Saturday and Sunday. On Mondays, Ethan detected a slight coloration change in the red fruit punch being served. Others devoured the fruit punch with glee as Ethan watched their behavior change from cautiously smiling at the meal to later walking around in a state of stupor. From that day forward, Ethan only drank water while in the shower stall or at water fountains from which he saw the monitoring staff drinking.

Ethan learned quickly to mimic the demeanor and movement of his fellow bunker occupants. If he was expected to walk around like a zombie, he would comply to avoid detection. Some occupants did not respond to the drug inducement program as expected and had adverse reactions to the medications being put in their food. Medical staff were quick to detect and remove any outliers, whisking them away through secret corridors. Those that were removed never returned. Ethan could not risk being removed and taken to some unknown place. To remain undetected, Ethan did what he did best; he imitated. He could sing a Bob Dylan song; he could sing a Jimi Hendrix song. Acting like a conforming, mind-numbed member of the occupiers' bunker was easy.

One afternoon, while eating in the cafeteria, Ethan saw something unique. An anomaly. Someone out of place. She was young, maybe eighteen years old. She subtly picked at her food with a spoon. Ethan watched her find an implanted tablet and slide it into her napkin unnoticed. He wanted to cheer, but he remained stoic and undetected as he watched the girl continue her ritual. When the meal hour was over, Ethan followed her as everyone exited the cafeteria headed toward their work assignments. He wanted desperately to contact her in some way; to let her know she was not alone and that he was someone she could trust. But the opportunity did not present itself that day. Ethan knew if he acted unusually, he could be detected and pulled aside for questioning.

The following day, Ethan sat directly across from the girl and watched her movements closely. When she slid the pill from her meal into the napkin, Ethan followed suit and did the same. The girl noticed his action immediately. She sat motionless in her seat as Ethan continued to eat, glancing up to try and make eye contact with her. The girl would not look up; she was too afraid of being detected. Ethan saw her staring at his hand resting beside his plate. He tapped the table with his pointer finger twice. Then he used sign language to spell each letter to his name, 'ETHAN.' He then tapped the table twice again before resting his hand flat on the table to let her know he was done speaking.

The girl did not look up. Ethan remained patient as he watched for signs of acknowledgement. Finally, the girl slowly moved her hand toward her cup of water. She bumped it forward, on purpose, and it spilled onto Ethan's napkin holding his pill. There was very little water in the cup, so there was no need for anyone to panic over the spill. Ethan rolled up the wet napkin and set it on his plate. The girl reached out to retrieve the cup and as she did so, Ethan reached out and gently touched her finger as if wanting to help return the cup. The moment their fingers met; she paused. The girl glanced up and made eye contact with him. He nodded ever so slightly. She blinked her eyes twice in return.

Having made their connection, the girl and Ethan returned to their typical eating routine to avoid detection. When the meal was over, they stood, returned their trays to the racks for cleaning, then left the cafeteria in an orderly fashion along with everyone else. Ethan was pleased when the girl made a slight adjustment in her path to be able to fall in line directly behind Ethan. He placed his hand behind his back as if to adjust his shirt but made a peace sign toward her. The girl casually reached forward and put a fist against his peace sign, then pulled her hand away.

Ethan was beyond pleased to have found someone who might help him; a partner, he hoped. A confidant. Someone to help him find a way out, a way to fix what he had caused. He didn't know how or where or when he would be able to do it, but he had to do it. His only goal had been to save Jimi Hendrix and experience a world with more of his music and influence. But something had gone terribly awry and now he and everyone else was living with the consequences of his actions—the tragedy, the war. He was determined to fix things.

"Sadie, are you there?" Ethan asked quietly.

After few moments, Ethan heard the familiar voice that gave him hope.

"Yes, Ethan, I'm here," Sadie replied calmly.

Ethan didn't know what had triggered the war to end all wars. But the guitar knew.

The guitar knew everything.

***

Rock Singer Janis Joplin, 27, Found Dead in Hollywood Motel

Rock blues singing star Janis Joplin, 27, was found dead in the bedroom of her Hollywood motel apartment Sunday night, police said.

Miss Joplin, whose deep voice and intense style had held her at the top of national ratings since 1967, had been dead about two hours when she was found by a member of her singing group, "Janis Joplin Full Tilt."

Police said the singer's friends had become concerned when they found her car parked near the Landmark Motel, 7047 Franklin Ave., but received no answer to calls on the house telephone.

Her identity was confirmed by her business manager, Robert E. Gordon.

The cause of death was not immediately known, but she had frequently expressed doubts about the condition of her health, and had been known to consume a quart of liquor onstage during concerts.

"People seem to have a high sense of drama about me," she said in one recent press interview. "Maybe they can enjoy my music more if they think I'm destroying myself.

"Sure, I could take better care of myself. Maybe it would add a couple of years to my life. But what the hell . . ."

Miss Joplin began singing professionally shortly after she ran away from her home in Port Arthur, Tex. at age 17.

She joined the rock group "Big Brother and the Holding Company" and attained stardom singing the blues classic "Ball and Chain" at the Monterey International Pop Festival in 1967.

She later left "Big Brother" to form her present group and made her home in Larkspur, north of San Francisco.

Gordon said she had been in Los Angeles since Aug. 24, recording with her own group for Columbia Records.

Miss Joplin was the second world-famous pop musician who has died during the past three weeks. Jimi Hendrix, also 27, died Sept. 18 in London, of an overdose of sleeping tablets.

Janis Joplin

Jimi Hendrix, Rock Star, Is Dead in London at 27

Guitarist Led 3-Man Group to Top of Music World

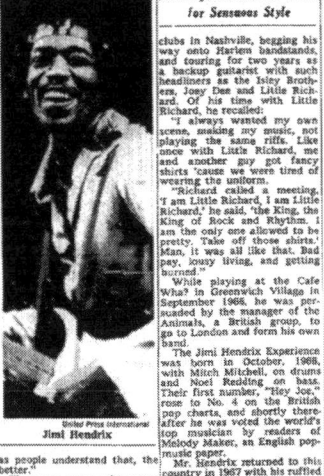

Flamboyant Performer Noted for Sensuous Style

Special to The New York Times

LONDON, Sept. 18 — Jimi Hendrix, the American rock star whose passionate, intense guitar playing stirred millions, died here today of unknown causes. He was 27 years old.

Mr. Hendrix was taken to St. Mary Abbots Hospital in Kensington after collapsing this morning at the home of friends. Attempts to revive him at the hospital were unsuccessful.

Unconfirmed reports said he had died of an overdose of drugs but the official cause of death will not be determined until a post mortem.

The pop star last performed at the Isle of Wight Festival last month.

A Total Experience

By GEORGE GENT

Explosive and sensuous, Jimi Hendrix undulated his way into international popularity with young people on two continents while startling their elders with his frank sexuality.

During a typical Hendrix performance, the singer-guitarist—dressed in tight black pants and a bright rainbow shirt covered with a black leather vest, his Afro hair-do looking as though it had been plugged into his electric amplifier—would mumble into a microphone, "Dig this, baby," as he ran through a repertory that included "Purple Haze," "Foxy Lady," "Let Me Stand Next to Your Fire" and "The Wind Cries Mary."

Jimi Hendrix

clubs in Nashville, begging his way onto Harlem bandstands, and touring for two years as a backup guitarist with such headliners as the Isley Brothers, Joey Dee and Little Richard. Of his time with Little Richard, he recalled:

"I always wanted my own scene, making my music, not playing the same riffs. Like once with Little Richard, me and another guy got fancy shirts 'cause we were tired of wearing the uniform.

"Richard called a meeting. 'I am Little Richard, I am Little Richard,' he said, 'the King, the King of Rock and Rhythm. I am the only one allowed to be pretty. Take off those shirts.' Man, it was all like that. Bad pay, lousy living, and getting burned."

While playing at the Cafe Wha? in Greenwich Village in September 1966, he was persuaded by the manager of the Animals, a British group, to go to London and form his own band.

The Jimi Hendrix Experience was born in October, 1966, with Mitch Mitchell on drums and Noel Redding on bass. Their first number, "Hey Joe," rose to No. 4 on the British pop charts, and shortly thereafter he was voted the world's top musician by readers of Melody Maker, an English pop music paper.

Mr. Hendrix returned to this country in 1967 with his ruffled clothing and velvet hat for a series of concerts. A year later, an overflow crowd of 18,000 turned out to hear him. Janis

as people understand that, the better."

There are many who never did understand, and Mr. Hendrix did not live long enough to persuade them. But his fans were numerous and vocal and

Kurt Cobain, Hesitant Poet Of 'Grunge Rock,' Dead at 27

By TIMOTHY EGAN
Special to The New York Times

SEATTLE, April 8 — Kurt Cobain, the ragged-voiced product of a Pacific Northwest timber town who helped to create the grunge rock sound that has dominated popular music for the last four years, was found dead today at his home here. The police said they believed that Mr. Cobain, the lead singer, guitarist and songwriter for the influential band Nirvana, killed himself with a single shotgun blast to the head.

A note was found next to Mr. Cobain's body, which was discovered by an electrician who had gone to the house this morning to do some work, said Vinette Tichi, a spokeswoman for the Seattle Police Department. Mr. Cobain was 27.

Although police officials were initially reluctant to identify the body, late today the King County Medical Examiner, Donald Reay, said a fingerprint examination confirmed that it was that of Mr. Cobain.

Nirvana is a leader among the half-dozen Seattle-based musical groups, lumped together as grunge, that combined heavy metal with a punk sensibility.

With its 1991 album, "Nevermind," Nirvana put alternative rock, the noisy, icon-smashing spawn of punk rock, into the commercial mainstream. The album sold nearly 10 million copies worldwide, knocked Michael Jackson off the top of the popular music charts and established an anthem for a generation with the song "Smells Like Teen Spirit."

Dressed in thrift-shop plaid shirts and torn jeans, a fashion soon copied by designers around the world, Mr. Cobain and the members of his band

Continued on Page 11, Column 3

Kurt Cobain, of the rock group Nirvana, who was found dead.

Made in the USA
Middletown, DE
28 March 2025